# Something Leather

ALASDAIR GRAY

# Something Leather

 RANDOM HOUSE  NEW YORK

Library of Congress Cataloging-in-Publication Data
Gray, Alasdair.
Something leather / by Alasdair Gray.
p.    cm.
ISBN 0-394-58963-7
I. Title.
PR6057.R3264S56      1991      823'.914—dc20
90-46250

Manufactured in the United States of America
98765432
First U.S. Edition

**FOR FLO ALLAN**

# Contents

One beginning and one ending for a book

was a thing I did not agree with.

A good book may have three openings,

entirely dissimilar

and interrelated only in the prescience of the author,

or for that matter

one hundred times as many endings.

Flann O'Brien, *At Swim-Two-Birds,* third and fourth sentences

# Something Leather

# CHAPTER 1

# One for the Album

June is intelligent, and honest, and very lonely. She is also strikingly good-looking, which does not help much. She likes admiration but most men's admiration becomes resentment when she refuses to let them bring it to a very ordinary sexual conclusion. She thinks slightly plainer women have an easier time. She was married once and that also ended for ordinary reasons. Her husband could not forgive her for earning more than he earned yet did not want her to stop work and have a child. At the time she was sorry. Now she is glad. Too many women, she thinks, use children to distract themselves from unsatisfying lives. Her salary from the civil service is now too big for her to risk losing the job, the job too unsatisfying to let her rest in it. She often dreams of taking a long break and finding work that pleases her, but perhaps (says her honesty) no such work exists. People who know what they want in life are guided to it by an obsession. June's only obsession is commonplace—she likes dressing well. When buying a garment which suits her rare kind of handsomeness she feels that life, after all, might become an exciting adventure. She has a large wardrobe of clothes to remind her of that wonderful, short-lived feeling. It does not stop her usually feeling like a Mercedes Benz forced to work as a taxi.

Her job has an advantage apart from the wage. By working overtime she can make Friday a holiday and walk about assessing fashions in shop windows and on the bodies of passers-by. Her favourite styles are those of the thirties and forties which flirt elegantly or luxuriously with the human outline. On this clear summer afternoon nearly everything she sees annoys her, the prevailing styles shout aloud that times are tough. Young men with money wear floppy suits and stubble on their chins. Jackets, waistcoats, woollens, shirts and skirts are worn in eccentric layers as if put on fast in an emergency. The commonest fabric is denim; the commonest garment a shapeless jacket with huge pockets suggesting a labour camp. This has been popular for years and makers have given it a new lease of life by dyeing it to appear dirtied by rough usage. Jeans and skirts are also made from this denim. Some young people (June is no longer young) wear jeans they have deliberately ripped; why? The only elegant garment she glimpses is made of the toughest fabric of all. Someone slim and neat passes in a suit of gleaming black leather with silver zips. June has never worn leather but some shops sell nothing else. She experiences a faint, familiar thrill: she will hunt down an exciting new thing to wear. The leather shop welcomes her with a scent she finds comforting and yet exotic—she has forgotten how good leather smells. But the skirts and jackets don't appeal to her and she does not even look

at the trousers—trousers are not her style. An assistant asks
what she is looking for.

"None of this, exactly," says June glancing discontent-
edly along a rack, "I would like something more . . . something
less . . ." She is going to say "conventional" but blushes instead.
She does not exactly know what she wants.

"Perhaps you should have it made to order," the assistant
says, briskly.

"Where?"

"The Hideout is quite near here—number 3798."

June wanders meekly into the sunlight. Her meekness is on
the surface. *Hideout* adds a spice of Wild West adventure to
this hunt for something she cannot yet imagine.

The place is further than the assistant suggested. Beyond a
crossroads June finds she has left the fashionable district. A
poorer lot of people crowd along the cracked pavement but they
look cheerful in sunlight. June is no snob, all that worries her
is the absence of any place called The Hideout or numbered
3798. Between 2988 (a loan office) and 4040 (a betting shop) is
a long row of boarded-up fronts. She walks up and down before
these, excitement cooling to a familiar disappointment till she
notices a car at the kerb: a cheap little Citroën with two wavy
blue lines on the side. To the canvas roof, with great ingenuity,
an arrow-shaped sign is fixed. A leather belt is stapled to the
sign in a loop surrounding the words HIDEOUT LEATHER-
WEAR. The arrow points across the pavement at a dark little
entry smelling of cat-piss and leading to steps worn to such a
slant that June feels insecure on them. They bring her to a
landing with a plank floor and three low doors, two faced with
rusty metal and padlocked, one coloured vivid orange with a
handwritten label saying PRESS HARD above a bell-button. June
presses it, hard.

She has gone through the shadowy entry and up these stairs with the uneasy excitement of a huntress following game into a dangerous thicket, but when the door opens her uneasiness vanishes. A bright ordinary little woman in a print dress opens it and says, "I'm sorry, come in, I can't attend to you right now because I'm finishing something for someone but if you can wait a minute I'll be with you in a minute. What sort of thing are you looking for?"

She leads June down a short corridor to a long, low-ceilinged bare-looking room with six dusty windows above the shop fronts on the street. A sewing machine, a rack of hangers empty of garments, a table with tools and samples on it are almost the only furniture. In a corner of the carpetless plank floor is an electric kettle plugged to a wall socket, two mugs, a jar of coffee powder, a bag of sugar, and a radio playing pop music. Beside the sewing machine sits a woman who scowls at June as if she were intruding. She is very like the woman who opened the door, though plumper and with thick black hair cut straight across the brow and shoulders like the wig of a sphinx.

"I think," says June hesitantly, "I want a . . . a skirt."

"Sit down and look at some patterns," says the woman and points to a fat album on the table, "I'll be with you in five minutes," and she sits at the machine and resumes putting something through it while the other woman talks to her in a low penetrating voice which sounds conversational yet complaining.

The album has cuttings taken from catalogues and fashion-magazines mounted on big pages under transparent film. As June turns these pages she grows more and more frustrated. They show all sorts of leather garments, some conventional, some bizarre, but nothing June would wear in the street. She is too old to enjoy dressing before a mirror. Why did she come here? She finds she is straining to hear phrases which penetrate the stuttering bursts of sewing-machine sound and the din of pop music.

". . . had her eye on me but I had my eye on her . . ."

". . . I said you don't buy what you don't like . . ."

". . . hotpants isn't just her middle name it's her first and last . . ."

June shakes her head impatiently, turning the pages faster and faster until she reaches blank ones at the end. She is going to slam the book shut and leave when she sees the corner of a loose photograph protruding from those last pages. Pulling it out she discovers she is holding two black and white photographs, but for a long time the one on top has her whole attention.

A black leather skirt, calf-length and with a rear fastening of silver studs from waist to hem, is worn by a woman who is photographed from behind. It would be too tight if most of the studs were not unfastened but a few top ones are fastened to hide an arse made proud by her high-heeled shoes. The shoes and skirt are all she wears as she presses against the wallbars of a gymnasium, stretching one arm up to grasp a bar just beyond the reach of her fingertips. Then June sees her wrist is handcuffed to that bar. Her free hand grips a bar at shoulder height, her legs are braced as far apart as possible to take all the weight she can off the steel bracelet round that wrist. Her head is flung backward. All that appears of it is a white line of brow and much unbound thick black hair cut straight across the shoulders in a way which reminds June of someone near her, but the reminder is not strong enough to break the dreamy enchantment cast by the photograph. If the woman gossiping by the sewing machine (". . . and I said to her, I said, . . .") is the woman in the photograph she is more interesting, more enticingly beautiful in the photograph. Then June notices she is alone in that room, the voices are gossiping beside the front door, which slams. She hears someone approaching her and asking cheerily, "Well? Have you found what you want?"

"Not . . . exactly," says June after a pause, and as she still cannot draw her eyes from the photograph or bear to lay it down she starts talking as if the skirt, nothing but the skirt is the thing she stares at, is all that interests her.

"A front fastening, I think, and . . ." She hesitates, having no other ideas.

"Pockets?" asks the woman.

"Well . . . yes."

"Big ones?"

"Perhaps . . ."

"Like hers?" The woman takes the photograph uncovering the one beneath. It shows a tall lean woman in her early thirties, her scalp shaved quite bald, standing arrogantly astride. She wears big baggy suede overalls with the legs rolled above the knee. Saddlebag pockets on the thighs make them bulge out like jodhpurs but more noticeable is her smile of greedy pleasure, the thin cane she flexes in her hands.

"That's Miss Cane, our schoolteacher. Her real name is Harry—she's an artist. Lots of goodies in her pockets!" says the woman encouragingly. June stares, then nods, blushing.

"I know exactly what you want!" cries the woman enthusiastically. She lays both photographs on the table, grabs a pad and sketches on it saying, "Like this? . . . and loops for the belt here . . . Why not a front *and* back fastening . . . ?"

June finds herself agreeing to a skirt she has no intention of wearing.

Then the woman slides the photos back into the album and says confidingly, "I nearly died when I saw you with those."

"Why?"

"They shouldn't be in that album—they're from an album my wicked clients use."

"Wicked?" says June, pretending not to understand.

"Not *horribly* wicked. But they enjoy games not everyone enjoys, so they like to be careful. I don't blame them! I'm a bit wicked myself—that's why they trust me. Now I'm going to measure you."

The woman kneels and as her light fingers put a tape round June's waist, hips, lower hip etcetera June looks absentmindedly round the room. She sees no sign of another album.

"It's in a wee safe under the table," says the woman, who is making notes in her pad, "You see these photos don't just show available dress designs, they show available . . . people, so they're rather tempting. Would you like a peep?"

She smiles at June who is too confused by having her mind read to say a word, but perhaps she nods because the woman shuts the pad briskly saying, "I'll maybe allow you a peep when you come for the fitting. When will suit you?"

"Friday?"

"Sure! Anytime next Friday will do. Give me your phone number in case something happens and there's a delay. But there shouldn't be."

June gives her phone number, asks the price of the skirt (which is reasonable) and offers a down payment.

"No need," says the woman, smiling, "I know you'll be back."


"You seem even more remote from us than usual," says June's boss to her in the office next Tuesday.

"I feel a bit peculiar," June admits.

"You look flushed. Take a day off."

"Maybe I will," says June, but she knows what her disease is. She is haunted by daydreams of a picturebook showing temptingly available victims and tyrants. Her heart beats faster at the memory. She feels—while knowing this irrational—close to a gladness and freedom she has not enjoyed since she was eleven and sex was a thrilling secret shared with a few special friends, not an anxious negotiation with a potentially dangerous adult. But that was long ago. To play truant from work and visit The Hideout before Friday and ask to see *the wicked album* will be admitting a sexual need. June has never in her life admitted a sexual need to another adult. She waits till Friday before returning to The Hideout, and forces herself to wait till mid-afternoon, instead of arriving like an eager little girl as soon as it opens.

And she stands on the cracked pavement between the loan office and the betting shop and stares at a space of reddish, brick-strewn gravel with a railway viaduct behind it. For a while she cannot believe the whole building has vanished. She fights the desolate frustration she feels by examining the rows of buildings on each side of the space, and going into a pub across the road from it, though it is the sort of pub where lonely women are stared at. She orders a gin and tonic and asks the barman, "What happened to the tailoring business across the road?"

"Those shops were pulled down weeks ago."

"Oh no—they were there last Friday."

"Could be. But nobody's been in them for years."

"But there was a . . . a leathercraft shop upstairs in one. Called The Hideout. A small woman ran it. She advertised with a sign on a parked car."

"She couldn't have. Parking's illegal on that side."

June finishes her drink then goes to the fashionable leather-wear shop which gave her the address. The only information the assistant has is a card a stranger handed in with The Hideout name and address on it. She says, "These small firms come and go very quickly. Will I give you the address of another?"

June goes home to her room and kitchen flat, buying a bottle of sherry on the way.

She has a very hot bath, washes her hair, then sits in her dressing-gown on the hearthrug, sipping sherry and listening to a record. This does not cheer her. She feels empty and old, with nothing much to expect from life. A second glass leaves her gloomier and fuddled. The telephone rings. She picks up the receiver.

"This is Donalda Ingles," says an unfamiliar, anxious little voice, "I've got your skirt."

"*Who* are you?"

"Donalda. We met in The Hideout last week. Your skirt's ready!"

"I went there today and . . ."

"Yes, you saw what they did to us. Listen, can I bring it round?"

"Bring it here?"

"Yes. You aren't busy are you? I mean, nobody's with you, are they?"

"No, but . . ."

"Give me your address and I'll bring it over right away, I'm sure you'll like it!" There is an odd, pleading note in the little voice through the receiver. After a pause June gives her address and the voice says, "I'll be there in twenty minutes."

June goes thoughtfully to her wardrobe. She is about to choose a dress when she changes her mind and puts on pants, bra and white cotton blouse with the dressing-gown on top. She will wear the skirt for the maker of it, if for nobody else. This decision makes her feel young again.

The entryphone rings. June presses the admission switch and goes to the door. A woman in a long waterproof coat and carrying a suitcase comes up the stairs to June's landing and stands before her saying, "Hello! Don't you remember me?"

It is the small plump woman with black hair like a sphinx's wig.

"Yes, but I didn't expect you, I expected—"

"Oh Senga couldn't come, she's very busy from having to shift, you see, and she thought you'd rather see me anyway."

"Why?" says June, letting the woman in and closing the door.

"Senga gets these notions. I never argue with her. This is a very nice room, do you mind if I take off my coat?" She asks this as if expecting to be refused. In The Hideout she seemed sullen and plaintive. Now she is an intriguing mixture of boldness and shyness, as if shoving herself forward against her will. When June says, "Of course take it off!" she hesitates before quickly unbuttoning and dropping it on the sofa beside the suitcase, then she stands gazing at June in a helpless, pleading way. With a white silk blouse she is wearing exactly the high-heeled shoes and leather skirt she wore in the photograph, and to prove it she lifts both hands to shoulder height and turns round till she faces June again, having shown the rear fastening more than half undone. And June knows she is being seduced and has partly wanted it. Her heart beats hard and fast, yet she is able to smile with perfect confidence at the plump, sexy-looking, nervous little woman. Though June has never been seduced by a woman before the situation is familiar.

"What about *my* skirt?" she asks. Donalda nods, opens the case, takes the skirt out. June slips off her dressing-gown and stands with folded arms before the wardrobe mirror. Donalda kneels and fastens it round her, buckling the belt, patting and smoothing the leather over waist, stomach, arse and tops of the thighs and all the time murmuring, "There, isn't it nice? Aren't you lovely?"

June looks down on her with some of the loneliness, some of the contemptuous superiority she always feels with people who greatly desire her, though looking at the mirror she notices wryly that her own skirt is far more challengingly whorish than the one Donalda wears. She also sees, as well as feeling, Donalda's arms embrace her waist, Donalda's face press into the angle of her neck and shoulder, Donalda's lips brush her ear and whisper, "There's a present for you in the right pocket."

June slides her hand under the pocket flap and pulls out the photographs which enchanted her in The Hideout. She stares at them as Donalda leads her to the soft rug before the fire, stares at them as she responds to the little beseeching murmurs and hand pats by which Donalda brings her to lie down and open to her. She even stares at them while absentmindedly, with her free hand, returning some of Donalda's caresses. Donalda sobs, "Oh you devil! You lovely devil! You don't care for me at all, do you? It's *her* you wanted Senga to send!"

"I'm not sure," murmurs June, looking from the photo of the tempting victim to that of the exciting tyrant. Which does she like best? Which would she like to be? She really does not know.

Much later June lies with closed eyes, half satisfied and half dissatisfied as she always feels after lovemaking. She is conscious of Donalda's body against her back, Donalda's hand resting on her thigh, Donalda's small voice explaining or complaining about something.

"You haven't once asked who I am or how I feel or what I want in life—I think you care for nobody but yourself but I must tell you about me. I come from a real big family, three older brothers and three younger sisters and I had to help my Mum look after the lot. I really loved my Mum, she was a really good woman who never thought of herself, she made herself old before her time slaving from morning till night for all those men and young lassies who never gave a damn for her. Well, when I turned fifteen I couldn't take any more—I was sick of helping her so I left home, I suppose because I'm wicked. We all have wicked dreams, don't we? And unless we bring one of our wicked dreams just a wee bit to life we live like zombies—the living dead—slaves like my Mammy, right? Right? Answer me! *Please!*"

"Right," says June, who feels too tired to disagree or think much and has begun to find Donalda Ingles a bore.

"I want to ask you another thing. Have you arranged something for this weekend? Are you going to see someone or are they coming here to see you?"

"I've made no arrangements," says June, and to stop Donalda suggesting one adds, "I like weekends to myself."

"Anyway," says Donalda, after a pause, "When I left my Mammy I got into big trouble. I won't go into details, they would only sicken you—I had a baby and all that. It was Senga who saved me. She's not much older than me, we were pals at school, but she's as sure of what to do as my Mammy is, though my Mammy is a slave and Senga is definitely a boss. When I help Senga I'm helping myself because . . . don't laugh . . . Senga is a fairy godmother who makes dreams come true. She's so good at it she earns her living that way. She told me to do this with you, please let me, it won't hurt," says Donalda, "Just turn over a bit."

June turns obediently over. She wears nothing now but the unfastened skirt and the belt, which has several straps and buckles. June lets Donalda draw her wrists behind her back, cross them above the belt and loop a strap round them. The pressure of the strap suddenly becomes almost painful and June finds her wrists fastened there.

"And now?" she placidly asks. Donalda stands, goes to the kitchen and returns with three clean glasses. These she lays on the table and fills from the sherry bottle.

"What's happening?" asks June, puzzled. Donalda dips into the suitcase and brings out a radio telephone and a wide strip of adhesive bandage. She says, "A couple in a car downstairs have been waiting to see you so I'm asking them up. If you start screaming I'll gag you with this bandage."

June is too astonished to scream. She tries to stand which is hard without hands and impossible when Donalda sits on her legs and puts an arm round her neck.

"Listen!" says Donalda, and her voice is not hard or cruel, "Please believe this, Senga and I make other peoples' dreams come true but we haven't *begun* to help you yet—you're so locked up in yourself you don't know what your dreams are. You're under a spell and we won't let you go till we've broken that spell, because you're the loveliest thing we've ever met. But first, before Senga brings the teacher here . . ."

She fastens her mouth on June's mouth in a kiss which is almost a bite, and for a moment June enjoys a melting delicious weakness like nothing she has known.

We will return to her later.

# CHAPTER 2

# A Distant Cousin of a Queen

Harry is a fœtus before the sexual scanning of them is practical. She is pulled from her mother's body through a caesarian section because the mother believes a surgical delivery will ensure her husband's presence. Just before the operation she is told that a local, not a general, anaesthetic must be used.

"I felt every bloody thing they did to me down thea," she tells friends, "It didn't hurt, but it was loathsome."

When Harry is held up in the air her mother says, "Oh God, a fucking little gel! For a boy I might have whipped up some maternal instinct but a gel is *not on.*"

She weeps passionately and the husband and father pays no attention to Harry, who is also weeping passionately. He pats his wife's hand and says, "Don't worry, dia, it isn't important."

Harry's mother compensates for disliking her daughter by wanting more from Harry's nurses than they can give. For nearly two years all those who do the job resign or get dismissed before a month passes, often before a week. At last a woman from Greenock is employed. Her voice strikes Harry's parents as comically coarse and ill-bred but her quietly servile manner is just right, and she can produce Harry any time looking as clean, pretty and passive as an expensive doll. Harry's mother wants Harry for coffee mornings, where she introduces her as, "My daughta, of cawse."

Harry sits with a straight back, hands folded in lap, looking hard at whomever is talking. This is usually her mother, but other visitors find the small girl's close attention disconcerting. When someone asks her genially, "What have *you* to say for yawself?" Harry looks straight at her mother who tells the visitor, "Let ha off the small talk. Amusing topics are still beyond ha grasp."

A week or two later when a handsome military man asks Harry, "What a small people like you being taught nowadays?" she replies in a direct, clear little voice, "Please let me off the small talk. Amusing topics a still beyond my grasp."

This reply appears to delight all but Harry's mother who pretends not to hear, but that day, before giving her back to the nurse, she kisses Harry more emphatically.

The nurse produces this perfect Harry by smacking and nipping her when they are alone together, not because Harry is bad but to stop her from becoming bad.

"If I hear *one word* of complaint about you from your mother," says the nurse, "I'll do *this* to you," and she systematically bruises parts of Harry's body which are usually hidden by a nappy and rubber knickers. (Harry needs these long after babyhood.) Sometimes the nurse says, "If you breathe one word about me to another soul I'll do *this* to you," so Harry learns to choose words carefully and avoid them when possible. By the age of four Harry's face wears an intense frown as if she were trying to remember the exact shape of something stolen from her. This expression, with slight variations, stays to the end of her life and though she is not aware of it, this makes strangers think she despises them. She grows tall, thin and wiry for her age. One day she unthinkingly answers a stinging slap from her nurse with a backhand blow of equal force, the first wicked act of her life. She and the nurse are equally astonished. The nurse has a cane she has often wielded as a threat but never used for a beating. In a mood of great excitement she goes to Harry's parents and asks for permission to use it. She has never brought them a problem before. They dismiss her and put Harry in a boarding school.

But a week or two pass before a suitable school is found. Harry is tended by another of her mother's servants who changes Harry's nappies and nearly faints when she sees what they hide. She shows it to Harry's mother who is less moved because she is pitiless.

"I'm quite pitiless because no-one eva pitied me," she tells her friends, but she agrees that the blue, black and red mosaic of bruises is an ugly sight.

"Paw kid," she tells Harry who is sobbing bitterly at losing the one person in the world she was allowed to depend on, "I *knew* that woman was too good to be true. Don't worry. We'll straighten you out."

The boarding school is an elegant little Georgian mansion with large garden, shrubbery and paddock near the city of Bath.

"Beway-a of me!" the headmistress tells Harry's mother happily, "I am a very dangerous liberal, and an atheist to boot. But if one of my little gels shows religious yearnings she is allowed to attend services in the church of ha choice and layta, if she stays firm, may receive instruction. The Ricardos a Jewish, though not awthodox of cawse. Their daughta is now a nun in Stanbrook Abbey."

"Harry might go that way. One of my in-laws is potty that way," says Harry's mother carelessly, "though he is a Buddhist of course. Yaw fees . . ."

"No school has higha fees," says the headmistress swiftly, "Not in Britain anyway. Everything the gels see, use and a taught is of the best quality. I have neva befoa taken moa than twelve pupils but of course Harriet is exceptional. She will *not* be an unlucky thirteenth. My small numba of gels lets me enshaw nobody suffas or is bullied during what can be a very difficult and highly formative few yias."

"I think most kids a improved by hard knocks in the early yias," says Harry's mother, "It toughens them. They learn to look to themselves, not to othas fo what they need, so in layta yias they make othas do tha bidding. That's my experience."

"Many books expound yaw theory at much greata length," says the headmistress, nodding and smiling as if she approves of brevity, "But I attended—" the headmistress mentions a more famous boarding school than her own—"It was and is a wondaful place with a wise and dedicated staff, but so big! We all made lots of valuable friends but I know for a fact that some gels had experiences which marked them fo life."

"And you emerged unscathed?" says Harry's mother softly, looking hard at the headmistress. Harry's mother believes all teachers are pæderasts: why else would they enter so loathsome a calling? She believes everyone but some people she knows belong to the servant class, so finds it hard to be polite to professional women who talk as if they were her equal. But the headmistress has agreed to take Harry so politeness is not now needed. After a pause the headmistress says in a slightly louder voice, "Yes. From what you tell me it is clia Harriet has suffad enough in ha short life. This is the first time I have agreed to take moa than twelve pupils and will certainly be the last, but I'm glad to help a child in Harriet's difficult position. She cannot help being exceptional."

Still staring hard at the headmistress Harry's mother's face settles into the brooding frown which is always on Harry's face. She has mentioned that Harry still needs nappies, but the bruises are healing so there was no need to tell more. She believes this teacher is only admitting Harry to her school because Harry is related through her father to a European royal family. Harry's mother finds the connection useful because, as she tells her friends, "It opens doas," but she hates those who remind her of it as she envies and dislikes her husband's family. She says at last, "I'm glad you think my daughta exceptional. Yaw old school wouldn't touch ha with a bargepole so hia she is! But I hia the guardians have given you Amanda's kid so yaw establishment probably instils the main decencies. I'm only sorry you've seen fit to admit new money."

*Amanda's kid* is a millionairess orphan, *new money* is the daughter of a popular singer. Speaking clearly and carefully the headmistress says Harry's mother ought to meet the popular singer one day—he is kind, courteous and highly intelligent. Moreover, she enjoys having one pupil with a Bohemian background because it teaches the others to mingle without lowering themselves. While the last remark is emerging from the headmistress's mouth she notices with horror that it is meaningless snobbery, that she is groggy with insults from a duchess she believes she is helping.

"I've not been to Bohemia so that sounds nonsense to me," says Harry's mother, smiling pleasantly for the first time today and rising slowly to her feet. Not many do this without seeming decrepit. Harry's mother unfolds her body in a graceful upward flow which seems to leave her taller than before she sat down.

"Goodbye!" she says, extending a high hand which the headmistress automatically reaches up to touch, "No doubt you do yaw useful job betta than most. If my daughta is spoiled by ha *very* expensive schooling nobody can blame me."

The headmistress was once a professional actress but finds she has been manoeuvred into talking and feeling like a caretaker with delusions of grandeur.

The headmistress was once nearly famous as a juvenile lead in a 1938 production of *Dear Octopus.* Her love of acting was not strong enough to survive the war so after it three things combined to make her a teacher. She likes small girls, finding it easier to behave like an adult with them than with anyone else. She has rich friends who want someone they know to manage their children. Her parents have left her a family home which she can only maintain by claiming the rates and cost of upkeep as expenses against taxation. Most of the servants live out; she and a housekeeper and a friend she met at drama school are the resident staff. They teach girls between the ages of four and fifteen how to keep clean, to eat, dress, walk and talk nicely, to read, write and count. Visiting tutors introduce them easily and without strain to singing, music, dancing, art, history, the French language, tennis, swimming and ponies—there is an adjacent riding school. None of these pursuits is compulsory but every girl develops a good appetite for two or three of them. No class has more than four pupils and on bright days it is easy for everyone to move outside and continue their lessons on the lawn, in the rose arbour, in the summer house or sunken garden. A few ordinary things are not taught. Each pupil learns to keep her room tidy but it is cleaned by the servants. To the end of her life Harry panics if expected to make a cup of tea or sign a cheque and pass it over a counter in a public building. The school teaches one great falsehood: that the pupils are finer than pupils of all other schools and much finer than people who could never pay fees their own people pay. Apart from that it does more good than harm to children whose parents, for various reasons, hardly exist for them.

There is a games room, a music room, a library and a lounge with a television set. On light evenings and at weekends the girls usually put on overalls or their oldest frocks and play in the shrubbery, which is really a wood thin in trees but thick in undergrowth. Here, playing mostly in couples, the girls make little nests and dens which they call houses, usually inside elder bushes because these have thickly overlapping outer leaves and a mainly hollow centre. Amanda's kid, nearly thirteen, has a gang of two or three smaller girls who have built for her a complicated wigwam called The Fortress. It is made of branches, turf, poles, tarpaulin and corrugated iron with a very low tiny door. The shrubbery is out of bounds to the teaching staff because, "It is important that children have freedom to invent private worlds of thea own," but the headmistress comes to know nearly all that happens in the shrubbery. At least once a fortnight each pupil is invited to a beautifully served dinner for two or a cosy afternoon tea for two. At these the headmistress chats about her problems and asks for advice.

"I'm worried about little Harriet. I call ha little, you see, to remind myself that she's only five even though she's much talla than you, who a a whole yia olda. She seems to have no friends. What does she do in the shrubbery? She's very fond of it."

"Climbs the tree, Efel."

"Try to call me *Ethel*. Which tree?"

"The conker beoind the ollies," says Linda, who was called *new money* by Harry's mother.

"The sweet chestnut. Not a bad tree fo a small wiry girl to climb," says the headmistress thoughtfully. "The boughs and branches a mainly horizontal. Is ha balance good? Does she take risks? Eat a strawberry tart while you recollect what you have seen. Chew it slowly so that you enjoy every crumb befoa replying."

Soon after these instructions Linda says, "She climbs very slow and careful. She goes very igh up, crawls out along a branch as far as she can get then just sits. If you wive to er she pretends she can't see. If you shout er name loud enough she goes back to the middle of the tree and gets onto a branch on the uver side."

After a while the headmistress says, "The tree is to Harriet what the piano is to Clara." Clara is an eleven-year-old who spends all her free time in the music room.

"Clara and Harriet a both very lonely gels," says the headmistress. "But it is now too late to help paw Clara. How can we help paw Harriet, Linda? The other gels avoid ha because she does nothing but frown when they speak to ha. The tyootas a lucky if she ansas them with moa than a monosyllable and so am I. The only thing she does in the gym is stretch haself for ouas on the wallbaas. Thank goodness she likes clay modelling, but it is a solitary art. How can we help ha, Linda?"

"The troof is, Efel, I'm too miserable to elp anyone," says Linda, weeping, "I'll allwise allwise allwise be a applicant."

The headmistress cuddles her, strokes her kindly then softly asks, "Is Hjordis still beastly to you?"

"I run errands for er, bring er all sorts of fings to add to The Fortress and she still won't let me in. Every week the ole gang examines me but Yordis says I'm still too young and must apply again next week. And the exams get arder and arder! Oh I'll never never see wot's inside!"

"Yaw in daynja of choking," says the headmistress, "Go to the lavatory and wash yaw face in *warm* wata, ending with a splash of cold. Then come back and eat this slice of excellent cheesecake. I will then tell you exactly what The Fortress contains, though I have neva entad it in my life."

When Linda is calm the headmistress tells her, "The Fortress contains a quite valuable Persian rug, a mirra framed in coppa, a large glazed photograph of Hjordis's motha with a very handsome man who was ha fatha for a while and some antique knick-knacks. All these vanished from Hjordis's bedroom soon after the central chamba of The Fortress was built. That was a yia before you came but they must be thea, apart from a few knick-knacks. She pawned these on a visit to Bath to raise money to purchase Turkish cigarettes. I will not interfia until she turns to marijuana. But the main thing you would discova in The Fortress is Hjordis in a bossia mood than you have eva seen befoa. I know you love Hjordis very much and no wonda! She is lovely, cleva and very charming when it will get ha something. But when she was very small—much smalla than you, Linda—some terribly sad things happened to ha, things so sad I refuse to talk about them and Hjordis refuses to rememba them. The result of these sad happenings is that beautiful charming Hjordis hates and fias everybody who is not unda ha thumb. She can neva have a friend of ha own age. That is why she needs a gang and why nobody wants to be in it but the twins and you. The gang is a good thing fo the twins. It teaches them to work with a slightly larga group than themselves. And how very important you make them all feel, Linda, meekly following them about, running errands fo them and continually failing the exams they set! Without you the gang would fall apart."

Linda understands some but not all of this. She says, "If I stop trying to get in I'll ave nobody to talk to. The uvers giggle whenever I opens me mouf."

"I can hardly blame them for that, Linda. I really think you *ought* to give me yaw fatha's record for a while."

Linda's mouth opens wide, her face whitens and she starts to choke. Her voice is like her father's, who talks and sings in the main dialect of Greater London. His new money has enabled him to buy a new wife and pension off the old one. Linda has been sent to this school to have the main dialect of Greater London rubbed out of her voice, the main dialect of the British rich stamped there instead. This has not yet happened because Linda cannot sleep unless she first plays one of her father's records, turning the sound low, putting her ear near the speaker and dreaming he sings just to her; dreaming also that he, she and her mother still live in a brick terrace house with two cosy rooms downstairs and two up, a house with a small park near by where she can run and tumble with children whose friendly voices sound like her own. If someone suggests to Linda that she part with the record she starts to suffocate.

"I apologize!" says the headmistress, flinging her arms up in a gesture of surrender. "I promise not to suggest that again. I will eventually destroy your father's record because you beg me to and then you can begin to speak the language of Shakespia and Docta Johnson. But Harriet is a lot lonelia than you, Linda, and *she* neva giggles at how you speak. *She* neva giggles at anything. If you made friends with ha you would be helping ha, and yawself, and—I confess it—me! I am a selfish business-woman, Linda. Mine is not a good school, it is a bad school if the cousin of a queen and the daughta of a famous singa a both lonely little gels hia."

Linda thinks hard about this, sighs and says wistfully, "I would like that a lot, Efel, but I wouldn't dare. The troof is, Yordis would do somefing orrible to me if I joined the enemy."

"Is Harriet the enemy? I thought I was that," says the headmistress cheerfully.

"You are, but there's two of you since Harry came."

"Let us have a glass of lemonade, Linda! I have not had so interesting a conversation fo yias."

The headmistress is not as surprised as she pretends by what Linda now tells her; it adds details to a picture she knows in its main outlines. Hjordis, like all leaders, uses frequent broadcasts to entertain her followers and impress the surrounding universe. On warm weekends, when the girls have collected well-filled lunch baskets from the kitchen and taken them to the shrubbery, Hjordis walks up and down in front of The Fortress, sandwich in hand, delivering between bites loud speeches which sometimes provoke a muffled giggle or derisive shout from the depths of an elder bush. The twins sprawl and munch and listen on a blanket on the grass near by, nudging each other whenever Hjordis uses a word they think rude. Linda, hands clasped on top of head, stands under a tree in the only spot where applicants are allowed to stand. She has paid for this privilege with her lunch, which Hjordis (who often declares she prefers birds to people) has crumbled and scattered for the tits and robins. "Oua enemy boasts she is a Liberal!" cries Hjordis, "What does that mean? Mr Pargetta fo history says it's to do with gun-boats and free trade—with freedom. What freedom does the enemy allow us? The freedom to choose a bush in ha rotten shrubbery!"

"You have a fortress!" sings a distant voice.

"I have a rubbish heap!" shouts Hjordis. "A sawdid rubbish heap when I should have a geodesic play-dome with a trampoline floa and walls of opaque or transparent panels in the pattern of my choice! One of my uncle's factories makes nothing else! The enemy soon shot his offa down! *In the shrubbery I prefer all my little gels to start as equals.* Lies! Foul lies! She doesn't give a damn for equality! In this world equality means just one thing: equal rights fo the equally rich. Do we have that? Do we, hell! Oua people a a bloody sight richa than she is, she wouldn't let us in ha school if they weren't. But whea does that jumped-up bourgeois bitch sleep and whea do we? She sleeps in ha motha and fatha's beautiful old bedroom on the second floa while we sleep in the attics! The old servants' quawtas! Each in a paw little room with a sloping ceiling that once belonged to a skivvy or housemaid or valet! And whea do we usually eat? In a cella off the kitchen, a cella that was once the servants' dining room. Don't be fooled by the Laura Ashley curtains and the windows above ground level, we eat in a putrid basement! And oua splendid modern classrooms and sculptcha studio and record lab, whea a they located? In the old stables and kennels, the outhouses whea a lot of animals and thea stinking grooms once lived! None of you object to that, do you? No, yaw all perfectly happy because now and then Lady Muck invites you upstairs to see how nicely she can handle the family silver and tinkle the teacups in The Land That Time Forgot—the breakfast room and dining room and drawing room which a *still* ha private property because of the *money* she gets from OUA people! OUA people! OUA people!"

"You'll bust a gut, Hjordis," warns an American voice. It belongs to a millionairess from Texas, the only pupil Hjordis fears apart from a tall gangling untidy girl who reads the *New Statesman.* One of the twins approaches and holds out a dish with a chocolate éclair on it and a thermos mug of sweet milky coffee. Hjordis lifts these and walks slowly round The Fortress, eating and sipping in an effort to calm herself. Her brain is teeming with the sort of notions which always come to her when she talks loudly.

"This rotten system has got to stop and I mean to stop it!" she announces, returning, "The enemy has told you the cousin of a queen is coming hia. She has *not* told you that my motha and Harry Shetland's motha were very very very close friends, so Harry is going to be *my* special friend, a closa friend than any two of you a! I am going to take ha unda my wing—my gang will protect ha."

"What from?" sings the distant voice.

"From exploitation!" screams Hjordis, "The British public don't give a tuppenny fuck fo how awdinry rich people like us get exploited by the middle classes, but they've a soft spot for royalty! Imagine the headlines! QUEEN'S COUSIN IN LIBERAL POVERTY TRAP! My uncle owns all the British newspaypas. He and I will make the govament investigate this school aw fawce it to resign."

"Bosh!" says a weary voice from nearby, probably the voice of the *New Statesman* reader, and elsewhere someone giggles. "All right!" says Hjordis querulously, "My uncle only owns nialy half the British newspaypas, but half is enough!" She flings the empty mug toward The Fortress entrance and faces her gang.

"At ease!" she tells Linda. Linda thankfully lowers her hands, sits on the grass and rubs her legs. Hjordis strolls about muttering in a discontented tone only heard by those in the clearing: "We aren't a propa gang, we haven't an ally. We have everything else . . . strong leada . . . powaful enemy . . . a Fortress . . . an army . . ."—she stares at the twins until they salute her—". . . a hopeless horde of frantic applicants . . ."—she grins sarcastically at Linda, who blushes guiltily—". . . but no ally. Don't worry. The ally will soon be hia."

But Harry disappoints Hjordis. Harry answers the intensely whispered message, *"My motha was yaw motha's best friend!"* with the same gloomy stare then turned-away face she gives everyone. Nor can Hjordis get her alone to explain things more fully. Harry is not given a bedroom in the attics, but one beside the headmistress's bedroom on the second floor. In the shrubbery she at once climbs to a high branch of the tallest tree, shifting to the opposite side when Hjordis tries talking to her from underneath. For two weeks Hjordis, like Hitler after the loss of Stalingrad, is too ashamed to make a public announcement, but she is braver than Hitler. One Sunday she declares to the world, "I was wrong, I admit it! The daughta of my motha's best friend has joined the enemy! The descendant of Teutonic warlords is now spying fo the liberals! I don't know what you get up to in these bushes of yaws and I don't care—it's none of my business. But Big Sista Is Watching You! These beady little eyes in the sky don't miss a thing that happens unda the leaves! Thank God my Fortress has a solid roof! And there's room in it for everyone! Why not join me in it? I've a big tin of lovely biscuits."

"Pipe down you silly sow!" says someone wearily.

"Dismiss!" Hjordis whispers quickly to the twins, then runs to The Fortress and shuts herself deep inside. She cannot weep when others see or hear her.

Linda is too young to hide grief. A week later, tear-stained and furious from yet another failed examination, she charges to the foot of the chestnut tree and yells up into it, "Come down, Harry Shetland! Come down ere to me you bloody bitch! You

gotta be my friend! You gotta ply wiv me now now *now!* Efel
says you gotta and I'm so lonely I want to kill meself oh!" She
bangs her brow seriously against the trunk until half stunned
and dizzy she falls to the ground. Reviving after a moment she
bangs the back of her head on the ground in a half-hearted way,
then sighs and dozes off for a while. When she at last opens her
eyes she sees the face of Harry frowning gloomily down at her
from very near. Most of Harry's weight hangs from a hand
grasping a branch among the leaves overhead, one leg kneels on
a low bough, the other dangles, she sucks the thumb of her free
hand. The pose suggests she is wondering whether to climb
lower or higher and has been wondering for a long time.

"*Will* you ply wiv me?" asks Linda, sitting up. After a watch-
ful moment Harry puts both knees on the bough and creeps
swiftly to where it dips near the ground before curving up into
broad-leaved branches. She sits in the dip with her back very
straight, ankles crossed and hands folded neatly on lap. Linda
approaches and stands before her, hopeful and awed.

"Let us consida the case!" says Harry suddenly and clearly,
"of a certain paw very dirty little gel. She has been wawned
repeatedly against dirt and against opening ha mouth about you
and me, dearie. She has been shown what will happen to ha if
she ignoas these wawnings. Yet she ignoas these wawnings. She
gets dirty. She talks. Quick! What must be done to ha?"

"The troof is," explains Linda, "I want to ply kings and
queens, though I don't know much about them. You must
know a lot, so you can tell me what to do. You're taller than
I am so *you'd* better be king. I don't mind if you boss me a bit."

"No royals please!" says Harry sharply, "Royals a just *not
on*. We have no time fo interloe-pas be they German, Greek,
black, brown or Irish. We do not speak fo the lost cause of racial
purity, we speak against boredom. Please direct yaw attention

to this paw little horrid gel who does not deserve ha great advantages. How will we punish ha? Smacking and nipping a the usual thing."

"All right," says Linda in a resigned voice. "You be queen and I'll be king. But I must sit beside you like we're on a frone togever. Will you elp me up?"

"We said *no royals!*" Harry reminds her, "We said *smacking and nipping a the usual thing*. We a prepared to hia anything else you propose, but ponda well befoa you speak! Just now you a the dirtiest and smallest of us. Yaw voice is comically coarse and ill-bred, it brands you as an interloe-pa from the start. Perhaps you a the paw paw paw dirty dirty *dirty* little girl of whom we speak!"

"No I'm not!"

"Then it must be me," says Harry, twisting round and hanging over the bough with her legs on the near side, arms and head on the other, the seat of her blue corduroy overalls level with Linda's face.

"Begin!" she commands in a muffled voice. But Linda's mind has not been shaped by dread of punishment. The idea of hurting someone puzzles and repels her.

"I can't!" she complains, and "Wy should I?"

"This very horrid little gel has been expecting it fo weeks and weeks and weeks," Harry explains, "and it gets worse the longa she waits. She'll be so glad and grateful when you stop. And then you may kiss ha and say *You and me ur still pals dearie ur we no? Ur we no?*"

"That's stupid!" says Linda.

Harry twists round and up then creeps swiftly along the bough toward the tree trunk. "Oh don't go awy!" cries Linda in alarm, trotting beside her. "Honest, I meant no arm!"

"Thank you fo a very lovely aftanoon," says Harry coldly,

gripping a higher branch, giving a little leap and disappearing quick as a cat into the upper foliage. Linda is left crying, "Come back, please come back! I didn't mean to annoy you!"

Linda's cries are not answered. She stands thinking for a while, then abruptly turns and trots quickly through the bushes to the clearing. The ramshackle conical tower of The Fortress vibrates with a muffled voice declaring that A Hard Rain's Going To Fall. The only other life is some small birds pecking the remains of Linda's lunch from the grass. She goes to the tree where applicants are allowed to stand, lifts up a half brick and bangs it on a sheet of rusty iron hung by a rope from a branch. The noise is loud. She drops the brick and waits. At last a twin emerges. She is wearing jeans and a bush shirt and smoking a slender brown cigarette. She strolls around the clearing until, seemingly by accident, she stops in front of Linda. After looking at her thoughtfully from the shoes up to the bruise on her brow the twin blows a cloud of smoke over Linda's head and says, "Well?"

"I got infomytion," says Linda in a small voice.

"About?"

"Enemy."

"Which?"

"One in tree."

"Don't move," says the twin, and returns quickly to The Fortress. The noise of the record stops, then both twins emerge followed by Hjordis.

Pupils who show interest in make-up are given lessons in it by the headmistress and usually learn to subtly accentuate their most pleasing features. Hjordis deliberately uses white face powder, scarlet lipstick, dark eye-shadow and eyebrow pencil to model herself on the Wicked Queen in Walt Disney's *Snow White.* She wears a black dress and black opera cloak lined with scarlet silk which flutters behind her as she goes straight to Linda and says, "What have you discovad?"

Linda tells her. Hjordis gets her to repeat it slowly, then questions her closely about tones of voice and exact positions, then says, "You a moa cleva than I thought, Linda. The time is nia when I believe you may be fit to join us."

"Oh!" whispers Linda.

"Don't get happy too quickly!" Hjordis warns her, "I have one moa test fo you. Pass that and you could be inside The Fortress befoa teatime with me yaw friend fo life. If you fail I don't want to see you again. Eva. You will be *entie-aly* friendless hia."

"Wot's the test, Yordis?"

She is told and trembles with fear and anxiety. It is a terrible test, but the reward for passing, the punishment for failing, is overwhelming.

She returns apparently alone to the chestnut tree and shouts up forlornly, "Arry, I'm very sorry I didn't do wot you said! Please come down! Please ply wiv me, please! I'll do exactly wot you tell me to do!"

She shouts this at intervals for a very long time, standing near the dip in the long low bough. After five minutes she would gladly stop but is now aware of Hjordis behind a nearby holly bush. Linda becomes so conscious of Hjordis that she is suddenly surprised to see Harry sitting upright on the bough before her, ankles crossed and hands folded as if she had never left it.

"What is wrong with this little gel?" asks Harry almost kindly, frowning at Linda in a puzzled way. Linda's mouth is opening and shutting, trying to tell Harry noiselessly to go back up the tree. Hjordis walks over to them saying pleasantly, "Hello, Harry Shetland! I hia my friend Linda failed to oblige you. May I help?"

Harry wriggles up to kneel on the bough, but a twin is sitting astride it between her and the trunk, and another twin approaching from behind. Linda gives a little wail and runs away.

Linda's terror does not stupefy but makes her sensible. She pushes as fast and straight as possible through a rhododendron clump, nearly tumbles down a steep slope to the sunken garden, charges across three flowerbeds, up a flight of stone steps, through the rose arbour and across the lawn. Passing two older girls in bikinis and dark glasses sunbathing on a blanket she gasps, "Efel! Where's Efel?"

"Boozing in her private apartment I guess," says the Texan millionairess. Linda toils up a slope to the terrace, runs across it to an open french window, charges through the music room (where Clara, a fine pianist were she not tone deaf, struggles with Rachmaninov) and into the hall. Only then does she start shouting.

The headmistress is enjoying a glass of sherry and a glance through *Encounter* when she notices the shouts. They make no sense until she goes to the head of the stairs, hears "Efelefelefel!" and sees a small sturdy figure striving up toward her.

"Well Linda?" she asks.

Linda halts and gasps, "Yordis Arry conker *stop* em Efel! *Stop* em!"

"Speak moa slowly."

"Arry asked I smack er I wouldn't Yordis is!"

The headmistress cannot move without dignity but can walk faster than many people run. She walks straight to the chestnut tree by the exact route Linda took from it, even striding over the flowerbeds. She is slowed by her height when pushing through the rhododendrons, so Linda catches up. They hear a wild wailing with several words in it but at first only *please* is distinct, *please* repeated very often. Arriving beside the tree they do not see exactly what they expect, though nearby the twins cling together as if afraid of something.

Harry lies flat on her front on the ground, head pillowed on arm and turned sideways so they can see her calm, absent-minded, no longer frowning face. Hjordis squats beside her, whacking at her bottom with wild windmill flailing of the arms and crying frantically, "*Please* beg fo mercy! *Please* beg fo mercy! Aw just ask! Oh *please, please, please* ask me to stop doing this!"

"I ask you to stop doing it, Hjordis," says the headmistress firmly. "Stand up. Stand up and take my hand quick quick quick! You too, Harriet. Help Harriet up, Linda. Good. Take my hand, Harriet. Linda, take Harriet's otha hand and don't let go. Twin one, hold Hjordis's otha hand. Twin two, hold Linda's otha hand. Now we must all hold tight to each otha and not let go fo I am taking you all to a wondaful place you have neva seen befoa. Follow me!"

The headmistress is perfectly happy. Such moments (she knows) bring out the best in her. Childish souls have ground each other into chaos and now she will strike a nobler order into them. Hjordis, mewing at intervals, (that is how she sobs) clutches her hand almost gratefully. Harry is relaxed, blank-faced and docile, Linda and the twins awed and excited. Like a goose at the head of a flight formation the headmistress leads them from the shrubbery by the easiest way, making a slight detour to pass the sunbathers on the lawn. She enjoys feeling she can still astonish older pupils. As they approach the terrace Linda says, "I'm sorry I told Yordis wot you said to me, Harry."

"No need for sorrow!" says Harry, absentmindedly quoting her mother's words to a guest who dropped a delicate porcelain cup he had been asked to admire, "You have taught me a lesson

I will rememba till my dying day. I am almost grateful to you."

Linda gasps. The headmistress squeezes Harry's hand and says, "That is the longest speech I have eva heard you make, Harriet, and a very good speech it is. Though a bit hard on paw old Linda. You and Linda don't know it yet but yaw going to be great friends one day."

Harry looks down at Linda with curiosity, Linda looks apprehensively up at Harry.

The headmistress leads them into the hall, up the broad stairs to the landing of her own apartments, round the stairwell past the drawing room and dining room, then stops beside a door they have not seen open before. She says, "Let go hands everyone and listen carefully, especially you, Hjordis. The Fortress is a thing of the past. Tomorrow Hjordis will take ha possessions from it and bring them hia, and in the evening we will set fy-a to it, perhaps letting off a few squibs and rockets at the same time. Yaw new gang headquartas, Hjordis (I speak as one leada to anotha), lie behind this daw. It is a very special place. No child has been in it since I was a child, no grown-up but myself and a cleaning-woman has seen it since my parents died. Am I correct, Hjordis, in thinking Linda and Harriet are membas of yaw gang?"

She stares hard at Hjordis, who at last sees she is dealing with an intellect greater than her own and murmurs, "Yes, Ethel."

"Then open the daw and lead us in, Hjordis."

The door opens on a staircase much steeper than that which rises to the attics, and unlike the attic stair it is windowless. It ends in a loft under the central shed of the roof, and is lit by big skylights through which nothing can be seen but the summits of surrounding chimneystacks and a small white cloud in the blue. Huge crossbeams and struts under the skylights cast bars of shadow on a floor whose centre is covered by six carpets lain edge to edge; they do not reach the loft's dark edges and corners. They are well-worn carpets; this loft has clearly been used as a lumber-room, box room and games room for generations. It contains so many things to play with, look into, climb over and hide behind that merely staring around from the same spot gives a minute of pure pleasure. Suddenly Harry walks to a rocking horse of the unsafe Victorian kind, its hooves fixed to wooden crescents. Sedately she mounts and starts rocking. Linda squeals and runs to a half-open wardrobe with a cracked mirror on the door, 1920s coats and dresses hung inside above a decade of footwear. The twins join her as she starts rummaging.

"I will show you something special," says the headmistress, leading Hjordis apart from the others, "In one of yaw public addresses you called me *bourgeois.* You wa quite correct. My family did not build this house. It was purchased in 1827 by my great-great-grandfatha, who made money by providing the betta part of London with splendid drains. This loft was the favourite haunt of his son, his son's son, his son's son's son (who was my fatha) and *his* son, who was my brotha."

They approach an eight-legged billiard table with a network of wee railway-tracks spread over the faded green cloth. The headmistress lifts and winds with a key the clockwork of a Hornby locomotive, couples it to a goods train with tiny cows, sheep and milk cans in the open trucks, and releases it. With small pistons churning it pulls out of a perfect tin model of Crewe station in the 1930s, snakes away between bright cardboard bungalows and factories of that period, then climbs an easy gradient through a cardboard pine forest on to a Meccano replica of the Forth railway bridge. This spans a looking glass lying flat, grey with dust, but made oceanic by a fleet of battleships on it beside a Spanish galleon in full sail, three

pleasure yachts, two china swans, a shore of real seashells
where a stuffed seagull stands. The sizes of these, in reverse
scale to the possible, seem a miracle of perspective. The train
slows as it leaves the bridge and comes to halt half in and half
out of a tunnel through the base of a rock with Edinburgh castle
on top, exquisitely modelled in papier mâché. A battalion of
bright little Gordon Highlanders is formed on the esplanade;
knights in mediaeval armour stand on the higher battlements
and turrets.

"This used to be *my* secret kingdom," says the headmistress,
sighing, "My brotha built it. I helped him. He was the only man
in my life. Most little gels worship tha olda brothas, I am told.
I may have worshipped mine too much. He fell at the retreat
from Dunkirk. Perhaps I am the only British woman living who
remembas a British soldia who died at Dunkirk. The British
public wa told the retreat was a sawt of triumph, to stop them
seeing it was an avoidable fiasco caused by addlepated senia
officas telling a dud government that the Germans would neva
try to fight us *seriously*. Do you like this place, Hjordis?"

"I do, Ethel. Yes."

"Then it is all yaws—on condition that you take nothing out.
I will not set foot hia again befoa you leave this school. What
you tried to do to Harriet in the shrubbery was pretty awful,
but if she and Linda play happily hia unda yaw supavision I will
forget that. It is very thrilling to deliberately rob a smalla
person of all dignity, but from now on you will resist that
temptation. You despise my brand of liberalism of cawse, but
did you know that on the island of Sark is a boarding school
even more private and expensive than this one? It is run by two
enthusiastic fascists with an insane, unscientific and highly
fashionable faith in shock treatment: also aversion therapy. In

my school, as you know, I learn everything that happens. If I eva again discovad you had made Harriet or Linda miserable *fo any reason at all* I would expel you. I would also give yaw guardians such a report, and such advice, that they would send you to that school on Sark, wha yaw very soul would be painfully twisted into a vile and unnatural shape to prove a shameful theory. The staff would be careful not to make a vegetable of you, but you would often beg them to do so—in vain. Look hard at my face, Hjordis. Do you think I am joking?"

Hjordis looks. The headmistress is smiling—all her large perfect teeth are visible. Hjordis shudders.

"*Am* I joking, Hjordis?"

Trembling violently, Hjordis shakes her head in urgent denial.

"Good! Now run away and enjoy yawself. I will go below and have a snack sent up from the kitchen. And you had betta wash yaw face, Hjordis. Those who use a lot of thick make-up should avoid strong sensations."

The headmistress skips downstairs, thankful for her dramaschool training and relieved that the school on Sark does not exist—for half a minute she thought it did. Her brother died a month before the Dunkirk retreat of a haemorrhage unconnected with military stress. She never knew or liked him much and still thinks his obsession with miniature worlds very unhealthy—why manipulate toys when there are so many *real* people to play with and rearrange? Several children have enjoyed the loft since the school started, for twice before she has used it to seduce or bribe a troublesome clique. And now her four youngest and most difficult pupils play in a secure place near by with her one bothersome teenager, and are grateful for the privilege.

Linda is so grateful that a fortnight later she brings the headmistress her father's record and says, "Brike it if you want to."

"No!" says the headmistress. "He is a fine singa and these songs delight millions. I will keep it fo a yia, and you will like it even moa when you get it back. It will no longa obsess you because yaw own voice will sound quite different then."

A year later Linda speaks in the main dialect of the British inheriting and investing class. She condescends to her father in an amused ironical drawl which makes him feel his money has been well spent, but it destroys her friendship with Harry. This develops slowly for a few months, giving both of them a new experience of confidence and hope, then for no obvious reason the friendship dies. Both feel sad, lonely and betrayed. Harry cannot be friendly with someone whose voice does not strike her as comically coarse and ill bred.

Twenty-seven years pass before Harry meets Senga.

# CHAPTER 3

# The Proposal

Senga is still a schoolgirl before contraceptive pills are cheap and widely used. In these years many girls under eighteen have no steady boyfriend, those with one are usually virgins, a popular girl can be friendly with several boys who do not necessarily dislike each other or distrust her. Senga at fifteen has a reckless gaiety which many find attractive. Instinctive caution usually inclines her to Tom who is not very amusing or good looking. He is tall but walks as if ashamed of that. He dresses well, but moves and sits as though to stop his clothes getting creased. He is two years older than Senga and her other friends find him dull. They belong to a small group who attend the same school and meet most evenings in a local café. Tom has more pocket money or is more generous than the others. He buys drinks for the group which it would not consume if expenses were shared equally. Senga's other friends think this is Tom's way of buying the pleasure of their company and the pleasure of sometimes walking home with Senga, though she never invites him inside. But Senga is not mercenary. What she likes in Tom is her power over him.

She feels it one evening on the stairway of a tower block owned by the district council. They come by lift to the fourteenth floor and instead of going to the door of her home she lets him persuade her on to the stairs, which can be used to compensate for the difference in their height. It is too late for children to be playing there and far too early for dossers or thieves. She lets him embrace her, and slip his hands under her jacket, then under her sweater. He lacks courage to pluck her blouse out of her jeans waistband and grope under that, but the most intimate sensation in his life is the warm soft feel of her back through thin nylon, also the softness of her neck beneath his lips, for he lacks courage to rise to her mouth. She is amused and intrigued by the changes in his breathing, by the fifth limb growing suddenly out from between his legs and poking at her thigh. Keeking down sideways at his closed eyes and mindless expression she feels slightly jealous of how overwhelmed he is. It seems an ecstatic state. Senga cannot imagine herself overwhelmed by any boy or by anyone not superior to her. The only superior people she knows are a few film stars (mostly women) and her mother, a widow who has endured several emotional adventures without losing her composure, her efficiency, her very observant daughter's friendship.

But Tom's hands, though still fearful of entering her blouse, are pressing her down toward the cold hard steps. She lightly slaps his cheek saying, "Time up, lover boy." He sighs and releases her, staring into her face with such wide-open tragic eyes that she chuckles and quickly kisses his mouth as a consolation prize.

"Do you *like* me, Senga?" he pleads.

"Of course! I'm crazy about boys. But it's time you were hame with your mammy and daddy."

He continues staring, astonished by so much pain flowing from whom a moment ago was his greatest source of delight. He once gloomily told the group that his parents influenced him too much. He now knows he is mocked for that. Senga decides to console him again. Slipping an arm round his arm she leads him briskly along the corridor to the door where he will get a last quick goodnight kiss, but tonight he refuses to be easily dismissed. He says awkwardly, "Senga, I got my prelim exam results today. I've failed my English. I won't be able to see so much of you for a while. I'll have to do more homework."

"Is that right?" she asks coolly.

"I'll see you twice a week," he assures her.

"I'll like that fine . . . if I'm free."

This worries him. He says, "Senga, you won't get fonder of someone else, will you, when I'm not around?"

"How do I know? It depends on who turns up."

"It's only three or four months to the exam, Senga! I can see you all the time after that."

"Aren't you going to the university?"

"Well?"

"Don't you have exams at the university? Won't you have to study when you're there?"

Tom gapes at her. He cannot understand how he has missed seeing this obvious fact.

"I like you, Tom," says Senga, "But I won't spend five nights a week at home because you're trying to be a doctor or something."

"I don't want to be a doctor."

"Well, whatever it is. What's wrong with you?"

An idea has occurred to Tom, an idea so enormous that he is ecstatic with his eyes open. He grasps her hands and says, "Listen, will you marry me?"

"What?"

"Marry me! I love you, haven't you noticed?"

She stares hard at him. He plainly means it. She cries, "Oh Tom, you're wonderful! You're daft but you're wonderful!"

He lets her hands go and says with a touch of anger, "Yes or no?"

"How can we get married?"

"We need a room to ourselves," he says, his mind working fast, "a rented room of course, a rented *furnished* room so first I need a job. And I've got qualifications! I've failed English but I'm fine in chemistry, maths and technical drawing. I'll see the careers teacher tomorrow. It won't be easy at first but at least we'll be together with no damned parents putting pressure on us."

"But what will they say, your mum and dad?" asks Senga, whose mother puts no pressure on her, or none she has noticed.

"It doesn't matter what they say! If you lo . . . lo . . . (ach I hate that word, it sounds stupid) if you love me, Senga, I can do anything! So yes or no?"

She is awestruck by her power over him and a bit awestruck by him too. She says, "Come here a minute." She takes his head between her hands and gives him a kiss she learned a month ago from a boy who walked her home from a dancehall, a boy she won't see again. It is a prolonged yet delicate kiss done with lips slightly apart and pouted forward as if talking French. Tom is pleased by it but more interested in what she will say when it ends. When it ends she has been most influenced by it.

"How *can* I say yes?" she asks in a voice so full of longing and of approaching tears that he suddenly feels very strong and cries, "Don't say yes. Don't say a word yet. Give me a day to work out how to do it. And I'll meet you tomorrow in the usual place at half-past six before the others arrive and I'll tell you how we're going to do it and *then* you'll say yes—I know you will."

She weeps at this, laughing and shaking her head at the same time. He embraces and kisses her, feeling stronger than ever, and for a moment she is almost overwhelmed.

Senga takes a long time preparing to enter her home after Tom leaves. Even so her mother, sitting before the television set, looks at her closely and says, "What's the matter with you?"

"Nothing."

"Who was tonight's lucky lad?"

"Tom."

"Tom again?" says her mother with a smile of friendly amusement. "Are you two getting entangled?"

"It's not as bad as that, Ma," says Senga, and goes to her bedroom.

Tom, elated, strides homeward through lamplit streets but grows depressed when halfway there. He used to like home more than most children like it. His parents were elderly, and treated him as one of themselves, and gave him all he wanted. He remembers happy evenings in the living-room, fitting together, sometimes with his father's help, increasingly expensive and elaborate models of aeroplanes, painting each one afterward with great exactness. But since the age of ten he has discovered wants and emotions which have no room in his parents' house. It, too, is in a building owned by the district council, but called a villa because it holds only four apartments, each with its own piece of a small surrounding garden. Most dwellers in villas feel more important than those in the tower blocks and tenements. Tom's parents feel this. His determined stride does not slacken as he nears the garden gate but (though he despises himself for it) he walks more softly on the tips of his toes. He knows that behind the orange-curtained living-room window his mother and father are quietly pretending to do different things while listening for sounds in the street and hoping every approaching footstep is his. Tom, like Senga, has had a door-key from an early age. He enters quietly and moves quietly toward his bedroom. Passing the living-room he hears his father say, "Come in here, Tom." He sighs and enters.

His father, a sturdy but not large man, sits with rolled-up shirt sleeves at the dining table, carefully copying receipts and invoices into an account book. Tom gets his height (not breadth) from his mother. She sits on the sofa, knitting with quick nervous jerks which stop when her son enters. In this house nobody looks straight at each other. She says, "Where have you been, Tom?"

"Seeing friends."

"That Senga, was it?"

"What if it was?"

"That is no way to speak to your mother, Tom," says his father, still writing.

"She's not good enough for you, Tom," says his mother plaintively, "And she's far too young. People must be laughing at you."

"Well," says Tom turning back to the door, "goodnight."

"How are your studies going?" asks his father.

"Not bad."

"Your English teacher thinks otherwise," says his father, "He was in the shop this morning. He told me you've failed preliminary English."

"Since you know about it why ask me?"

"Tom!" says his mother, shocked, "That is no way to speak to your father."

"Well I'd better go and study, eh? Goodnight," says Tom. He turns to the door.

"I'll bring some cocoa and a biscuit in half an hour, Tom," says his mother cajolingly.

"Thanks a lot, Ma, but don't bother," says Tom quietly but distinctly. "I'm not hungry and not thirsty but thanks very much all the same." He leaves the room with the bitter satisfaction of knowing his mother now feels what the mother of a noisier family would feel if her son seized her offerings of cocoa and biscuit and smashed them to the floor.

Tom's room would be bleak without the model aeroplanes which hang by threads from the ceiling. He shuts the door and sits on his bed, breathing deep because he wants to howl with rage. Instead he pulls a wallet from his pocket, removes a strip of small photographs taken in a coin-operated booth and stares at them. The first shows Senga's naturally smiling face, the rest are more or less comic distortions of it. He gazes at these until he sighs with relief, relaxes and smiles back. A minute later he lays the photos on a table beside school books and walks up and down muttering, "The trouble with you two is you cannae *enjoy* life. You do nothing for fun, nothing for fun at all but watch TV or go to a show. You've no friends and you're so damned snobbish you won't even ask your relations in for a drink in case the neighbours think we're low class or something. Well, I've got friends, I've got a girl who likes me, I like her and . . ."

His door is tapped and opened by his father who peers in grinning and says, "Talking to yourself again?"

Tom looks back without speaking.

Tom's father is more relaxed with his son when his wife is not near. He enters, closes the door, sits on the bed and says, "I know what you're thinking."

"Do you?"

"Of course! You work all day at school and probably hard. No wonder you want some freedom in the evenings. Do I give you enough pocket money?"

"Yes Dad. Thanks."

"I'm not asking for thanks! Like half the folk around here my own dad was unemployed between the wars. I left school at fourteen to work as an errand boy and every penny I earned went to my mother. Son, I *want* ye to have money. I also want you to do more with your life than I've done with mine."

"You havnae done badly, Dad."

"All right, I keep a paper shop and make adequate money by it. But with a decent education I could have been a, a, a lawyer, a doctor, a teacher even! One of the people who give something important to the world and who never lose their jobs when a depression comes. Because the professional classes know how to protect themselves. And that's the chance I'm giving you!"

"I don't want to be these things."

"When you get to university you can choose to be anything you want! Even a shopkeeper if you think that's fun. But it isn't."

Tom suppresses a sigh. They have discussed this many times, usually in the same words, so he is surprised when his father adds, "And don't get entangled, Tom."

"What do you mean?"

His father, pointing to the strip of photos on the table says, "Why are you keen on this wee dolly bird?"

"She likes me," says Tom defiantly.

"Wait till you're at university, Tom. You'll meet girls of your own sort there."

"What sort is that?"

"Dependable?" suggests his father.

"I am NOT dependable!"

"Then you're well suited to Senga!" says his father, grinning, "I hear a lot of things in the shop, you know, and I can tell you—"

"I don't want to know anything you have heard about Senga!"

His father stands up to face him and says just as fiercely, "Then don't get entangled!"

They stare at each other. The father is first to look away. He says, "If she's keen on you she wants you to make something of your life. If you're keen on her you want to provide her with a decent home. Does that make sense?"

"Oh yes it makes sense!" says Tom bitterly. His father frowns at his shoes and mutters, "Your mother is worried sick about you."

Tom says uncomfortably, "Tell her not to worry, Dad."

"Then you'll work at your English?" his father pleads, "You'll start tomorrow night and really grind at it? It's only four months till the Highers but four months at your age can make or break you for life—I only want what's best for you."

"I want what's best for me, too!" says Tom desperately. "I've only done badly in one subject! Won't you trust me to do what *I* think right?" He too is pleading. He has never before pled with his father, who first stares astonished, then smiles thankfully, pats Tom's shoulder and says, "Thanks for setting my mind at rest, son. I'm sorry if I'm hard on you at times—I can't help it. My dad was like that with me. But I'll tell your mother not to worry. I know you won't disappoint us."

He leaves. Tom wants to howl again, but instead thinks very hard about what he must do tomorrow. He sleeps very little that night.

Neither does Senga. She has never before been given the chance of completely changing her life. She cannot help loving Tom for giving her this huge chance, though at the moment he gave it she saw he is not a man she can live with, not even a man who attracts her: hence her hysteria. In bed she fantasizes about what might happen if Tom were more interesting. In sleep the fantasies become delicious nightmares which shock her awake. Tom Dracula's horde of lovely victims pursue her, begging her to join them. Next morning at breakfast her mother asks, "Is it your time of the month again?"

"Nearly, I suppose."

"Take a day off school, I'll write you a note."

"It's not as bad as that, Ma," says Senga crossly. She cannot yet reject the gift of Tom's proposal. Her mother's sensible mirth at the idea would destroy it at once, so she tells nobody but a friend whose credulity prolongs it, one she meets in the girls' lavatory during the morning interval and first swears to secrecy. But the secret is too exciting to be kept. No other girl of her age has had marriage proposed to her in that school, and proposed by a tall, well-dressed older boy who has never before surprised anyone. At lunch break in the playground a crowd forms around Senga, a quarter of it composed of very little girls who ask to see her engagement ring.

"I'm not engaged!" says Senga with angry annoyance which is only half pretence. "He proposed to me, I haven't said yes yet, Dona shouldnae have told anybody, she promised not to."

"But you will say yes?" ask girls who have admired Tom from a distance and a number who have not.

"I havnae made up my mind yet. I might and I might not. I mean, I don't *need* to marry him, I'm not *pregnant,* for God's sake."

This causes silence. Most of the girls find *marriage* an excitingly romantic word and *pregnant* not. Several of the small girls do not know the connections between marriage and pregnancy, and most older ones now suspect she must be pregnant since she mentioned the possibility. Senga's reputation for boldness comes mainly from a speech-style learned from her mother. Tom never uses words boldly, another contrast which makes their affair interesting to the general public.

The school has three playgrounds: one for boys, one for girls, and a playing field with entrances from the other grounds where both sexes can mingle. By the afternoon interval Tom's proposal is general knowledge among all the girls and most of the older boys, also the fact that Tom, after an early morning visit to the school careers adviser, left the building and has not returned. Only two girls and a boy in Senga's group know the café where he has arranged to meet her at six-thirty. They tactfully offer to stay away. She says, "No, don't. I'll need all the support I can get."

She is now frightened by the publicity she has gained. She enjoys being the star of a small group but now an audience of three or four hundred expects her to perform. This audience will be satisfied by an engagement or elopement, otherwise it will boo or applaud Tom's humiliation by a girl who has made his honestly loving proposal public before refusing him. She fears that if Tom comes to the café with a practical marriage plan she will not have the courage to refuse him. She is glad to have her ordinary pals beside her in the café, especially the group humorist who treats the whole business as a joke. Senga smiles at his jokes but is unusually quiet. Her two girl friends watch her closely.

At seven o'clock the joker says, "Mr Romeo seems to have run out on you, Juliet. He's probably at Scotch Corner on the A1, hitching a lift to London."

"I don't think so," says Senga firmly.

At quarter to eight the joker suggests that Tom has been locked in his bedroom by his mother and offers to lead an expedition to free him. Senga laughs until she cries real tears. Tom's arrival and non-arrival are now equally dreadful to her. Between eight-thirty and nine it dawns on them that Tom will not come tonight and at once all of them grow happier, Senga especially. She feels she has wakened from a colourful but embarrassing nightmare which can now be treated as a joke.

" '*Yes or no?*' he demands and I go really tragic, real tears pouring out of me. '*How can I say yes?*' I cry and he rises to the occasion. Tom can easily do the dramatic Hollywood thing when he wants. '*Don't say yes! Leave all to me! I will save us from our evil parents,*' no he didnae really say that but—"

They are all laughing but eventually quieten. At quarter past nine, shortly before the café shuts and when the group are the only customers, Tom enters. He walks taller than usual but looks worn and tired and so, untypically, do his clothes. He says, "Hullo" to the group and to Senga, "Sorry I'm late. Can I have a word with you?"

He goes to an empty table. Senga's limbs tremble. For a moment she feels too weak to stand. The feeling passes. She gets up, gives a little smile and shoulder-shrug to her observant companions and follows Tom to the near by table, relieved by his subdued manner but also saddened. She assumes he too has realized they must not marry.

She sits facing him. He says, "Sorry I'm late, I had trouble with the room. But it's all right, the deposit is paid. It isn't a very nice room but we can shift to another if you find a better one at the same rent. That's your problem, however. At eight tomorrow morning I start as a window cleaner."

"What are you talking about?"

"Tomorrow I start work as a window cleaner," says Tom patiently, "Twelve pounds five shillings a week or seventeen with overtime. It won't be for ever. Five months from now I can start as an apprentice technician with Colville's or Scottish Electricity, or Dexter Delvers, or Shedden Maguire. It will mean, at first, a drop in our weekly wage, but after four years I will be earning a far bigger wage than my dad earns so I'll be able to support you. Until then you'd better think of getting a job, too. I mean, what I earn will feed us and pay the rent, but you may want a few luxuries on top of that like clothes and a fancy cooker. Anyway, you can collect the marriage form from Martha Street registry office as soon as you like."

"I can collect the marriage lines?" says Senga, faintly.

"Senga," says Tom more patiently than ever, "I apologize. I am very sorry that just now I am unromantic, and practical, and very very tired, but I have had an exhausting day. I have visited three government offices: the Youth Employment, the Labour Exchange and the Ministry of Pensions. I had to queue for more than an hour in every one of them and they were no help at all. The only good news I got was from the school's careers teacher who told me about my apprentice technician prospects. But he would not believe I needed to start earning money *now*. I couldn't tell him that I'm going to marry you and you are not the waiting kind. If I'd done that the news would have been all over the school in a couple of hours. He would also have told my mum and dad. So I looked for a job in the newspaper adverts and I got one, didn't I? Didn't I? Yes I did, a job where they don't want to know my National Insurance number or anything else if I start first thing tomorrow at eight. But of course I couldn't wait for my first week's wages before I got us a room. I went to the only man who might lend me money, my uncle the bookie who's never asked to our house. I told him everything and asked for twenty quid. He gave me sixty straight away as a wedding present. He probably did it to annoy Mum and Dad, who'll disown me when they hear about it. And then it was half-past seven and I still had to find the room. Well, I've found one. It's wee, you'll hate the wallpaper, I wish we could have looked for it *together,* Senga, but of course I can't expect you to go to a bother like that. So now you know what I've done for us today and I honestly think I deserve some thanks, even if you are incapable of gratitude."

The possibility of a completely new life now opens its jaws in front of Senga like an enormous trap. The sight makes her shudder. She says, "I don't think I like you, Tom. You're trying to bully me and we're not even married."

"Am I a bully just because I expect you to go to Martha Street to collect our marriage lines?" asks Tom querulously, and she suddenly sees that though he has worked amazingly hard to make the new life possible he too now feels it a trap. She says, "I don't want to marry you, Tom, and you don't want to marry me—not if you've to work as a window cleaner and live in a poky wee room."

This is more truth than Tom can at once swallow. A great rage enters him which would drive a noisy man to shout and a violent man to smash things. Tom gasps, nods and says grimly, "That's what you think, is it?"

She says, "Yes. That's what I think."

Tom puts his elbows on the table and rests brow on his fists.

Then looks up and sees the three at the other table craning their heads to listen. He sees by their faces that they know all about his proposal. He leans across the table and whispers to Senga, who now looks like and is a frightened little girl, "You've made a right fool of me, Senga McGuffie. You must be right proud of yourself."

She stares at him dumbly. He stands and says aloud, "You and I are finished now. Done. Totally and completely and absolutely and . . . and totally finished."

"You said that before," says a voice from the other table.

"Said what before?" demands Tom.

"Totally. You said it twice."

"Shut your face or I will shut your face," says Tom ominously, "And here, Miss McGuffie, is a wee present for you." He takes the strip of photographs from his inner breast pocket intending to rip it and fling the bits at her, but he likes her too much to do that. He hesitates, lays it gently on the table and hurries out. Senga has another fit of hysterics. Her girl friends rush to her, cuddle her, stroke her, wipe her tears with handkerchiefs and make soothing noises.

"He's daft! He's daft! He's utterly daft!" she raves between fits of weeping and laughter, and "I never *wanted* him to ask me to marry him!"

"Then why get upset about it?"

"Because he isnae really daft."


Tom enters his home with no attempts at quietness. "Tom! Come here!" calls his father. Tom enters the familiar living-room where his father stands glaring and pointing and shouting, "Tom, last night you asked me to trust you, asked me to tell your mother you would resume your studies! And you have not even come home for your tea!"

"Good news!" cries Tom, flatly and bitterly. "Senga and I are finished with each other."

After a moment his parents' faces, struck suddenly blank, brighten a little though they are too polite to smile. His father strokes his chin. "Finished, eh?"

His mother says quietly, "Tom, do you know what I'm going to tell you?"

"Yes," says Tom, "you are going to tell me yet again that she isn't good enough for me, by which you mean that her mother works in Woolworth's and my dad owns a paper shop."

"You're completely wrong," says his mother firmly, "I was going to say she's a *flirt.*"

"Why should she not be?" cries Tom passionately, "She's full of life, she wants to enjoy it, a lot of men are keen on her, why shouldn't she flirt? She was the best thing that ever happened to me, and she liked me a lot better than the others."

"Then why have you finished with her?" asks his father.

"Because she's refused to marry me!" screams Tom through clenched teeth. His parents look to each other for support and see nothing in each other's faces but bewilderment. Tom masters his emotions and speaks more calmly: "Another thing, I'm starting work in May as an apprentice technician, probably with Colville's. I've spoken to them at school about it and the careers teacher says it will be the best thing for me. So the university notion is out, done with, totally scrubbed and I must say it's a relief."

His father stares at him in such a stricken way that Tom in tenderness and pity goes to the smaller man and places a fatherly hand on his shoulder saying, "Ach, don't worry, Dad! My job will be as good as anything folk are taught to do in university and just as well paid. And it will be work I can do with no bother, so there's no use worrying about it. Life's too short. I'm also very hungry just now." He goes to the kitchen door, pauses and asks them wistfully, "I'm going to make some sandwiches. Would anyone else like one? And a cup of cocoa maybe?"

But his father stares at his shoes, his mother at the wool on her lap, as if searching for something in these. He sighs and leaves them.

After a while his father mutters, "I've got to speak to him but I don't know what to say."

His mother, who is trying to knit, flings the needles down and cries, "How dare that Senga refuse our Tom! The CHEEK of her! The CHEEK! The CHEEK!"

During Tom's last months at school he finds his proposal to Senga has done him good. Girls of his own age now look at him with interest. He stops wearing his suits as if afraid of creasing them, stops feeling ashamed of his height and starts finding it an advantage. He and Senga never become close friends again though he never quite manages to stop loving her. Even after they have left school he keeps informed of her doings. Five years later he learns that Senga is engaged to a cranedriver in a shipyard. Tom is now an expert in precision grinding. His abilities are useful to several companies. He invites her to a meal in a good restaurant, expecting her to look older and more working-class than he remembers her, but he can see no difference, she is as attractive as ever, so he proposes again. He explains that he wants to start a family because a family is the only thing he lacks. His bullying nature is now obvious. Senga finds this second proposal purely comic and cannot hide the fact. She marries the cranedriver, a man with many friends who talks a lot about politics.

Two months later Tom marries a woman who looks like Senga but was bred in a wealthier home and wants to be kept in another one.

# CHAPTER 4

# The Man Who Knew about Electricity

Donalda is usually met through other people. Today this is an old man who trots up and down a busy pavement, showing a light bulb to passers-by and asking them if they know about electricity. Most pretend not to see or hear him. A few pause for a second with pained smiles then shake their heads and hurry on. The old man is not discouraged. He is a peculiar little man with the bent back and knobbly joints of somebody who was once big. He wears black canvas gym shoes, a shirt printed with orange and purple silhouettes of palm trees, a fine tweed suit so large that the trouserlegs are turned up three inches at the ankles, the sleeves turned back as much at the wrists. Apart from these folds his clothes are neatly pressed and very clean. Maybe people are repelled by his voice. He has the accent of a city in north-east England and the pavement is in a city of the Scottish west.

At last the old man says, "Dost thee knoo aboot electricity, John?" to a boy with a new leather briefcase full of books and with the badge of a new university on his blazer pocket. The boy knows a lot about electricity. He asks the old man to repeat his question and answers, "Yes."

"Good, John! Good!" says the old man approvingly, "So thee can change a light boolb?"

As if offering a gift he holds up the bulb in its rectangular cardboard wrapper, new from the shop. The student sees the old man's hand has a thick bandage round it secured by a safety pin over the palm, but the fingers sticking out look sufficiently flexible.

"Anybody can change a light bulb," says the student.

"Good, John! Then thee'll step roond the cooarner and change me boolb? I'll pay thee, John! Nowt for nowt, I know the rooal, I've got a bob or two. Thee can spare a minute shooaly?"

The student ponders. He is going to the railway station an hour earlier than usual because a lecture has been unexpectedly cancelled. Trains which can take him home leave every half hour. Also, his parents have taught him to tell the truth and give help when folk ask for it. But he lives where everyone, even shopkeepers, are equally prosperous, or pretend to be, so by telling the truth and helping people he has made good friends without being inconvenienced. He is sure his parents would think it unwise to help beggars of the old man's sort, though the old man is not, apparently, begging. The old man's face staring hopefully up is brown and deeply lined by rough experiences, but the expression is the opposite of sinister.

"Change the bulb yourself," suggests the student.

"Nooah, John, I knoo nothing aboot electricity. Shooaly thee can spare me a minute?"

The student admits he can and is led round a corner into a street between soot-blackened stone warehouses.

The old man's home is more than a minute's walk away though the student walks so fast that the old man only manages to keep a fraction ahead of him with quick wee skipping steps that are more like a dance than a walk. They turn a second corner into a street which seems part of a city bombed by powerful enemies. The ground on each side is mostly torn earth, weeds, rubble and rags. Some remaining tenements have windows broken, or boarded up, or blind with dirt. The student did not know there was such a street near his university. Behind the warehouse roofs he sees the summit of a glass and concrete tower. A window on the second floor from the top has a white rectangle in it, a poster facing inward which he fixed there a week ago. It advertises a students' Christian society he belongs to and he tries to recall what he saw through the window when putting the poster up. He remembers a wide view of various buildings which did not interest him, he had preferred to look at the surrounding hills.

"Here it is, John," says the old man leading him into a tenement close, and he sees one upper window is unbroken and raised a little. Through the opening a hand is using a teapot to water marigolds in a window box, so the building is not wholly derelict, and when the old man leads him downstairs to the basement he sees it is not wholly abandoned by the local government. A gas lamp glows and hisses in a dirty passage with no other light. The student is fascinated. Before now he thought gas light belonged to the nineteenth century when Robert Louis Stevenson wrote about it. He sees too a dingy door with five or six keyholes. The old man stealthily turns a single Yale key in a hole he stoops to reach. Before pressing the door open he places a finger to his lips and whispers, "Be very quiet, John! Me landlady is a woman and gets queeah ideas."

The door opens on what seems a dusty cupboard. The old man steps in and with another key opens a door in the far wall. The student, amused and curious, goes through.

He enters a room with a window on to a sunken area between the tenement and street. A thick blind covers the window and at first the dark brown light through it lets the student see nothing but egg-boxes, the sort that hold half a dozen each. Piles of them cover a sideboard, add height to a wardrobe, form a pyramid on the corner of a table in the middle of the floor. Growing used to the poor light the student notices he stands under a web of wires radiating from a black mass in the centre of the ceiling. Wires go to a television set among the boxes on the sideboard, to an electric radiator on the floor, to a radio on the chair beside a bed, to something under a mound of coats on the bed which must be an electric blanket, to an electric hot-plate and an electric kettle on the table. After the old man has cautiously and quietly closed the doors behind them the student says, "Have you no wall-socket?"

"Of coorse, John, of coorse! Boot it gives off sparks and shocks and flames and things. Doan't thee worry, I'm no fooal."

"That light fixture is overloaded—a fire hazard. Your landlady could be prosecuted for it."

"It would only oopset her, John. Women are like that."

The student decides to put in the bulb and leave quickly. He lays down his briefcase, climbs onto the tabletop and peers at the cluster of adaptor sockets hitched to the light wire. A low-wattage bulb sticks sideways from it. He says, "I'll see

better if you raise the blind." "Oo noo, John! Lots of valuable
stoof in heeah, John, lots of bad people aboot. They'd brack in
and steal me stoof if they could see in heeah!"

"Is the light switch on or off?"

"Not working, is it, John?"

The student points to the wireless set and says, "Switch it
on."

The old man does. A loud blast of rock music happens. The
old man jigs about to it. The student points to the light switch
beside the door and yells, "NOW SWITCH THAT OFF."

The old man hurries to do it. The music dies. The student
unscrews the spent bulb saying, "Give me the new one." He
hands down the old one, tears the cardboard wrap from the
new, clicks the new into the socket. The old man presses down
the light switch and several things happen quickly. The light
and music go on very bright and loud then die out at once. A
door bangs then the door of their room is slammed open by
someone dumpy, furious and female who shouts, "What the
hell is going on here?"

Near by a baby has started screaming.

"I'm changing a light bulb," says the student calmly. His
stance on the table gives him a feeling of power. The woman
is smaller than her anger at first makes her seem. Her hips and
breasts are matronly but her face childish, thin and desperate.
She wears a nightgown, dressing-gown and slippers, every lock
of her hair is twisted into a tight helmet of pink plastic rollers.
She turns to the old man shouting, "I telt ye! I warned ye not
to bring folk here! Remember what happened last time! I think
you're trying to kill me!"

In an embarrassed way the old man grins, shaking the light
bulb beside his head as if listening to it. She turns back to the

student saying, "Clear out. Clear out of here this instant and mend the bloody lights first. You've fused everything in this place."

"Relax," suggests the student.

"How *can* I relax? I've a yelling wean next door that cannae sleep with the light off. Listen to it!"

"Where's your fuse-box?"

"Behind the front door."

"Any spare wire in it?"

"Aye. Mibby. I mean, I think so."

"Then attend to your kid and I'll attend to the fuses."

She heaves a huge sigh and hurries out.

"Good, John! Good!" whispers the old man, smiling and nodding encouragingly. The student says sternly, "Before I get down from here tell me which you want: light, heat or entertainment. You can't have all three till your wall-socket is fixed."

The old man looks astonished. After a while he mutters miserably, "Wouldna mind soom light, John."

The student unplugs the wires from the adaptors, the adaptors from the light socket, clicks the light bulb into the socket, jumps to the floor and lifts his briefcase.

Though the doors are now open into the cupboard-like lobby it is very dark. Working mostly by touch the student opens the fuse-box, discovers and pulls down the main switch, removes the fuses, also a small card wrapped round with wire. Laying them on the briefcase he carries it like a tray into the brightest room. This belongs to the woman. The window here is hidden by thin print curtains pinned together in the middle. There is an old wooden sink with one brass water tap below the window, a rusty heavy iron gas cooker beside it, an iron fire range, a recess holding a double bed beside the door, a rope slanting up from a wall-hook to the wheels of a pulley on the ceiling, wheels with spars between them on which hang some stained triangles of yellowish brown linen. There is a faint smell of lavatory. The woman sits near a table pushing backward and forward a carrycot pram with a baby in it. To the student this baby looks indecently small, red and wrinkled. Its wails have sunk to a fretful mewing which the woman soothes by saying softly, "Cool it, Theresa, you're fine. Shut up. Pipe down. Pull yourself together."

The student lays his briefcase on the table and asks, "Have you a screwdriver?"

"I had but I lost it."

"Have you a nailfile?"

"Naw."

"Have you a tea-knife?"

"There's knives in that drawer and hurry up. This one needs her sleep."

There is a drawer at the end of the table. The student opens it and rummages through a mess of cutlery, saying, "Why can't the kid sleep with the light off?"

"Nobody likes the dark."

"Open the curtains, there's sunlight outside."

"This is a basement and I've had trouble enough with nosy parkers. Whenever anyone looks in here some rotten thing happens."

"Like what, for instance? . . . I've found your screwdriver, by the way."

He sits on the table edge and deftly loosens screws on the fuses. After a moment he says again, "Like what, for instance?"

"Well," says the woman, almost unwillingly, "When the old boy in there burnt his hand the SS came to see him and . . ."

"SS?" says the student, puzzled.

"Social Security. Anyway they looked in here too and they cut my allowance right out. Just like that."

"Why?"

"Nothing to do with you," says the woman in a very low voice. He works away quietly. He notices that in the lengthening intervals between the baby's cries she has begun glancing at him furtively. At last she says, "Where are you from?"

"Helensburgh."

"One of the snobs, eh?"

"Not really."

"A student?"

"First-year physics. Not all of us are practical men with our hands. But I think . . . this is just about . . . right."

He is on the way to the lobby with the fuses but stops and looks back at the briefcase.

"Ach leave it!" she says impatiently, "I'll no' steal your books."

He wishes she had not read his mind but nods and enters the lobby.

The lights go on and the baby closes its eyes and mouth. The student returns for the case saying, "That will hold for a week or two but not much longer. Your wiring is no use at all, a real fire hazard. Get it seen to."

"You really know about electricity!" she cries.

"A bit."

"Could you sort my iron? It conked out three weeks ago and I really need it for drying the wean's nappies. I mean, she's got a rash."

He glances at his wristwatch and is astonished to see that less than fifteen minutes have passed since he met the old man. He shrugs and nods. She says, "You're a pal," and lays the iron on

the table. He pulls a chair up to it, sits down and begins unscrewing the plug. She goes to a mirror and starts removing her
curlers. She says, "Sorry I yelled at ye in there."

"It didn't worry me."

"You see I've had trouble with that auld bastard—excuse the
language."

"I've heard worse."

"I suppose you think I'm . . . I suppose you think I'm a bad
lot."

"No. Why?"

"Living here. Like this."

He glances around. The room strikes him as messier than it
need be. The bed is unmade. Dirty plates, crumpled clothes lie
on and partly under a dusty sideboard and two sagging arm-
chairs. He says, "Maybe you can't help it."

"I can't. That's right." She lays down the last of her curlers,
shakes her head and wanders nervously across the room. She
shuts the door to the lobby saying, "Do you believe in God?"

"Of course."

"So do I but he hasnae helped much."

The student senses something queer in her manner but thinks
the best way to handle queerness is not to attend to it. There
is nothing wrong with the plug so he starts unscrewing the iron.
She says, "Life can be hell sometimes, can't it?"

"We have our ups and downs."

She stands so near that her dressing-gown touches his cheek.
He bends over the work, sure she is going to ask for money and
determined to refuse it. She says in a small quick voice, "Have
you the time for a short time?"

He is relieved by this simple question, glances at his wristwatch and says, "Ten to four."

She moves away and sits in an armchair. He looks at her. She sucks her underlip like a small girl trying not to weep. Her mop of curly black hair reminds him of a girl he knew at school. She hugs her body tightly below her maternal breasts. This makes them more prominent. For the first time his voice has an uncertain note. He asks, "Did you . . . I mean, you *did* ask me for the time?"

"Right!" she says in a hard voice with a hard little smile and nod. He cannot stop looking at her breasts. She asks bitterly, "Is something wrong with me?"

"No but . . . but I need a . . . thing with a thin end. Like a needle."

She stands and plucks thoughtfully at her lower lip. "Will a kirby do?"

"Eh?"

"A hairgrip." She takes one from the pocket of her gown, holds it out and walks toward him, her mouth and eyes wide open in a vacant frightened way. He stands to face her, reaching out his hand but not to take the grip. He does not exactly know what he wants to take for he is more sexually stupefied than sexually excited. A voice in his brain is asking, "What should I do first? What should I do first?"

At that moment the door of the room bangs open and a huge man steps in. He stands then announces in a hoarse Irish voice, "I'm interruptin' yous."

"No you're not," says the student, taking the kirby grip.

"He's mending my iron," says the woman disgustedly, "And you've wakened the wean."

She pulls the pram to the armchair, sits down and pushes it back and forward.

"I say I'm interruptin' yous!" declares the Irishman. He shuts the door behind him, goes to the table and sits slowly down in a chair facing the student. The lavatory smell increases.

"Don't mind me, young fella!" he says, "Carry on with what you were doin'."

The student sits. His heart still beats fast from recent surprises but he sees the Irishman is not dangerous. The hugeness is all in his height. His face and hands are so thin and white that his weight seems mainly a matter of clothes. The four garments are almost buttonless and the student sees a plastic raincoat, black overcoat, corduroy jacket, tweed waistcoat, knitted cardigan and striped pyjama jacket. There are probably some shirts and vests under these for his chest looks far too broad for his very long narrow neck, which has a clean silk scarf wound round it. Nothing else he wears is clean, not even the woollen balaclava helmet with a flat cap on top, the rimless spectacles which give his gaunt face a clerical look. Despite these clothes he often shivers as if terribly cold. He removes the spectacles and wipes them on the end of the scarf muttering, "Don't mind me, don't mind me."

"I don't mind you," says the student, busy with the iron, "The old boy next door got me in to change a light bulb then she asked me to sort this."

"He knows about electricity," says the woman offhandedly.

"Yes, there's big futures in electricity," says the Irishman. He takes a flat-sided bottle from the overcoat pocket, is about to swig from it but pauses, to say in an apologetic note, "You'll not be offended if I offer you none? This stuff is right for the likes of me, in fact it's indispensable. But it wouldn't do for a young fella who still had his health . . . Make the man a cup of tea, Dona!" he shouts at the woman, who obediently stands and fills a kettle at the sink.

The student now wants to leave as soon as possible. He

concentrates on mending the connection while the Irishman drinks, coughs then says, "I trust I amn't upsettin' you? I'm a disgustin' spectacle, that's true. Well, I'll leave in a minute."

"You don't disgust me," says the student easily.

"Still, judgin' by your clothes you don't often sit in a room with a coupla cases like us."

"It might interest you to know," says the student after a pause, "that my grandfather was a riveter with Harland and Wolff."

"Indeed! So you feel a degree of solidarity with the workin' classes?"

The student thinks about this. People who speak for the working classes are supposed to be socialists and the student distrusts left-wing organizations. But his father once told him that most of the British working classes vote Conservative. At last he says, "I think I can say that."

"Good for you!" says the Irishman, raising a triumphant forefinger, "But you see, we are NOT workin' class, we are . . . how can I put it . . . casualty class."

"There's no such thing," says the student crisply.

"No?" says the Irishman, holding his bottle to the light. It is nearly empty. With a sigh he puts it down and says, "This used to be a workin' classes district. Casualties lived here too, but the majority were decent labourers and tradesmen. Not people I always see eye to eye with, though the best of them were Irish like meself. One day the area is scheduled for redevelopment, somethin' to do with a ring road or a college, I don't rightly recall which. So the landlords stop repairing the properties and the workin' classes shift to expensive homes in posh new housin' schemes like Easterhouse, Castlemilk, Drumchapel. And now the entire area—the part not knocked down— is full of the unemployed and elderly, and moral casualties like me, and sentimental casualties like her." He points at the woman beside the cooker who stands holding the handle of the kettle, waiting for it to boil.

"Leave me out of this!" she tells him.

"It's her own fault, of course. Before she had the child she was earnin' seven pounds ten a week in a Bridgeton lemonade factory."

"But can she not—" begins the student. The Irishman interrupts.

"Exactly! Of course! I tell her that myself. 'If you loved Theresa,' I say, 'Give her to the social workers. Have her adopted. Get rid of her and do both of yous a favour.' She refuses to listen. She is one mass of utterly disreputable primitive instincts."

"For Christ's sake, hold your bloody tongue!" shouts the woman, and adds for the student's benefit, "Excuse the language."

"We'd be lonely people if it wasn't for my tongue, Dona," says the Irishman quietly. The student, resting an elbow on the table and chin in the palm of a hand, finds the conversation interesting. He says, "What sort of casualty is the old boy next door?"

"Temporary. He is a trusted nightwatchman of many years standin' and will be back on the job when the hand heals. Of course he's nearly seventy and won't last for ever. Besides, this buildin's condemned, they'll knock it down soon and we'll all be hard put to it findin' a place to stay. Why, I hear that even quite *prosperous* people have trouble gettin' new houses."

"Well, my parents aren't exactly prosperous, but when we moved to a new house last year we had to pay *twice* what it would have cost ten years ago."

"Exactly!" says the Irishman with a pleased air, "So you will understand that things are *equally* difficult for the like of us. Strange isn't it, the vast improvements we've seen in recent years, new towns, more cars, more roadways, bigger buildins. Yet all the time the casualty class grows bigger, too. Is there a connection, do you think?"

"Couldn't say."

The woman puts the mugs of milky sweetened tea on the table saying, "Sorry there's no biscuits."

"You're a lovely girl, Dona," says the Irishman. The woman goes to the pram and bends over it.

"Just look at the way she moves! Isn't she a lovely girl?"

"She's not bad," says the student, glancing and sipping the tea.

"Do you hear that, Dona?" cries the Irishman, "The gentleman thinks you're *not bad.* When a laconic fellow like him says that about a woman it's better than a whole cargo of compliments from the like of me."

The woman turns and shouts, "You're a pimp! You're a pimp!"

"Well if I am," he says strongly, "I'm the worst paid pimp in Glasgow."

They glare at each other. The student, afraid to hear more, devotes himself to the iron. The woman sits down in the armchair with arms folded and legs crossed. The Irishman again examines his bottle, sighs and sips tea instead.

A moment later he addresses the student on a confiding note. "She doesn't really think I'm that. I'm not a pimp. Pimpin' is a middle-class occupation. A pimp is a sort of employer and I haven't the dynamism, the qualities of get-up-and-go to employ a whole woman like Dona. My feelin' is mainly fatherly, and she thinks she's safer with a man around, an undemandin' fella who doesn't lose his temper and can be trusted with the baby when she needs out for a breath of air. I am alcoholic, you see, but am not, and have never been, a drunkard. Liver, lights, stomach, genitals, circulation, they're crumblin', slow and sure. But the brain is in control. The brain will stay in one piece for another year at the least . . . What am I talkin' about?"

"Why you live with her."

"We need company, you see, and I'm the best she can find in the circumstances. But she deserves better and despite what she called me a moment ago there is no financial bond between us, none at all. And would you believe it, her Social Security money was cut off a week ago because someone decided she was *cohabitin'* with me. Whatever that means."

The student has almost put the iron together again. He feels the Irishman stare at him as if expecting a response. He says crisply, "Bad luck."

"That's it in a nutshell!" cries the Irishman enthusiastically, "Bad luck! That is what a Frenchman would call *le mot juste.* Education has certainly given you a way with words young fella."

The student smiles slightly. He is too wise to be upset by the mockery of unimportant people. The Irishman says, "I am in danger of borin' you. Tell me this, have you a girlfriend?"

"Yes."

"Goin' steady?"

"Nearly a year."

"But you live with your parents?"

"Yes."

"Who does the girl live with?"

"Let's not talk about her, eh?"

"You are a gentleman sir, and I apologize for my intrusion. It's just I have a theory, you see, that a lotta nonsense is talked nowadays about what they call permissiveness. If you read the papers, sir, you'd think those in their teens are indulgin' in all sorts of startlin' practices. Now I believe that most young people are just as respectable, and cautious, and unadventurous, and miserable as we were in my own young day. Here a minute!" He leans toward the student and beckons. The student cocks an ear toward him. He murmurs into it, "Dona there— hardly seventeen—been to bed with a young fella nearly twice in her life and *that* was almost a year ago. *And* little good it did her. So when I came in and saw the pair of you—well, I misunderstood the position entirely and for a moment I felt . . . hopeful, you might say. I like her. I like her. And she needs a bit of healthy appreciation from someone in her own age group. She's a fine strong girl you see. She needs . . ." His voice has grown louder.

"Money!" shouts the woman, "Money for food and rent!"

"Oh Dona, you need an awful lot more than that!" says the Irishman reproachfully. "Don't be put off by her rough tongue, sir. That is a temporary consequence of superficial economic tensions—she's afraid of bein' chucked out into the street. Solve these tensions and you'll find her the most docile creature imaginable. *You'll be able,*" he whispers, *"To do anything you like with her."*

"Well," says the student rising to his feet, "I think I've fixed it. Where's your wall-socket?" he asks the woman. She points to one beside the fire-range.

He carries the iron to it but pauses before plugging in. "Does this give off shocks and sparks and flames and things?" he asks with a slight smile. She shakes her head.

"Just testing," he says, and plugs it in, and stands for a while without looking at her.

"How much do you need?" he asks suddenly.

"Six pounds," she says in a low voice, not looking at him.

"That's not a lot," says the student, "Can the old boy next door not help? I mean, if you lose this place so will he."

"He's already paid me three weeks in advance. And I still need six pounds."

"Not a bad owld fella," mutters the Irishman, and drinks the last of his bottle.

"Well," says the student, bringing out his wallet, removing two pounds, showing them and laying them on the mantelpiece, "at the moment this is all I can spare. Sorry."

"Thanks," says the woman stonily, "I'll get the rest somehow."

"Good," says the student. He touches the iron lightly, says, "It's working," switches it off and unplugs it. The woman sighs and says, "Thanks, mister."

Then she smiles as if putting worry behind her and suddenly she looks like any young woman thanking a friend for a bit of help. The student is glad things are ending well. He picks up his case.

"You're surely not leavin'?" cries the Irishman, shivering.

"Goodbye," says the student to the woman.

"But you'll be back? It's a lonely life for her here by herself all day—she'll be glad to see you anytime—"

"Will you shut up?" says the student. The Irishman does.

"Cheerio. You've been a pal," says the woman in an ordinary friendly way, and looking at her now without embarrassment the student is startled by her likeness to the schoolgirl he once knew, and by how attractive she is. He hesitates, nods and steps into the lobby.

And is confronted by the old man smiling and nodding and whispering, "Good, John, you did it! Catch this, John! Catch this!" He thrusts two tenpenny pieces toward the student's face.

"What's that for?" asks the student staring.

"Thee mooney, John! Thee changed me boolb. Nowt for nowt, that's the rooal, ye ken!"

The old man drops the coins into the student's blazer pocket and skips back into his room, slamming the door. The student makes to open it but hears the lock snibbed. He starts knocking and shouting, "Open up! This won't do! It's silly! I don't need . . ." He hesitates, then speaks in a voice which is even louder. "Listen, I'll come back tomorrow and look at your wall-socket! In the afternoon, say about two-thirty! Don't forget, two-thirty I'll be here. Remember that." He looks back to make sure the kitchen door is still open. He opens the front door, stares amazed at the gas lamp (it seems years since he last saw it) then runs upstairs. He also runs along the streets to the station, not because he is late for a train (the whole episode took less than forty minutes) but to use some of the great power he feels inside him. He also feels the world is a more exciting place than he realized, and will allow him delicious experiences he secretly dreams of but had never expected to make realities.

In the kitchen the woman and the Irishman, who have heard him of course, sit for a long time as still as if they had heard nothing. The woman is Donalda Ingles twenty-two years before she meets June.

# CHAPTER 5

# Mr Lang and Ms Tain

J une meets Tom Lang when she is in her middle twenties
and he can afford entourages. Outside the film industry
most modern bosses distrust entourages. They like to see
their underlings one at a time, or round a table where they
sit at the top holding agendas to control proceedings; but
Tom enjoys having people near by who depend on his
wishes and must not intrude on him. With heels on desktop,
heavy muscular body tilted back in a solidly crafted swivel
chair, he talks loudly over the phone in the presence of one
actual and one potential employee.

"We dispatched exactly what you asked for, Mr Cockport,"
he says, "Our correspondence shows it. The only item missing
is your original order form which I will have to hand when the
last of our filing cabinets arrive. But why not consult your own

records? You'll see the problem is not mine but yours. Good day." He puts the phone down, yawns, stretches and asks "Anything else, Ted?"

"The storage racks in the loading bay," says his under-manager, "The head joiner wants overtime."

"The hell he does! Send him in." The under-manager leaves. Tom tells a young woman standing near the door, "Not long now, Miss er . . ." The head joiner enters and Tom puts his feet on the floor. The two men talk truculently. Tom is aggressive, the joiner obstinate. A verbal bargain is struck and the joiner leaves. Tom phones his under-manager and says, "I've sorted out the joiner, Ted. He'll finish the job at the agreed price and he'll finish it this week. He thinks that next week he'll be putting up shelves in the basement, but find another firm for that job will you? We can't trust this lot." Tom puts the receiver down and says, "I've been a bad lad leaving you standing here all this time though I must say you stand well, Miss er . . . ?"

"Tain," says the woman.

"June Tain," agrees Tom, nodding at a letter on his desk. "The agency has told me all about you. You've had experience as a receptionist, I see, but in a receptionist experience counts a lot less than appearance so let's have a look at you."

He looks at her.

Ms Tain has subdued her appearance in a charcoal grey suit and sweater, low-heeled shoes, no jewellery. Her dark brown copious hair is fixed in a bun on the nape of her neck. She wears just enough cosmetic to make her pale skin look ordinary. She cannot subdue her finely shaped figure and face which strike some people as romantically Spanish, some as classically Greek. Her expression is gloomy and patient.

"You look well and you stand well," says Tom cheerily. "How do you walk?"

She stares at him, not understanding.

"*Walk* for me, June!" he explains. After a moment she strolls across to the window and looks out at a street with the high wall and cranes of a dockyard on the other side.

"Top marks for walking," says Tom cheerfully. "Now it says here you've done some book-keeping."

"Not much and only for my last employer," says Ms Tain, turning round and looking worried. "He was a dentist."

"Well that might be useful to us. You see receptionists always have time on their hands," says Tom and summons in a neat middle-aged woman in black.

"Tell me about Marian, Mrs Campbell. Why does she always seem to be polishing her nails? Is she lazy?"

Mrs Campbell says that her assistant book-keeper is not lazy but has only enough work to occupy her two or three hours a day. The work is a simple record of invoices and receipts, nothing needing concentration. A receptionist in a business like their's should easily manage it between dealing with phone calls and the occasional visitor. Ms Tain agrees to try.

"Wonderful!" says Tom. "I need coffee. This is *not* the coffee break but coffees all around, Mrs Campbell. How do you take yours, June?"

Ms Tain takes hers black with one spoonful of sugar and asks if she can sit down.

"You were free to sit where you liked the moment you came through that door," says Tom magnanimously.

Mrs Campbell enters a small adjacent kitchen and Ms Tain, looking gloomier, sits on a low easy chair beside a low table. Tom lights a cigarette and says, "Cheer up, June, I've only one more hurdle to put you across and that's a matter of overtime. We pay twice the usual rate for it, there isn't a lot of it but it's erratic."

After a moment Ms Tain says, "If you could give me a day's notice . . ."

"Sometimes. Usually not."

"If I had *some* warning . . ."

"Can't guarantee it. How do you like the decor?" He flaps his hand toward the walls. Each is occupied by a green dragon on a scarlet ground or scarlet dragon on a green ground. Doorways to the kitchen and a cloakroom-washroom have curtains of coloured glass beads. The lights are disguised as Chinese lanterns.

A corner of Ms Tain's mouth twists in a small smile. She says, "Very colourful."

Tom grins and says, "You think it's ghastly. Admit it."

She smiles symmetrically and admits it.

"It's like me!" says Tom happily. "Rich-looking, loud, vulgar and you can't ignore it, right?"

Ms Tain smiles and agrees.

"I always wanted an office like this," says Tom. "You should have seen our last premises. A dirty little shop with two back rooms and a basement you couldnae swing a cat in. Now, suddenly, boom, we've arrived, we're expanding, even big firms buy equipment through me. Know how that happened?"

"A Scottish Industries Development Grant?" suggests Ms Tain. For a moment Tom is taken aback.

"Well, yes, we got *help* from them," he admits, "but the real reason is that firms can order from me at short notice and I deliver on the dot. They can phone me at twenty-five past five on Friday, ask for thirty gross two-point-two tungtanium needle bits and the consignment will be on their doorstep on Monday morning." He looks at an ebony statuette beside his telephone. It represents an ancient man with flowing robes, very long whiskers and a sly grin which from some angles makes him look like a buffoon. Tom places an affectionate hand on the bald bulbous head saying, "This old chap is the Chinese god of wealth. I sometimes burn a joss stick in front of him."

"Mr Lang, it will be difficult for me to work overtime without *some* notice," says Ms Tain in a distressed voice.

"You got a kid?" asks Tom, looking at her hard.

"You have nothing at all to do with my private life!" she tells him sharply. He grins approvingly and says, "Quite right! Quite right! But ten minutes' warning is all I can promise you—enough time to make a few phone calls."

Ms Tain stares at the floor, sighs and murmurs, "All right."

Mrs Campbell returns with coffee.

"Meet June Tain, our new receptionist," says Tom, receiving a mug from her.

"Glad you're joining us," says Mrs Campbell, setting the two other mugs on a low table by Ms Tain, who thanks her. Mrs Campbell also sits on a low chair facing the desk.

"So when can you start?" asks Tom.

"Tomorrow?"

"That's the spirit!" says Tom, and sips coffee, and leans comfortably back. "Better make it Monday though. Mrs Campbell, put the bullet into Marian for Monday will you? I personally will see to Alice. Alice, our leetle receptionist. It wasnae her refusal to do overtime that decided me to get rid of her. I can forgive a girl a lot if she's decorative. But Alice is *fat*. I came in yesterday, looked at her and said to myself, 'No! No, that is not the image I want to greet the customers of *Lang Precision Limited.*' "

Suddenly Mrs Campbell and Ms Tain start speaking at the same time. Both stop, glance at each other. Ms Tain nods, meaning *you first.* Mrs Campbell says, "Mr Lang, just now Marian takes over from the receptionist during lunch and coffee

breaks. Who will take over from Miss Tain? There's only me
or the typist."

"Don't worry about it," says Ms Tain, quickly swallowing
some coffee then standing up. "I'm not taking this job."

Both women look at Tom who frowns slightly, pondering a
response consistent with dignity. At last he asks on a note of
vague curiosity, "Why?"

Ms Tain, giving him a sudden lovely smile, says "Personal
reasons," and walks out of the room.

A moment later he strides after her down the corridor calling, "June! Wait a minute June!" She keeps walking. He says,
"Please, Miss Tain! Please stop and hear me a moment!"

She keeps walking. He walks beside her and says quietly,
"Listen! I need a receptionist and you need a job."

"That's no reason why I should eat dirt!"

He sighs, slips in front of her and blocks the way, hands
clasped as if in prayer. He says, "Please, Miss Tain! I want to
explain something. All I ask is five more minutes of your time—
they won't be wasted—I can promise that." He ushers her back
along the corridor knowing she is partly moved by curiosity and
partly by the coercion of his bulk.

In the office Mrs Campbell is gathering the mugs on to a tray.

"Leave them, don't wash them, Mrs Campbell!" says Tom.
"Just check our orders from Newcastle. We should have heard
from Newcastle by now." He sits upright, not sprawling behind
his desk. Mrs Campbell leaves, exchanging with June a perfectly neutral glance which means *that man!* It would be a smile
if he were not watching them closely. He says, "Sit down,
June."

"We're not on first-name terms, Mr Lang," she reminds him,
not sitting. He nods and says, "You think I'm a bastard."

"You invited me to your office," she says in a thoughtful

voice, "you kept me watching you for minutes while you acted the great big boss, then you made me parade like a mannequin. You were going to sack another woman because you thought you'd talked me into doing two jobs instead of the one you advertised, then you leaned back chuckling and gloating and expecting to be admired!" She looks at him with an astonishment she seems keen for him to share. He nods seriously and says, "I recognize the picture, Miss Tain. Yes. A dirty pressurizing bastard. That's how I get the world to work for me. All bosses are like me, you see, though some of them fool folk into thinking otherwise. I think foolery's a waste of time—that's my trouble."

"All bosses are not like you."

"No? Perhaps you're right. Of course you're right. I read in the papers that the Duke of Westminister is the most charming man in Britain, besides owning most of it. All his servants love him, it seems. The charm was probably inherited along with the servants, *and* his first hundred million, *and* central London, *and* half of Scotland. Or is it Wales? I can't remember. I know this though, I'm a small business man struggling to get bigger. If I acted like the Duke of Westminister I'd be done for. Folk would laugh at me. So I act like a businessman in an American movie: not the golden-hearted kind nobody believes in, but the pressurizing bastards everybody believes in."

"I don't like working for bastards. May I leave?"

"Wait a minute! I'm a *clever* bastard. I won't try to pressurize you again because you've shown you won't stand it. You'd be a great receptionist. I need one and you need a job. Try me for a week or two, I improve on acquaintance. While you ponder that proposal I will make us another cup of coffee with my own fair hands—please don't tell Mrs Campbell, she's a very jealous lady."

Tom busies himself in the kitchen. Ms Tain yawns, slumps back in a chair and closes her eyes until he returns. He puts a mug on the table near her but sits on the far side saying, "So what do you think?"

She says, "I'll be your receptionist if you don't fire anybody."

"Right, Marian stays. But you'll do overtime for me? You won't go back on that?"

"What work can a receptionist do outside normal office hours?"

"Help load a van," says Tom chuckling, "We all muck in sometimes—even me. It speeds delivery and means we all get home earlier. *And* everyone's paid double rates for the full hour, even if we finish the job in ten minutes—which is frequent in the circumstances. It's also healthy exercise after sitting at a desk all day."

She smiles and says, "Then I'll put up with it."

He gives her a quick, almost shy glance and says, "Why aren't you a secretary? You're clever enough."

"I can't type and don't know shorthand."

"Take lessons."

"If I ever go back to studying I'll try to learn something interesting—law, perhaps. And while we're being honest I'd better tell you—I may stay here as long as a year, but six months is all I can promise."

"You little bitch!" says Tom, greatly amused.

"Please don't swear . . . You understand me, don't you?"

"Can't say I do."

"There aren't many interesting office jobs for women, you see, and after a few weeks you're either harassed for sexual favours or taken for granted like a piece of the furniture. Those who get bored with a job usually change it."

Tom points a finger and prophesies: "You will work here longer than you think!"

She looks at him sceptically.

A great certainty moves his heavy big body to rise and stroll lightly round the room, happy with an audience who deserves him: an attractive woman with an independent mind. He says, "Lang Precision bores nobody who works for it—we're changing too fast for that. Six months ago I had a staff of eight. Now I've twice that. What'll we be like in another six months? A lot bigger, I say. You'll work bloody hard, Miss Tain, but I promise you won't be bored. And I'm sorry, you'll have to get used to my swearing." He stops by the window, hands in pockets, and looks kindly at the dockyards.

She says, "Yes, it's a dangerous time for you."

He turns and stares.

"Most successful small firms go bankrupt when they try to expand," she reminds him, adding, "I worked with one. A boss easily manages a small staff personally, but a big one is different. Unless you learn to delegate you go under. You can't be everywhere."

"Can't I?" asks Tom in an odd voice, then grins, chuckles and announces, "I must be mad, but you're such a bloody little know-all I want to tell you everything. Can I trust you? With a secret, I mean?"

The question worries her.

He says, "All right, don't answer, I do trust you. Come and see this. When you said I can't be everywhere you forgot the miracle of modern science." He goes behind his desk. She rises and follows puzzled and curious. He pulls open a very deep drawer, but the inside seems only deep enough to hold two pairs of light earphones. He lifts these out and points to dials and switches on the surface underneath. "Where to?" he asks. "Reception? Accountancy? Loading bay? There was trouble in the loading bay, we'll go there." He puts on the earphones and presses switches. Beginning to understand but still curious, she too slips on the earphones. A hissing reaches her, some tweets and hiccups then a vast roaring which settles into the noise of wood being sawed. A distant voice bellows, "I hate that big bastard."

Someone sounding close behind her shouts "Nae wunner."

"Know what the accountants call him?"

"Naw."

"The Great I Am. The Great I Am."

"Good, they're on the job," says Tom cheerily, removing his headphones and switching the sound off.

"What a cheap, nasty trick!" says Ms Tain, handing back hers. Her voice conveys distress more than rage.

"Not cheap! The wiring alone cost more than five hundred. Say it, though—I'm a bugger!" He grins.

She is distressed and says, "I feel like walking out of here and not coming back."

"But you will come back," he tells her gravely, "because you're interested, and need the money, and I trust you."

She does not deny this but walks away, murmuring, "Sickening. Sickening."

And hears a sigh and turns. He sits behind the desk, elbow on top, chin propped on the thumbs of interlocking fingers. He says, "You're right, of course. This is a difficult time. I've been bankrupt already for exactly the reasons you mentioned. I hate delegating. I don't trust people and why should I? Most of them are a gang of lazy, lying cowards without an ounce of imagination. If I didn't boss them they would do nothing—nothing at all. So I pile loads on them, loads *I* can easily carry, but they havenae the sense or guts to tell me when it's too much for them. Then suddenly without warning they walk out. It's infuriating."

"I'll give you at least a fortnight's warning before I walk out on you."

"Don't plan too far ahead. You'll be more than a receptionist before you leave Lang Precision Limited."

Ms Tain starts work the following Monday at five of nine. At ten of eleven Marian takes her place at the reception desk and she has coffee in the accountant's office with Mrs Campbell and young Teddy, the under-manager. Her conversation with these two does not flow smoothly. There are strange pauses when there should be explanations, and Ted conveys so many states of feeling by facial and bodily gestures that at last she stares openly at him and starts to laugh. Mrs Campbell hands her a note with *We are being taped* scribbled on it, and says, "Where are you lunching today, June? I usually eat in The Tempting Tattie on Argyle Street. It's quite near and not expensive."

"Then I'll go there too, today," says Ms Tain, and adds, "Where does our noble employer usually eat?"

"On days like this, when the firm needs him at his desk," says Mrs Campbell primly, "Mr Lang orders his luncheon by phone from the kitchen of the Central Station Hotel. A taxi brings it."

"Only the best is good enough for TL!" says Ted, laughing every way except audibly.

In The Tempting Tattie Mrs Campbell says, "This is our third week in the new premises and we've already lost two new members of staff. The last receptionist, Alice, had to go. She was useless on the phone, and lost us an order. And Tom had a secretary all to himself for two whole days. She walked out at the start of the third."

"The usual reason?"

Mrs Campbell nods and says, "It was partly her fault. She was young and silly, just out of typing college, and dressed and wriggled in an 'I'm all yours, sir' way though she wasn't that type at all. He wouldn't have pestered a sensible girl. It's a pity his wife isn't sensible. She's a disaster—a doormat."

"Will the firm last?"

"It may if he keeps away from the office. In a firm that's just starting a lot of office work is intelligent waiting, but Tom can't bear that. He tries new arrangements to keep us working all the time, so we interfere with each other and will be in a real mess if a lot of work suddenly arrives."

"But he isn't a fool."

"I know! Such a gassy big windbag ought to be a fool, but he knows everything about precision tools, he's good with buyers and suppliers, he'll go anywhere to chase up business."

Tom's business trips sometimes take him to south Britain. On one of these Ms Tain gets a call from a voice which sounds like Tom pretending to be a Yorkshire man. The speaker says he has a complaint and blabs of it in a rambling way, ignoring her patient efforts to learn if he is an unpaid supplier who should speak to Mrs Campbell, or a displeased buyer who should talk to Teddy. The voice suddenly becomes distinctly Tom saying, "You handled that well June, I mean Miss Tain. I wasn't joking, just testing. I'll explain tomorrow."

Next day he tells her he needs a personal secretary, one the receptionist puts clients on to at once, whether he's in the building or not. He says, "Believe me a lot of important people are going to be phoning this place and I want them to be impressed by a clear firm voice which seems to know its business. You've got that."

"But I can't—"

"Shorthand isn't needed now. You dictate letters to a machine and give it to the typist. The job won't be a sinecure—that's why you'll get a twenty per cent wage rise. When I'm away you'll be handling the business from my angle."

"But surely Teddy—"

"Teddy has enough work with the deliveries. Besides, I'm always going for more customers than I'll ever get. The ones I get make us richer. Why need anyone but you and me know about the others?"

"Where will my office be?"

"Here. There's no room for another office in the building, and that desk was intended for my personal secretary." He points to a desk across the room from his own. Ms Tain does not look at it, but looks questioningly at him. He blushes slightly, and says, "You'll have heard in The Tempting Tattie that my last secretary and I had a misunderstanding. There's no danger of me misunderstanding you. Try the job for a week or two and see how you feel."

The employment agency sends a new receptionist and Ms Tain moves into Tom's office. The job and Tom are more interesting than she expected. Normally, or when things go badly, Tom is brisk, friendly and cheerful. Successes bring out the worst in him, making him almost comically pompous. Since Ms Tain does not always hide her amusement he learns to watch her warily at such times. He inclines to forget the morning and afternoon breaks. The best way to remind him is to make coffee in the small kitchen and put a mug of it on his desk while carrying one to her own. This greatly pleases him though he tries not to show it. He sometimes breaks off a phone call saying, "I must leave you now—my secretary has just brought the coffee in and she's a very jealous lady." Then he stretches his arms, takes the mug and talks about his problems or ideas for improving business efficiency. She offers suggestions which lead to some ideas being modified and the rest forgotten. He says, "I see things more clearly when I bounce them off you."

As he expected, she has an excellent way of talking to clients. The firm also works more smoothly when his orders to the staff are passed through her. This he did not expect, but very soon thinks he did.

Her only relief from Tom during working hours is when he is away on a business trip. The first time it happens she sends for Teddy, meets him at the office door and hands him a note saying FIND IF THIS ROOM IS TAPED TOO. She shows him the drawer with earphones. He puts them on, fingers switches, opens a panel in the side. Suddenly he announces indignantly, "We're not being taped at all—this is nothing but a bugging device! We could have said what we liked whenever he was out of the building!"

"I still want you and Mrs Campbell to have coffee here today," says Ms Tain consolingly.

They do, and Ms Tain finds them boring. As they can now discuss Tom openly they discuss nothing else—not even Tom talks as much about Tom Lang as they do. On a later occasion when he is away for nearly a week she gets so furiously bored that she calls in an electrical firm to remove the bugging system.

"He must have discovered we knew," says Teddy, staring at Ms Tain, "How did he find that out?"

"Not from me," says Ms Tain quietly.

"But I bet you got him to do it," says Mrs Campbell, "You're the only one he listens to around here. Fancy him having all those expensive hidden microphones ripped out of the walls before the van driver's very eyes! I'll never understand that man."

Teddy stops a chocolate biscuit halfway to his mouth and says, "I hear footsteps."

"When the cat's away the mice will play," says Tom gloomily entering and dropping his briefcase on Ms Tain's desk. He trudges toward his own with the tragic gait of a statesman ruined by his services to an ungrateful nation. The others nod to each other. The trip has been successful.

Ms Tain asks crisply, "Coffee? Tea, Mr Lang?"

He slumps into his chair, tilts it back, heaves heels onto desktop, folds hands on stomach, yawns and says, "No coffee. No tea. I have not slept six hours in the last forty-eight. I have driven over seven hundred miles, seen a dozen firms and am shagged out. Finished. Done for. Go on eating your biscuits. Nibble biscuits all day if you like. In ten minutes I'll be off home to my kip and that's the last you'll see of me till nine. Sharp. Tomorrow." He closes his eyes. Teddy and Mrs Campbell get up and leave. They know he dislikes them having coffee in his room and are intrigued that Ms Tain can pretend not to know.

She starts putting utensils on a tray. Without opening his eyes Tom says drowsily, "June!"

It is the first time in three months he has used her first name without correcting himself. She says, "Yes?"

"Pour me a whisky. Please!"

From a cocktail cabinet she takes bottle and glass, pours a measure from first into second, places both on desk before him. He sits up, sips, sighs, looks at her and asks, "Well?"

She stands with arms folded and back to her desk, half leaning, half sitting on it. She says, "No special correspondence. The orders from Colville's Clugston Shanks went through as planned. A late order from Lairds caused a strike among our one available van driver. Teddy ironed that out."

"A good lad, Teddy."

"You don't pay him enough."

"I know. He stands for it."

"Unless you pay him more he'll leave you. He's talking about it."

"Then I'll raise his wages. Thanks for the tip. I've missed you, June." He is watching her, solemnly. She smiles back and says lightly, "Have you, Tom?"

"I've missed you very much."

"All the same, you're probably going to fire me."

"Why?"

"I've had your bugging system removed. The firm which unwired it took it away as part payment for doing the job quickly."

Tom opens his desk drawer, looks inside then slams it and looks hard at Ms Tain, his face and hands growing very red. He whispers, "Why?"

She is suddenly frightened. She says, "It's wicked to spy on people," her voice quivering a little.

"*Wicked!*" he shouts, jumping up, "*Wicked!* What a childish thing to say! Every government in the world does it!"

"They don't."

"They do!"

"Well if they do they're wicked and rotten and it made you ridiculous, Tom. Everybody knew about it. They were all laughing at you."

"How could they know? Who told them? You?"

"The electricians who installed it drank at a local pub and told a barman who told our drivers. Things like that can never be hidden, Tom. You were being laughed at!" She still leans against her desk. He walks up and down shouting, "Let them laugh at me all they like! I don't care if they're doing what I tell them! That system worked for me even if they did know about it, in fact it worked better, yes of course it did! They had to keep their mouths shut about me or talk in sign language so

they felt I was always beside them, always listening! It kept me
in their thoughts—like God!" His glaring face is an inch from
hers, his fists hammer the space on each side of her body.

She whispers, "God?"

He has never been so menacing or she so subdued. He clasps,
kisses her and is embraced. Her mouth yields to his, which is
hard at first then softens as he starts to tremble, feeling he is
losing all control of things. Still holding her tight he withdraws
his face, gasps for breath and demands, "Who did you tell them
ordered that unwiring?"

"You, Tommy! I told them you ordered it! They were tre-
mendously astonished and impressed!" Her voice and face are
eager, submissive and amused. He groans and they kiss again.
Full of wonder he says, "I know nothing about you! Nothing
at all."

"I'm very ordinary, Tommy."

"Do you like me, June?"

"You're a very impressive man, Mr Lang."

"But do you like me?"

"I . . . I'm not sure. I like this, though."

A few minutes later they separate. He pulls his crumpled
clothes straight and says soberly, "I want you down on the
carpet with me."

"A bad idea," she says, going into their washroom.

"Listen!" he calls through to her, "I'm going to phone my
wife and tell her I'm still on the M1, that I've had a breakdown
and I'll be back tomorrow, right? She's used to that happening.
Then I'll drive to Renfrew airport and book a room for us in
the hotel. You finish here at five-thirty as usual, lock up and go
to Central Station where you take a taxi straight out to me,
right?"

"I don't think we should be hasty," she says, emerging. "My

mother expects me for tea and I've arranged to meet a friend afterward."

"Does that mean we discuss it tomorrow?"

"Yes, at nine. Tomorrow. Sharp."

"You've a sense of humour," he tells her, sighing. They kiss and cling again for a moment, then he tells her to photocopy the orders in his briefcase and pass them to Teddy. They look at each other for a moment. He leaves.

Three days later they stay overnight in the airport hotel. Next day a kiss before lunch break leads to a coupling, interrupted by a phone call, on the carpet. Ten days after that they spend another night in a hotel. Ms Tain finds he has just one short way of pleasing a woman intimately, and likes doing it three or four times a night. This makes him perfectly happy ("Oh I needed that!" he exclaims, almost every time) but she feels hardly any intimacy at all. For over a month Ms Tain gives her mother's poor health as a reason for not meeting Tom privately, and there are no more carpet fucks. Then one weekend he takes her for a two-day holiday to Paris.

The season is not spring but the weather is spring-like and fresh. They do not sit together on the plane in case someone recognizes him, but the flight, taxi-ride and arrival at a fine little hotel on a narrow street near the Arc de Triomphe make her happy and hopeful; their first fuck in the bedroom ten minutes later even enhances that mood. She would now like to drift about, gazing at things, exploring without urgency the quais and parks beside the Seine, chatting about what they see, reminiscing about childhood and getting to know each other better. But Tom cannot enjoy looking at things. Drifting makes him uneasy. He assumes every stroll needs a destination and a schedule for reaching it. He takes her to Versailles and examines it with an offended frown, sometimes muttering, "Oh very nice, if you could afford it."

He is jealous of the monarchs who once lived here, not at all consoled by it now being public property. He talks a lot about his unhappy marriage. He is paying for this holiday so she murmurs sympathetically, feeling guilty that she can hardly stand his company now, guilty that the first thing she will do when they return to work will be hand in her notice; but beside guilt she also feels hopeful. She is dressed beautifully, her hair hangs freely down her back, she draws several admiring glances. These gradually make Tom feel enviable and secure. At dinner that night he is amazed by the splendid woman across the table from him and says solemnly, "This is the happiest moment of my life."

She manages to smile. He drinks nearly two bottles of wine and three large brandies without apparent effect, but when they go to bed falls asleep at once. She is glad, although she does not sleep for a long time. She feels her first holiday in Paris, like Tom Lang in private, should be better than this.

Next morning he wakens her by satisfying himself. He would do it again but she says she has a headache. He becomes gentle, apologetic, says, "I know I'm too much sometimes. Will I get you a cup of tea? Or coffee, maybe?"

She realizes Tom does not know there is more to love than he learned in his teens. Given time, a tactful and experienced woman could make a very satisfying lover out of Tom, but he will never give a woman enough time and luckily he is not the only man in her life.

They return by an afternoon flight. It is Sunday. On Wednesday she hands in her notice. He is appalled, offers to double her wages, declares the firm needs her, proposes marriage, announces he will buy a house for both of them anywhere she likes while the divorce is going through. She leaves and six months later marries someone who is rather like Tom Lang, but fonder of home and less obviously selfish. She has a habit of getting entangled with the same sort of man and only discovering it later.

Lang Precision Ltd receives a Scottish Industries Award for being the most successfully competitive small firm of 1975, but it supplies tools to factories in a land where heavy industries are being closed or shifted south and light industries are sending their labour to factories in Taiwan and Thailand. Tom, with the assistance of an expert accountant, goes profitably bankrupt. He moves to London where his ability to deal with buyers and suppliers is found useful by a subsidiary of a gigantic company whose directors will never know his name or face.

# CHAPTER 6

# In the Boiler Room

The boiler room is entered from a dirty little yard behind an old hotel with a grand big front. The room has a concrete floor and walls of unplastered, unpainted brick. It is windowless and lit by a bare bulb hung from the ceiling at the end of the room not occupied by the boiler—the end with the door. The boiler is like the engine of an old steam locomotive without wheels and cabin. It has the same circular front of riveted steel plates, the same large dials indicating water level and pressures, the same small grim furnace underneath. It eats the same sort of fuel. Near by is a heap of small coal and a heap of coke. A long-handled and short-handled shovel lie on these, an iron-handled rake and a stout sweeping-brush with very coarse bristles. In a corner a heap of tumbled-together chairs slopes up to the ceiling, chairs too old or damaged for the hotel and sent down here for use as kindling. There is a stack of expensive but out-of-date fashion magazines sent down for the same purpose. These heaps are all close together because the boiler fills most of the room.

It may not seem a comfortable room but some find comfort here. The boiler pipes are old and leak a bit, so the hot air is neither too moist nor too dry and on this late January afternoon the heat is welcome after the freezing slush of the yard and the streets beyond. Even the thin sharp fume of burning coke smells pleasant by association, and after a while has a slightly narcotic effect. Three gold-lacquered basket chairs, chipped and soiled but with wicker frames too difficult to break up for kindling, stand in a small space before the boiler for the convenience of visitors. The boilerman prefers a plain wooden chair on which he sits by the furnace door, smoking his pipe and reading a library book. He is tall, lean, craggy and old; he wears a black boilersuit, big boots and flat cap, also spectacles with a fractured earpiece bandaged by electrical insulating tape. He does not hear a faint distant sound of dance music until it swells louder as the door opens and a small determined woman walks in, followed by a worried little boy. She wears a plastic headscarf and plastic raincoat and carries a heavy suitcase in each hand. The boy wears a thick duffel coat with the hood up and clutches a doll wearing the clothes and equipment of an American soldier in Vietnam. The boilerman looks at them blankly then says, "Hullo, Senga."

She says firmly, "Yes, hullo, Granda. I'm finished. I'm through. I've had all I can take." She puts down her cases and tells the boy, "Shut that door." He does.

The boilerman, nodding thoughtfully, stands and points to a chair near his own. He says gently to the boy, "Sit down, son."

He does not ask the woman to sit. She is clearly in no mood

for that. She takes a packet from her pocket, removes a cigarette, asks for a light. The boilerman hands her matches. She lights the cigarette and returns the matches saying, "Thanks. Yes I've had it, had it up to here"—she makes a slicing gesture across her throat—"I'm leaving him and this time it's final! . . . Take your coat off and sit down like your granda says," she tells the boy, who is staring at her uncertainly. He obeys. The boilerman looks thoughtfully at the bowl of his pipe then pockets it with an air of decision. He says, "I'll get you a snack from the kitchen, we've a wedding reception tonight . . ."

"Huh! *Wedding* reception! Save your trouble, I don't need a snack."

"Did he lay hands on you?" asks the boilerman quietly.

The wife, smoking in quick little angry puffs, grins grimly and says, "Hit me? I'd like to see him try. I'd have him in the Marine Police Station before he could blink. His feet wouldnae touch the pavement."

The boilerman glances at the boy, who seems not to be listening, and murmurs, "A woman, maybe?"

"Oh I wish it was! I wish he'd do something I could take him to court over, but no. No it's because of something ordinary. He went out for a drink last night, as usual, and said he'd be back in forty minutes. As usual. And as ususal he comes rolling in at half-past eleven. Met a pal and went up to his house for a chat about the future of socialism while muggins here is left alone in the house with the kid and the telly. As usual."

"Does he never let you out by yourself?"

"Oh aye! All for sweet human reason is that man of mine. 'When you want a night out just tell me,' says he, 'I'll sit in with the wee chap, no problem.' Where can I go for a night out? I've no pals to talk politics with. The only folk I know are a lot of silly women with nothing in their heads but babies and food prices and bingo. I married that man for his *company* and the bastard won't stay in the room with me for more than an hour at a time if we're no in bed with the light off. That's the only time we're together and it isnae enough." She is close to weeping, so he takes a deep breath and says, "I shouldnae call him a bastard, Granda, because he's your son. You know what I mean, but."

"I think so, Senga."

"Funny. I can say anything I like to you and you never take me wrong."

"That's because I'm neutral, Senga."

"Aye, you keep saying that, but I know you're on my side. Listen, I'm leaving the kid here for half an hour while I see about a room. I met a friend last week who needs a lodger. I havnae seen her for years, she's not very bright but she's got a good heart and she lives three streets from here."

"Would you like a cup of tea first?"

"Definitely not." She goes to the boy and makes small adjustments to the collar of his shirt, the sleeves of his pullover. She tells him quietly, "I won't be long, Hughie," and leaves.

The boilerman strokes his chin and studies the boy for a moment. The boy, hunched over the doll on his lap, seems to be studying the furnace door. The boilerman quietly coughs. The boy looks at him. The boilerman raises a forefinger, says, "Hughie, I'm going to get you something," and walks out. The boy turns back to the furnace door and frowns thoughtfully, sometimes moving his lips as if talking to it.

The boilerman returns with a plate containing triangular sandwiches, vivid pastries and a glass of green liquid under a layer of white froth. He lifts a crate from the floor, stands it

short-end-up beside the boy's chair and lays the plate on top.
He says, "That's for you."

"Not hungry."

"Then we'll let it rest there." The boilerman sits down, lights
his pipe and resumes the library book. After a while the boy
says, "Granda, what's the worst trap you were in?"

The boilerman looks at him closely.

"I mean in the war," explains the boy, "the first war."

"Passchendaele, I suppose."

"Did you kill many Germans?"

"You're keen on war, eh?"

"I've got three action men," says the boy earnestly, "An
infantryman, a paratrooper and a frogman. Of course they're
just toys but you can learn things from them, can't you? I mean
the wee weapons are all to scale. Look at this! Look at the wee
grenades." He holds up his doll. The boilerman glances at it
briefly then blows a smoke ring.

"Tell me about the first war!" pleads the boy.

"Yes," says the boilerman and lays his book down, "Well.
You know the big greenhouse with the palm trees in it behind
the museum on the Green? The one they call the People's
Palace?"

"Aye."

"That was where I slept on the night of the day war was
declared."

"Why?"

"When I read about the war on the placards, you see, I joine
at once. I was seventeen, you see, and I'd been working as
clerk on a weighbridge at the docks. Oh yes, my parents h
great hopes for me, but it was not a job I liked. As a hob
had joined the volunteer reserve, which was a free kind of 1

classes in soldiering. So when war was declared, I was prepared.
I signed on like a shot and bought my first tin of pipe-tobacco
with the shillings they gave me. So many of us signed on they
had to billet us in all kinds of queer places. So there was I, lying
on my palliasse on the walkway of the People's Palace conserva-
tory, under a tree with a label on it saying *Phoenix dactilifera.*
That was the very first night I ever slept outside a house with
my parents in it, and every hour I wakened to a queer dank
jungle kind of smell and saw that label with the words *Phoenix
dactilifera.*"

"Yes," says the boy, "but—"

"Next day!" says his grandfather, lifting a forefinger. "We
were sent up to Dunfermline and billeted in a whisky bonding
warehouse. Three months later twelve of us marched down
Queensferry Road to the railway station and marched onto the
Glasgow train, just as if we were a picket. Now what do you
think of that?"

"What's a picket?"

"A small group of soldiers with a special warrant to travel
on a train without tickets. But we had no warrant."

"Why?"

"We had been three months without leave, you see, and felt
justified in taking what was called *French* leave, which is without permission. Well, just before the train came into Queen
Street station it halted in the shunting yards of Saint Rollox.
The money in our pockets added up to just less than five shillings, which was judged too little to bribe the ticket collector at
the barrier. So we jumped out of the carriage, ran across the
lines, climbed the fence and . . . walked back to our proper
homes. Now listen!"—the boilerman points a finger—"The
next evening, at ten to nine, two polis-men knocked at the door
to ask if Private MacLeod was at home. He was. A laggard

among us had been caught skipping over the fence and had clyped on us. I was taken down to Old Dalmarnock Road polis-station—"

"Someone maligning the police again?" asks a policeman who has quietly entered.

"Aye, there you are, Fergus," says the boilerman but pays the policeman no other attention, so the boy ignores him too. The policeman enters a dark space between the coke heap and the boiler-room wall. He does something with his arms inside a tea-chest while the boilerman says, "They took me to Old Dalmarnock Road polis-station, where it was discovered they had no food, and that I was hungry, for they'd arrested me before supper-time. So a polis-man went back to my mother's house and she gave him food for me, and to spare. I was put in a cell with a stone bed and stone pillow, both painted red. There was also a fine fire blazing in the hearth—"

"There is not, and has never been, a Scottish police-station cell with a fireplace in it," says the policeman firmly, returning to the space before the boiler. He carries a paper cup of clear liquid, sits down and sips from it. After a pause the boilerman tells the boy mildly, "As I was saying, a fire in the hearth. I sat there with a couple of friendly inspectors, eating my mother's scones and . . . just talking. Just talking. I slept that night wrapped in a blanket on that stone bed and the next day I was marched to Tobago Street where I met the others, all twelve of us. Two unarmed polis-men walked us to Maryhill Barracks, where a small company of fixed bayonets marched us to the train back to Dunfermline."

"What did they do to you? The officers, I mean."

"Sixty days confined to barracks," says the boilerman promptly.

"That's not a *real* war experience," mutters the boy.

"It could have happened at no other time."

The policeman says, "You should ask about my war experiences."

The policeman is not a young man but has an unlined, indefinite face which at first sight seems boyish.

"Were you—?" the boy asks hopefully.

"Yes indeed, Son. You see before you one of the original desert rats. North Africa nineteen-forty. And so on."

"You fought for General Montgomery?"

"Monty?" says the policeman. "A big balloon! There was only one general the British soldier respected in that concise arena of conflict. Will I tell you his name?"

The boy nods vigorously.

"Rommel."

"Did you *see* Rommel?"

"I had not that honour. My own North African campaign was passed in a supply depot: a fuel-tank of the military apparatus. All kinds of armaments and food and drink passed through our hands, and furnishings, you know, for the top brass." The policeman sighs nostalgically.

"Our tents had wall-to-wall carpets in them with dressing-tables and three-piece suites. Crazy paving was laid up to the front flap of each, and every morning my barber wakened me sharp at eleven with a bottle of champagne."

"Fergus," says the boilerman, "I am aware that strange things happen in supply depots but I find your crazy paving hard to take."

"It was a fact!"

"Were you a . . . a major or something?" the boys asks, awed.

"A humble lance-corporal."

"But how did *you* have a barber?"

"We were in a very poor part of the world, you see, and there were always a lot of homeless children hanging around to do anything you liked for a coin or a half-bar of chocolate. One of them attached himself to me—two or three years younger than you he was, an orphan, but intelligent. I trained him to shave me in bed in the mornings. I would waken to the warm lather going on to my cheeks and I would be shaved and dried without my head once leaving the pillow."

"But did you never *fight?*"

"Indeed!" said the policeman, nodding, "Yes, each day after lunch we swept the horizon with our binoculars and if we saw anything unusual we reported it to the commanding officer. 'Beg to report sir, a duck has appeared beside the palm tree at half-past three o'clock.' 'Right! That duck is our enemy! Open fire!' Whizzbang, whizzbang. Ten thousand pounds of explosive missile waste their sweetness on the desert air."

"But *why?*" asks the boy, exasperated by such a waste of explosives.

"There was a *war* on, son! If we hadn't exploded a certain number of shells per week the brass at headquarters would have thought we weren't doing our bit. Of course it wasn't a typical situation—not everyone did well in that war. In fact I've heard that in the thirty-nine—forty-five affair it was the civilians who suffered most."

"There you are *wrong, Fergus!*" cries the boilerman forcefully, "I know the blitz was gey hard on the Londoners and Clydebankers, but life here in Britain during the war was far kinder and more decent than before or since. We had a working government then, controlling the industries and regulating the prices. Full employment for all! And food rationed, and clothes rationed, so the rich got no more than they needed and the poor no less. Even the king was eating Spam off his gold plate in Buckingham Palace. No petrol for private cars then—we *all*

used the trains and trams and buses. People with big houses had
to give rooms to bombed-out kids from the slums, and the
miracle is, hardly anyone grumbled! Even the advertisements
had a democratic look. WORK OR WANT, they said. MAKE DO
AND MEND, COUGHS AND SNEEZES SPREAD DISEASES, DIG FOR
VICTORY. People with gardens were encouraged to plant vegetables in them. Now listen to this!" From the stack of fashion
magazines he seizes one, leafs through, then reads aloud: "*The
young admire it for its reckless good looks. Their parents like it
for its thrifty fuel consumption. Not everyone can afford the
life-style indicated by a Blenheim table cigarette lighter, but
those who can usually own one.* What is that but a sneer and a
gibe at working people who could pay three months *rent* with
the price of their fancy cigarette lighter? Here's another advert
for a holiday in the Bahamas. It is aimed at young working
women and is a straightforward invitation to them to prostitute
themselves! *Rich boys know how to enjoy life,* it says. *They have
the money and time. Meet them in their favourite playgrounds
for . . .*"

The policeman, who has been smiling and shaking his head
at the boilerman's vehemence, laughs aloud and raises his hand.
"Cool it, Mr MacLeod, cool it!" he says. "Less of the commu-
nist manifesto and a bit more judicial calm."

The boilerman becomes calm instantly. He puts the magazine back on the stack and says quietly, "Quite right."

Another man has entered and sat down with them, a no-
longer-young man wearing neat but not expensive clothing. The
boilerman and the boy pay him no special attention though he
is the son of the first and father of the second. But perhaps his
arrival stimulates the boy to say with sudden vehemence,
"Granda, did you never, you know, stand waiting with your
bayonets fixed till the order came to go over the top and then

you charged across no-man's-land and jumped into shell-holes
to miss the shells and then came to the German trenches and
jumped down into them and . . . you know what I mean? You
*did* do that didn't you?"

"I did as little of that as I possibly could!" says the boilerman
firmly.

"Nobody will tell me about fighting," mourns the boy.

"Why do *you* want to hear about fighting?" asks his father.

"Because I might pick up useful tips—useful for school, I
mean. I don't always know what to do, you see. I mean, what
can you do when they chase you into the lavatory, and you're
holding the door shut, and two of them are shoving it to try to
get in, and one is reaching his hands under the door to grab at
your legs, and another starts climbing in over the side wall?
What can you do?"

The men glance at each other, thoroughly disconcerted. They
do not want to tell the boy he is in a world which cannot be
improved, but only the boilerman has a suggestion for improving it. He says softly, "Take a cake, Hughie."

The boy looks at the plate and selects a tight spiral of yellow
crumbs and scarlet jam. He bites it and talks mainly to himself.

"James Bond is full of tricks: guns and explosives inside
fountain pens and the heel of his shoes. I don't want to *kill*
anybody, but it would be great if I could give them an electric
shock whenever they touch me. Or what if I flashed a light that
blinded them—not for ever, but for an hour or two. That would
be all right, wouldn't it?"

The last question is another appeal to the adults. The policeman is the least embarrassed by it. He says, "Wait till you're
a bit older, son, then you can send for *me* if thugs get on to you.
Oh yes, we know how to handle thugs. When you first arrest
these big tough guys they're very sure of themselves, calling you

all kinds of names. But the nearer they get to the station the quieter they become. And by the time they're inside—if they've sense—they're as mild as wee lambs." He imitates a cringing whine: *"Don't give me the stick! Not the stick!"* He chuckles as if it is a cheerful memory.

"What bothers me," grumbles the boy, "Is that you've all been in the army and none of you talk about the killing you've done."

*"You* were in the army?" the policeman asks the father, surprised.

"Yes. National Service. Cyprus."

"Kill any terrorists?" says the policeman, interested.

"No, but I broke an old woman's china teapot."

They stare at him. He sighs and says gloomily, "We were stationed in this village for a while—nice enough folk, they seemed, and they liked football, so we got up a team to play them. It was a good game. They beat us two–nil but there were no hard feelings. Afterwards one of our boys went to a well for a drink. It was booby-trapped. His head, legs and other bits travelled a long way in different directions, a sight to sicken you. Then one of us remembered that during the game a young kid had gone to the well for a drink and a woman—an ordinary housewife—had called it away. We saw that the whole village had known about the booby-trap! Well, we had to search the place then and of course we made a right meal of it. There were quite a few breakages, and lots of pillows, mattresses and cushions got ripped. Oh, they didnae sleep soft *that* night, I can tell you! I didnae enjoy doing that. It was a relief to be doing *something* of course but I felt bad afterwards. I mean, they werenae all bad people, but when the soldier went for a drink at the well could the woman not have warned him away, too?"

"If she had, the terrorists might have . . . done something to her," says the boilerman quietly.

"I know!" says the father with a hopeless shrug.

"You have no cause for self-recrimination!" says the police-man loudly, "In certain circumstances the forces of law and order cannot afford to be mealy-mouthed. You were defending your country, defending an artery of trade that was essential to Britain's survival as a nation."

The two other men look at him. The boilerman says, "What artery is that, Fergus?"

"Gibraltar. Cyprus. Suez. Aden. India."

"Fergus, the Suez Canal was blocked for three years before my boy was sent to Cyprus, and for about six after he came back."

"Is that right?" the policeman asks the father, who nods. The policeman frowns then remembers something which cheers him up again: "Without the British presence the Greeks and Turks would have torn each other apart, like the Irish in Ulster," he explains, "If they now live in peace it is because we taught them to. If they're still carving each other up it shows they needed us."

"Everybody talks about *politics,*" grumbles the boy.

After a silence his father says, "I loved Cyprus."

Nobody asks for an explanation so after more silence he says, "If you take a walk in the countryside here, what do you see? Cows and sheep looking over fences. But in Cyprus . . . I remember being on sentry go at the edge of a camp up in the hills. Stony bare hills they were, hardly any green, but lots of gnarled kinds of bushes with big leaves. I was the only one awake when the dawn came up. You never see colours like that in dawns nowadays—I mean, not here. No sound but a few birds cheeping and some sheep-bells or goat-bells clanking down in the valley. And this slight feeling of danger keeping you alert to it all. Because the Eeky-Oakies might be somewhere near."

"We all had moments like that," says the boilerman thoughtfully. The policeman nods.

The door bangs open and the wife enters. Her lips are pressed very tight together. The boilerman stands up and says, "Senga."

She says, "Give me a light, Granda." She lights a cigarette with his matches and returns them.

"Any . . . luck?" he asks delicately.

"Luck? For me? You must be crazy. Donalda Ingles used to be a decent wee girl but she's turned into a slut. Her sink's full of dirty old bean tins, the place stinks like a lavatory, she's living with a tinker and smells like a midden. She needs help, poor soul, but I cannae give it. I cannae stay in a place like thon."

The husband rises and walks to the suitcases his wife brought in earlier. He says crisply, "So are you coming home?"

"Oh!" she jeers, "You want me *home* do you?"

"I didn't say that," says the husband. "When you have a place to live in, go there and good luck to you. Meanwhile, are you coming home? I'll carry the cases." He bends to lift them. She cries, "Don't you touch my things! I'll mibby spend the night here. It's a hotel, isn't it?"

"Senga," says the boilerman gently, "the cheapest room here will cost you ten pounds a night."

"Senga," says the husband, "if you're leaving me you cannae afford that sort of money. You're far too impetuous—you'll never get away from me by charging out the house like a madwoman. You must plan things calmly. If you do I'll *help* you for godsake. It will mean less damage, especially to . . .

to . . ." With a small gesture he indicates the boy, then stoops to the cases again, saying, "Do I take these home?"

She says coolly, "Take them where you bloody like."

He lifts them and says to the boy, "Come on, Hughie."

The boy stands up looking worried. He says, "Do I go with him, Ma?"

"Up to you, intit?" says his mother, blowing out smoke.

"I'll stay with you, Ma, if . . . if you want me."

"Hm! And who do you want?"

The boy stares at her looking terribly lost. Her husband says in a low voice, "Senga, that isnae fair."

"Oh go with your dad!" she cries impatiently. "I'm coming soon enough. Just clear off both of you and let me finish a fag in peace."

The father with suitcases, the boy with his doll, go to the door. Before leaving the man turns and says, "One thing, Senga! Don't think I've apologized to you. I've done nothing I'm ashamed of, nothing I'm sorry for, nothing I won't do tomorrow night. Come on, son."

They leave.

The wife walks up and down, puffing angrily.

"You heard them, didn't you?" she asks the two others.

"He wasn't exactly brutal to you, Mrs MacLeod," says the policeman.

"And would he be with two witnesses here? And one of them a policeman?"

The drink is giving the policeman a pleasant sense of extended intellectual powers. "Well, you know," he says, "a husband is entitled to beat his wife to the point of correction. That statute is graven on the foundation stones of the British Legal Constitution."

"You're blethering, Fergus," says the boilerman, "There is no such thing as a British Legal Constitution."

"The Scottish legal system is the finest in the world," the policeman announces to nobody in particular, "And I am fifty-five per cent *certain* that it permits a man to beat his wife *up to,* but not *beyond,* the point of correction. But where do we locate that point? Aha! That is the point!" He chuckles at his wit. The wife throws the cigarette down and stands on it, saying, "I'm getting out of here."

The boilerman goes to her saying, "Fergus is drivelling, Senga, at least stay for something to eat."

"No thanks, Granda. I'll see you when you've more . . . privacy." She leaves.

The boilerman wanders back to his seat murmuring, "Poor souls."

"I'm sure you were wrong about the Suez Canal," says the policeman. "Britain did not fight in that war for nothing. I shall look into it." He throws the empty paper cup onto the coke heap, stands and pulls his tunic straight. He says, "Aye aye. Everyone goes about saying how much they want war, and they're right to want it, because war is a very fine thing. But in my humble opinion war keeps manufacturing tensions which can only be resolved by a thorough-going peace." The policeman notices the boilerman watching him and stroking his chin. A sudden doubt occurs to him. He asks, "Did I say that the wrong way round, Mr MacLeod?"

"I honestly don't know, Fergus."

"Neither do I. Well, duty calls." He leaves. The boilerman looks at the dials, opens the furnace door and flings three shovelfuls of coke along a red-hot gullet of flames. Then he shuts the door, puts the shovel away, sits down, lights his pipe, and continues reading.

# CHAPTER 7

# Quiet People

Doorbell rings. Mrs Liddel opens to Mrs Mathieson who says, "I took my pain to the doctor—I've just got back from him."

"Would you like a cup of tea?" asks Mrs Liddel. Mrs Mathieson enters the sitting-room. Mrs Liddel enters the kitchen where Mr Liddel reads a library book, a kettle of water steams gently over a low flame.

"Mrs Mathieson!" explains Mrs Liddel, preparing tea and biscuits. Her husband says, "Mhm."

In the sitting-room Mrs Liddel pours two cups of tea as Mrs Mathieson draws a deep breath and announces, "The very first thing he did was tell me to strip myself naked all over."

"Oh dear!" whispers Mrs Liddel. As the story continues her kind, alert face expresses wonder, sympathy, dismay and dread.

These expressions are genuine. Mrs Liddel, her husband and two grown-up daughters have never been painfully ill, drunk or quarrelsome, or accidentally involved with criminal or indecent or eccentric behaviour, so most people's lives strike them as surprising. They have no television set because the things shown on it strike them as too surprising for comfort. When a visitor has no more to say Mrs Liddel can only shake her head and say, "Fancy that!" or "That should not be allowed."

When the visitor leaves Mrs Liddel takes the tea things back to the kitchen saying, "Mrs Mathieson took her pain to the doctor this morning. The first thing he made her do was strip herself naked all over."

While talking she washes and dries the tea things and restores them to exact places in cupboard, sideboard and drawer, sometimes pausing when the gravity of the news makes movement impossible. Mr Liddel is slightly ashamed of being the only one who knows his wife gossips. A casual observer might think he was ignoring her—he has raised his eyes only a fraction above the book held open before him. When the recital ends he says, "Well well!" and resumes reading, or else, "I see. So that's the way of it. I'd better take a wee walk. Come on Tippy."

Their old dog follows him to the park where he strolls up to the flagpole in dry weather or through the museum when wet. He broods deeply on what his wife has told him. It usually confirms what he deduces from newspapers and wireless broadcasts: Britain is getting worse.

Mrs Liddel is small and pretty, Mr Liddel massive and handsome. He is asthmatic. This shows if he moves quickly so he never moves quickly. A tram-driver from 1928 to 1961, he fails the army medical exam and is promoted to ticket inspector a year before trams are replaced by buses. He never learns to love the buses as he loved the trams and his worldview is shaped by this. He remembers when Glasgow tram lines reached to Loch Lomondside and most of industrial Lanarkshire; when the head of Glasgow Public Transport was invited to cities in North and South America to advise them on the running of municipal light railway systems. The scrapping of Glasgow tramcars is mingled in his mind with the Labour Party's retreat from socialist intentions. His favourite reading is biography and novels which present a rich social variety in a strong moralizing sauce. Dickens and Victor Hugo are his favourites, and only the confusing Russian names stop him enjoying Dostoevsky. He has read Upton Sinclair, J. B. Priestley, A. J. Cronin and Grassic Gibbon, but compared with Dickens and Hugo most twentieth-century writing strikes him as feeble. His detailed knowledge of modern existence now depends mainly on his wife, who is too busy to read.

Since marriage the Liddels have lived in a ground-floor flat in Minard Road, a street of tenements which offers better-paid workers most of the domestic amenities of the wealthy, apart from spaciousness. An entrance porch as large as a doormat has a double outer storm-door and an inner door which is two-thirds frosted glass. This opens into a tiny lobby which the Liddel daughters (shortly before they married and left) insisted in calling The Hall. Here are doors to a cupboard with a coal-bunker in it, to a lavatory two feet wider and four feet longer than the bath, to a back kitchen with a bed recess facing the window and sink, to a front bedroom one and a half feet wider and five feet longer than the bed, to a front sitting-room with enough room to walk comfortably round a heavy three-piece suite which boxes in the fireplace. The sitting-room also has a bed recess facing the window: a bay window divided from the street by a garden filled by a privet hedge round two small rhododendrons. The gardens and bay windows give Minard

Road its prosperous look, but Mr and Mrs Liddel would feel well housed without them. They are glad that each of their daughters has a whole bed of her own: indeed, the eldest has a whole bedroom. When the eldest marries and leaves, the youngest inherits the bedroom and the kitchen bed recess is converted to a dining alcove. When the youngest leaves the older people move to the bedroom, returning after a week to the bed in the sitting-room recess because they sleep uneasily without a wall on three sides of them. They are slightly ashamed of this lack of sophistication, but Mr Liddel says, "We must accept ourselves as we are."

The furnishings of the house are got when the Liddels marry and carefully kept, cleaned and polished ever since. In the mid thirties they purchase an electrically powered vacuum cleaner, and nearly thirty years later a refrigerator and washing machine. By the seventies it is evident that the sitting-room needs a new carpet—they can no longer turn it round so that the worn parts are hidden by furniture.

"I am loth to dip into our savings," says Mr Liddel, "since the cost of living is increasing at a rate faster than our pensions, and despite what Harold Wilson says this trend will continue, since the blighter will not tackle the problem at the root. But a new carpet is essential. Shall we consider letting the bedroom? If I hunted the Barrows for a wee secondhand fridge and hotplate and electric kettle we could turn it into a bed-sitting room."

"Oh dear! Would they not need to come into the kitchen?"

"That would be subject to negotiation. And remember, we need take in nobody who strikes us as unsuitable."

So Mr Liddel, who once did unpaid secretarial work for his branch of the Transport and General Workers Union, writes on a plain postcard that a small bed-sitting room with homely atmosphere is available for £5 per week c/o Liddel, 51 Minard Road, use of shared bathroom and kitchen between stated hours subject to negotiation, and two minutes' walk to nearest launderette. On payment of half a crown this is displayed in the nearest newsagent's window. The first to respond is a smartly dressed man who calls late next evening when the Liddels are about to have supper.

"Well now!" he asks briskly, "what can you show me?"

Mrs Liddel ushers him into the bedroom with a meekness which is half pretence, for she is very proud of how neatly they have fitted everything in. The stranger glances round and says, "A lot smaller than I expected for the price. Never mind, this is a good district, I'll take the room. I'll only want it for a fortnight—you don't mind?"

"Oh, no!" says Mrs Liddel thankfully, for there is something about the man she does not like. He steps to the door, closes it, opens it and rattles the knob saying, "Where's the key?"

"I'm afraid it hasn't got one—the tenants before us must have lost it and we never felt the want of it—all the other doors have keys."

"Hm! That isn't exactly satisfactory now, is it? Five pounds a week for a room without a key! I'll tell you what I'll do. I'm starting work with a firm of locksmiths. Tomorrow or the day after I'll put on a really good mortise lock. Don't worry about the labour—I won't charge you for that. You won't even need to pay the full price of the lock, I'll give you a trade discount of thirty-three and a third per cent. The cheapest you'll pay for a good quality mortise lock is seven pounds ten shillings, two-thirds of which is a fiver—exactly my first week's rent. How about that?"

Mrs Liddel is appalled to hear herself murmuring, "Thank you."

"Don't mention it. Well, I've had a hard day and feel like an early night," says the man, removing his coat and jacket in one piece and casting them over the bed foot, "Don't wake me tomorrow. I'll probably be up and out before anyone else has opened their eyes."

"But your luggage!"

"I travel light. I'll get what I need tomorrow," says the man, removing his necktie.

"I'd better introduce you to my husband—he's in the kitchen."

"No introductions tonight!" says the stranger firmly, unbuttoning his shirt and walking toward Mrs Liddel until she retreats before him into the lobby. "Tomorrow will be time enough!" and he closes the door on her.

Mrs Liddel enters the kitchen and tells her husband of this. He says, "Was that wise?"

"I'm *sure* it wasn't wise!" she says, almost tearfully. "I don't want a lodger who goes to bed without even brushing his teeth."

"Did he tell you the name of the locksmiths he'll be working for?"

"No. I wanted to ask who they were but it didn't seem polite."

"I'll have a word tomorrow with that lad!" says Mr Liddel darkly, "Thank goodness you didn't give him the key to the front door."

They eat Welsh rarebit on toast with a cup of warm milk, then Mrs Liddel cleans up and sets the table for breakfast while her husband uses the bathroom, then she uses the bathroom and follows him to bed. She lies as still as possible beside him till three in the morning then says, "I can't sleep for worrying."

He says, "Nor can I."

She rises and makes two cups of cocoa. They drink them with

an aspirin pill which they think good for nervous states, then they sleep soundly till half-past ten. They have never wakened so late since their youngest daughter was teething.

"Perhaps he's left for work?" says Mrs Liddel hopefully.

"We'll soon see!" says her husband. He washes, shaves and dresses with even more care than usual, then knocks firmly but quietly on the bedroom door. No answer. He opens it. The door opens inward but not far, because the bed is behind it. Peering round the edge Mr Liddel's eyes meet those of the stranger who lies on the quilt in his trousers, vest and stockings, looking straight across the top of a paperback book in his hand which has an indecent picture of a woman on the cover.

"Now you know why paying guests prefer doors with keys," says the stranger, smiling unpleasantly. Mr Liddel is too embarrassed to reply.

He closes the door, returns to the kitchen and after an hour of closely reasoned thought returns to the bedroom, knocks once loudly and enters with a firm tread. He says, "It is customary for paying guests to give rent in advance."

"But your wife and I agreed that . . ."

"My wife agreed to nothing—it was you who did all the talking. If you are not prepared to observe customary procedures I will not tolerate your presence here."

"Are you suggesting I am a cheat?" cries the stranger indignantly.

"I suggest nothing because I know nothing!" says Mr Liddel steadily, "I know neither your name, nor occupation, nor antecedents, nor destination. You may be a cheat. You may be an honest man. The burden of proof lies with you."

The stranger sighs then says frankly, "Mr Liddel, it is clear that you and I have kicked off on the wrong foot. I feel it will be better if I seek accommodation elsewhere."

"I agree."

"However, I don't see why I should be penalized for a lack of communication between you and your wife. It may take several days for me to find a room as convenient as this at such unexpectedly short notice."

"You may stay here rent-free for one night but no longer!" declares Mr Liddel, and next morning the stranger vanishes taking nothing with him but a bathroom towel, leaving nothing but some stains on the bed-sheets and the pornographic book.

Mr Liddel spends an hour tearing the book into small pieces and flushing them down the lavatory pan—if he put it in the midden a cleansing worker might find it and think a tenant of the close had been reading it.

"Shall we take the postcard out of the window?" asks Mrs Liddel after airing the bedroom and changing the sheets.

"Goodness me, I forgot it was still there!" says Mr Liddel, astonished. The doorbell rings.

Outside a whimpering little girl is held up with difficulty by a woman who seems not much bigger, and who says, "Is this the place that has the room?"

Mrs Liddel is so full of wish to take the child into her bathroom and wash it that she does not answer until the question is repeated.

"Yes!" she says, glad to feel her husband looming behind her. "But it's too small for more than one lodger. Look!" She opens the bedroom to prove she is telling the truth. The small woman not only looks but edges inside and gives a cry of delight: "But this is a great wee room! I've no seen a room as nice as this for years—it's got everything! Look at the wee fridge! And that picture of a horse! And that lovely quilt on the bed! My man will like this fine."

"We are not prepared to let so small a room to a family of

three," says Mr Liddel heavily, "It would be fair to neither the family nor ourselves."

"We're very *quiet* people," explains Mrs Liddel anxiously.

"Oh we're quiet people too!" cries the small woman. "And we're in a basement in Cessnock just now and it's damp, dead damp and Theresa has this cough which won't go away and a lovely clean room like this is just what we need and MacFee my man is a real hard grafter out all day and half the night you'll hardly ever see him *please* can we *please* can we stay I mean oh Mister what if Theresa died I don't think she'll ever get better in that place and nobody wants a couple with a wee wean och Mister be a sport!"

Mr Liddel is alarmed to find three female faces looking up to him, his wife anxiously, the small woman eagerly, the small girl (who has fallen silent) with open-mouthed astonishment. He clears his throat but it brings no ideas. At last he says, "You may stay here for a week—or a fortnight at most—while you search for alternative accommodation of a more suitable nature. But the rent, the rent will *not* be five pounds, it will be . . . it will be six! In advance!"

"Oh thanks Mister that's great I'll just run off now and we'll come in an hour or two it's a great relief getting a room in a nice quiet clean place for a change I don't think we'll ever find a more suitable place then this cheerio see you later!" She leaves. The Liddels stare at each other.

"The agreement I proposed was a purely temporary one," says Mr Liddel. "Did I not make that plain?"

"Oh yes!" says his wife, nodding. "But I'm not sure she took it like that."

After dark that evening the mother and child return with a small man who shakes Mr Liddel's hand and a bigger man who stands behind the small man, watching.

"Thanks a million, you won't lose by this," says the small man. "My pal here is helping with the flitting. Mum's the word—you won't hear a thing."

Mr Liddel watches from the kitchen doorway with Mrs Liddel keeking round his arm as the men deftly, swiftly, almost furtively carry into the bedroom old suitcases tied with rope and a variety of bulging sacks, some hessian and some plastic. When the bedroom door is finally closed with all the luggage and visitors inside, the Liddels shut themselves into their kitchen. Mrs Liddel prepares supper. Mr Liddel sits at the table, drums his fingers on it then says ruminatively, "I wish our paying guests would tell us their names and occupation, discuss procedures for sharing the bathroom, and pay their rent in advance. Shall I go and talk to them about it?"

"Perhaps not tonight—let them settle in first," suggests Mrs Liddel, spreading mashed sardines on buttered slices of hot toast. While eating these they gradually hear a faint slithering rustle. It comes from the bottom edge of the kitchen door. In little jerks the point of something brown and triangular is creeping across the linoleum, growing larger as it advances. Mrs Liddel shudders with dread. Her husband slowly rises, goes to the door, stops, grips the point of the thing between thumb and forefinger, pulls the whole of it out and lifts it up. It is a cheap envelope with six crumpled pounds notes inside.

"Goodness!" sighs Mrs Liddel thankfully. "It just goes to show."

"Show what?"

"That if you leave people alone they usually do the right thing."

"Mibby. Time will tell."

Before dawn the next day the Liddels are wakened by their front door stealthily opening and closing. Seconds later departing footsteps sound from the street. "That'll be him going to work," says Mrs. Liddel. "He must be on an early shift."

She suspects she hears two pairs of departing men's feet but is not sure of this and has no wish to alarm her husband. "Mhm!" says Mr Liddel, who suspects the same thing and has no wish to alarm his wife.

That morning the only sign that the Liddels have guests are three visits from enquiring neighbours. At one o'clock a strong smell of frying spreads through the house from the bedroom. At two Mr Liddel goes a thoughtful walk with the dog and ten minutes later Mrs Liddel taps the bedroom door. After a while it is opened wide enough to show an inch-wide vertical slice of face with an eye and corner of mouth in it.

"Is something wrong?" asks the mouth. Mrs Liddel had meant to ask that. Instead she says, "When would you like to use the bathroom? For a bath, I mean."

The small woman is so astonished she opens the door wide enough to show her whole face, saying, "I thought you didnae want us outside this room."

Mrs Liddel blushes because this is almost true. She says, "Will I put the immersion heater on? You can have a bath in forty minutes."

"Aye. Sure. Thanks a lot."

"And would you mind raising the blinds and opening the curtains?" asks Mrs Liddel, noticing the woman is fully clothed, "Three neighbours noticed they were shut this morning and called to ask if Mr Liddel or me was ill. You needn't be afraid of people looking in from the street when the blinds and curtains are open—the lace half-curtain and rhododendron make that impossible."

"Sorry, I didnae know. I'll open them now."

While the woman does this Mrs Liddel peers in and sees the

wee girl sitting on the bed staring at her with an astonishment
she shows to everyone but her mother. She wears a frilly nylon
party frock much too big for her, and most surfaces in the room
are covered with a huge variety of cheap colourful children's
clothing. Mrs Liddel wonders if the mother has spent the day
dressing and undressing her daughter like a doll. She says carefully, "Mr Liddel has gone for a walk in the park—would you
like a cup of tea?"

"Oh, yes!"

"On Thursday Mr Liddel changes his library book. He won't
be home till five. Would your wee girl like to play on the kitchen
floor? I keep it very clean."

Under the influence of strongly sweetened tea and Mrs Liddel's talent as a listener the small woman explains that her name
is Donalda, that MacFee her man is a scrap merchant, that he
is not Theresa's father.

"Oh?" says Mrs Liddel.

"No," says Donalda, "definitely not. Do you like sex?"

"It is not something I'm able to talk about," says Mrs Liddel
gently.

"I'm not surprised—it's not a nice thing. In fact it's nasty.
I hate it most of the time. MacFee's different—he's very keen
on it. He'd thump me if I didnae give it to him once a week.
I wonder if he does it the right way. I mean, if that's all there
is to it why is there all this fuss about it?"

"I've sometimes wondered that," admits Mrs Liddel.

"Still, give sex its due—I wouldnae have met MacFee if it
hadnae been for sex."

"Oh?"

"No. You see I was once a very bad girl—a real hard case.
I went on the streets—know what I mean?"

"I . . . think so."

"The SS had cut my money and were after Theresa so I parked her with my mammy who's a very decent spud if you don't try her too often, then I went to Bath Street and sort of stood about. Some other lassies were doing it too but they were bigger than me so I kept well away from them. Then a guy comes up and says 'Hiya, honey, how's tricks? Where we gonna go?' He wasnae a Yank, he just talked that way. I says 'I don't know where to go. Do you know a place?' He says, 'Deed a do' and takes me round a corner into a lane, then he pushes me into a doorway and starts acting like a lunatic. He slaps me real hard and says, 'Don't scream or I'll murder you! Who are you and what do you mean? What do you mean?' Then he slaps me again and says 'Who's your man?' "

"Oh, no!" cries Mrs Liddel, who has never heard anything so appalling. Donalda is pleased by this reaction. She says, "Well of course I was bubbling and greeting but I was too feart to scream so I says, 'I'm nobody! I'm nothing! I don't mean anything at all! I don't have a man!' That made him madder than ever. He says, 'How can you be nobody when you're taking bread out of decent people's mouths? My woman's a professional and you're nothing but a stupid cheap wee amateur, I hate you!' and he slaps me a lot more. And I girn and greet and say I'm sorry and promise if he lets me go away I'll never come back and never do it again. He says, 'Life is not so simple as that hen. The polis are pals of mine. If I call the cops and charge you with soliciting they'll put you in jail.' So I beg and plead till he says he'll give me another chance, then he takes me to Mrs Mitchel."

"Who was she?"

"She lived near the start of Parliamentary Road," says

Donalda, "I was to bring guys to her place and she'd lend me
a bedroom and handle the money. She helped me tart myself
up a bit, then he took me back to Bath Street.

"Well, the next guy who comes along says, 'How about it,
dearie, are you game?' I say, 'Yes, Mr Sandilands,' because he
was my old history teacher. He says, 'Oh, God, Donalda *you*
aren't doing this are you? Go home to your mother, girl!' I says,
'I'd like to, Mr Sandilands, but it's no possible and I really need
the money.' He looks from side to side then slips me four quid
and says, 'You shoulnae be here and neither should I but I'd
like to see Lorraine. Do you know if Lorraine's around?' I says,
'No, I just started tonight,' so he groans and rushes away. Next
second the man who slapped me is beside me taking the four
pounds off me. He says 'Four pounds for two minutes chat is
nice work, doll. Maybe you've talent. Try leaning against the
wall with your legs crossed.'

"Well, the next guy who comes along is MacFee who says,
'Have you a place?' I say, 'Yes, near the start of Parliamentary
Road.' He says, 'I know that place. I have wheels. Let's go.' He
takes me round the corner to his van. I get inside and he drives
me to a place near Parkhead Cross. 'Oh, God!' I think, 'another
lunatic!' He takes me up to a room and does it to me, then says
it was very nice and did I like it too? 'Oh yes!' says I, 'Lovely.
But can I please have some money now?' 'Before we discuss that
I think we should eat something because I feel distinctly peck-
ish,' he says. 'There's the cooker, there's the sauages, there's the
eggs. Do your best.' Well, I was starving, really starving, so I
made a really big fry-up. I fried nearly everything I could see
because I'm thinking, 'If I get nothing else out of him at least
I'll get a decent feed.' I use half a pound of margarine and most
of a white pan loaf. When we've scoffed it he says, 'You are a
first-class cook. You fry like a duck takes to water.' I ask him

for money again and he says, 'I will not deceive you. I *have* money—a lot of money—but I need it for petrol because in my business I must keep on the move. But there are more important things in life than money. Why do *you* want money?' he says. I tell him about Theresa and he says, 'The man's back is broad. Let's pick her up.' So he drives us to my Mammy's house, we pick up Theresa and that's that. I've kept well away from Bath Street ever since. MacFee is not a bad soul. He never gives me money but if I need something he always manages to get it, eventually."

Mrs Liddel rests her head on her hand for it feels heavy with the news inside. She is so stupefied by this news that she lets slip a sentence which sounds like a judgement:

"You're not married."

"Oh, I'm married!" says Donalda glumly, "Married for three years, though I havenae signed anything. I wouldnae mind a real wedding with a white dress and organ and cake and confetti—it would be a day to remember but who would pay for it? *The man's back is broad.* I wonder who he was talking about? There was nobody in the room but him and me."

"I think" says Mrs. Liddel cautiously, "he was referring to himself."

"But MacFee's back isnae broad—or no very."

"I think he meant he was able to carry burdens."

"So MacFee thinks me and Theresa are . . . That's not fair! I don't like that! MacFee is a decent enough provider but it's me who always finds us places to stay, especially nowadays when he's in trouble. *Oh!*" Donalda claps a hand over her mouth, removes it and says, "I shouldnae have said that."

After a long pause Mrs Liddel says faintly, "You'd better tell me about it."

"I will. MacFee would thump me if he knew but you are

definitely not a clype—you're a decent spud, like my Mammy. Anyway, MacFee is very good at stripping lead and copper and zinc and iron from old factories and houses that are going to be demolished—folk pay him to do that, and when work is short he never goes on the burroo. 'If I registered with them I'd be done for,' he says, so he sometimes takes stuff out of places whose owners arenae easy to contact and mibby don't want it taken away. I'll give you an example. Like, he sees this old tractor in the corner of a field he keeps passing—it's been there for years so he goes there one night with his brother-in-law (no my brother—his sister's husband's brother) and they take it to bits and go off with it. But someone sees the number of the van, so there are enquiries. Personally, I think the brother-in-law shopped him, but never mind. Everywhere we stay for a while police come sniffing around and we have to move on. I'll hate having to leave this place. As soon as I saw you and your man in the lobby out there I felt *safe*. I havenae felt safe for years. But maybe they'll not find him here, or not for a long time. Anyway, thanks for the tea and chat, it's fairly cheered me up. Do you think the bath-water's ready?"

Mrs Liddel is so overwhelmed by this story that when her husband returns she cannot repeat a word of it and alarms him by sighing and shaking her head. She tells him when they are both safe in bed that night and then she falls asleep. He cannot sleep for he cannot now doubt that Britain is getting worse. He remembers the thirties and the prostitutes he saw when on the tramcars, especially nightshifts. Some were hard and aggressive, some gloomy and passive. None seemed happy with their work, but who ever is apart from removal men? For a while Mr Liddel ponders why men shifting furniture seem cheerier than other manual workers, with the possible exception of house-painters. He comes to no conclusion, but is sure that in the forties and fifties he saw very few prostitutes and hardly any brawls between poorly dressed youths. In those years the country was mobilized to fight Hitler or repair the damage of having done so. There was full employment, working-class leaders in the Labour Party, Tory leaders who had promised that Britain after the war would be better for everyone. But in the sixties unemployment climbed past the million mark again and has been growing with inflation ever since. Inflation, of course, has benefited those who can increase their annual incomes without striking: lawyers, doctors, most managements and directors, brokers, bankers, higher civil servants, the police, members of parliament, the monarchy: also electricians. For a while Mr Liddel ponders why the electrical workers are better off than miners, dockers, seamen, railwaymen, postmen. He sighs, recalling a time in the fifties when he was a loyal member of the local Labour Party. An election was approaching and the branch secretary suggested that if Mr Liddel put himself forward he might be chosen and elected. He did not put himself forward. A gas board official was elected who is now in the House of Lords. "Perhaps if I had stood I could have tipped the balance," thinks Mr Liddel, and starts imagining the Britain he would have helped to create. It would have a decent minimum wage for everyone, a sensible maximum one too. Unemployment would be abolished by forbidding all overtime work and introducing the Australian system of giving a whole year of fully paid holidays to those who have worked for seven years. Such thoughts have almost soothed Mr Liddel to sleep when he is roused by a nearby clicking.

Someone outside the bay window and very close to it is tapping discreetly on the glass, the glass of the bedroom window. Mr Liddel remembers the new lodgers have no house key, so this is MacFee returning. The time is half-past one in the morning. Mr Liddel hears Donalda stealthily open the bedroom and front doors. They click shut again after what sounds like several people have crept softly through them, but he may be wrong about this. Mr Liddel knows that people who spy on others are likely to exaggerate what they hear. However, Britain is getting worse again. Mr Liddel fears he may see again before he dies the hateful things he took for granted in childhood: undernourished children in the streets; nurses with tins begging passers-by for money to keep their hospitals running; well-fed voices explaining that the poor have caused their own poverty by being too lazy, greedy or selfish to work longer hours for less pay; unemployed youngsters fighting, even killing, because of religious and racial differences that don't matter a damn. He is glad he and his wife belong to the true middle classes who will not grow much richer or poorer through the mismanagement of the nation.

Meanwhile, what should he do? He cannot enter a police station and say, "My wife tells me our lodger tells her that her lodger's man sometimes steals scrap metal—a tractor, for example." To knowingly shelter a criminal is a criminal act, but nobody should be suspected of crime on the basis of gossip and hearsay. And if the police did investigate and arrest MacFee what would happen to the mother and child he supports? The mother would probably lose her daughter or return to prostitution or both. A queer question strikes Mr Liddel: is the bedroom next door being used just now as a brothel? Yes, that seems possible, but he has no evidence, and he has always been sorry for people who snoop after such evidence. He has not forbidden his lodgers to invite guests to their room—a landlord who made such a rule would be a tyrant. All a good landlord should expect of his tenants is quiet and orderly conduct, especially at night, and his lodgers have been as quiet as possible, in the circumstances. Tomorrow he will give them a door-key.

Having decided this, a relaxation which is almost happiness pervades Mr Liddel. Cautiously he moves his large pyjamad body backward until it touches Mrs Liddel without waking her. Instinctively she nestles close against him, placing an arm as light as a ribbon across his waist. They both sleep.

# CHAPTER 8

# The British Bum Garden

arry is an odd but elegant girl, strikingly tall, thin, supple and strong. This comes from solitary acrobatics in the school gymnasium where she often hangs upside-down on the wallbars for many minutes. She normally walks on tiptoe with rapid little steps and knees close together, body and neck and head so erect that viewed from the hips upward she seems to stand still while the world slips past her. She has no conversation. Her few brief remarks are in a clear little voice which seems to arrive from a great distance. Any question which cannot be answered by yes or no she answers with a slow gloomy nod. She reads every book the tutors give her very fast, with the brooding concentration she brings to comic papers and film magazines. When asked to write essays on her reading she quickly covers many pages with lines which look like different lengths of knotted string. If told to write slowly so that her words can be read she takes half an hour to form a sentence, often stopping to consult a dictionary and ponder, so her occasional eccentric spelling reads like subversive criticism.

PRIDE AND PREJUICE IS A STUPID BOOK UNLESS YOU LICK MR DANCY.

All her readable sentences are a simple statement with one reservation, laboriously written in minute, widely spaced capitals.

MOBY DICK IS A GREAT BOOK UNLESS YOU LACK WHALES.

HUCKLEBERRY FUN IS GREAT FUN UNLESS YOU LOCK CIVILIZED PUPIL.

"I spy intellect hia. I hope it is conscious intellect," says the headmistress, "I feel on the verge of knowing what she means."

In another child Harry's mannerisms would be thought signs of a damaged mind, but they are fascinating in a cousin of a queen. Even older girls would gladly be her friend but she treats everyone with an equal aloofness they think truly regal.

Harry is happiest when modelling clay. Her character has been shaped by two people: a mother who wanted a passive bit of female cleanness on which to exhibit some astonishingly expensive and fashionable little frocks, a nurse who worked to make her exactly that. She overcomes it all when she puts on denim overalls and grapples with a wad of cold, grey, tough but yielding muck. In her first year at school she likes the clay as wet as possible, splashing as she moulds until her own surface is like the surface of the sloppy mound on the stand. One day in her second year she achieves a smooth dome, cuts a groove across it and works on each half, pinching it rough and stroking it smooth until the art tutor, delighted to see a distinct form, cries, "That is the best thing you've done! Let's pop it in the kiln."

Two days later the work has been fired and cooled. Harry takes it to the play-loft, returns to the sculpture studio and starts again.

"Are you making anotha of these?" asks the tutor. When modelling clay Harry's voice sometimes loses its distant bell-like tone and sounds almost drowsy.

"I am besotted by a dream of total privacy," she murmurs. "You cannot imagine how much a paw woman sometimes craves fo absolute, uninterrupted privacy."

Later that day she asks the headmistress if she can do her modelling in the play-loft. This is the first time she has asked anyone for anything since she asked Linda to smack her. The headmistress says, "Why not? I'm shoa Hjordis won't mind."

Hjordis is no longer a hysterical dictator who thrives by rejecting people. She allows a modelling stand and bin of clay to be brought to the loft and placed near the space where the others play. Harry starts work at once. Hjordis watches her for a while then asks, "Is that a bum?"

Harry pauses and looks at the cleft dome on the stand as if expecting it to reply for her.

"It could be fatta," says Hjordis, and goes to play with the others.

Harry makes many cleft domes, eventually using cement fondu as that dries solid without needing to be fired. She also shapes energetic waves which bend into loops or twist together like snakes, but she always returns to the serenity of domes, partly because Hjordis also likes them. "I wish you would make me five really big ones," says Hjordis, "bums big enough to sit on. And a lot of small supporting bums, as many as you can."

"Material," says Harry.

"I'll arrange that. And I'll organize extra help too, if you want it."

Very few young artists are given such an opportunity. Harry is inspired. The five big ones she makes by herself, but shows the twins how to build up rough globes and slice them in two with a wire. With a trowel she swiftly gashes each hemisphere, and Linda smooths the surfaces of the result. Hjordis meanwhile strides around a space cleared for the first British bum garden, sometimes stooping to mark the floor with chalk. The small domes are placed to mark the edges of a lane spiralling inward through nine revolutions and ending at a small arena protected by the five big ones.

"And now I want a HUGE bum fo the very middle!" shouts Hjordis, "A bum as big as me!"

"No," says Harry, and refuses to be persuaded. Hjordis falls back on another idea.

"Every Wednesday afta dinna the gang will come up hia, march to the middle with me in front, sit on a bum and talk about very rude things. I want you all to think very hard and come up with a very rude thing to talk about next Wednesday. Make it as sawdid as you can."

On Wednesday they march to the middle as arranged but find the central bums far too hard to sit upon. Only Hjordis insists on doing so. The rest squat on the floor and lean against theirs.

"Right! Who starts?" demands Hjordis.

Twin one, after nudging from twin two, says Ethel should be covered all over with her own poo-poo then made to lick it off.

"Very good!" says Hjordis approvingly, "Yes, that's a highly satisfactory rude idea. Next!"

Twin two's rude idea involves the assistant headmistress and is otherwise the same as twin one's. Linda says suddenly, "Wouldn't it be great if we all—" then goes white and can't be persuaded to say another word. Nobody expects Harry to speak.

"What a dull lot of wets you all a!" says Hjordis bitterly. "I have some wondaful dirty things I meant to tell you, all about Christine Keela and boy scouts and Lawd Mota Museum and the queen and Harold Wilson and President Kennedy and Marilyn Monroe, but I won't tell you a thing if that's all I'm getting from you. Anyway, yaw too young to undastand me. You don't know a thing about biology."

But the bum garden has social consequences. Older girls hear of it, make discreet enquiries, and are one at a time invited up to look. Near the door Hjordis introduces the visitor to her artist and workers, then escorts the guest round the lane to the bum centre. Both sit on cushions, nibble liqueur chocolates, smoke Turkish cigarettes and sip very strong black sweet coffee. These refreshments are served by Linda, who wears a turban and beaded Edwardian ball-gown pinned up round her to look oriental. When she withdraws Hjordis says, "I'm afraid Linda is a bit of an eye-soa."

"Don't apologize!" says the *New Statesman* reader, "You've worked wondas. Last yia you wa an obnoxious little prat, but Hjordis! You a now an intelligent woman who can get things done. You *a* a woman, ain't you? Biologically, I mean."

Hjordis nods, willing herself not to blush.

"Then you should start seeing less of these little gels and mingle moa with yaw own age group. You won't find that easy at first. Yaw so filthy rich the othas can't help envying you a bit, but I am a socialist," says the guest, whose father is a Labour cabinet minister, "I loathe class prejudice in all its forms. You can no moa help being a millionay-a than the pawest slum-child can help being a paw-pa. I am willing to be yaw friend."

If Hjordis could weep openly she would shed tears of relief, joy and gratitude. Instead she gulps and nods.

Then takes her things from the loft and never returns. Linda and the twins find it an unglamorous place without her and go back to playing in the shrubbery where they can glimpse the exciting older girls. Surveying the solitude of the loft Harry's slight sensation of abandonment is gradually replaced by a lovely feeling of power over space. She shifts all her favourite objects into the centre of the bum garden: the modelling stand, clay and cement bin, rocking horse, stuffed seagull and a bust of Garibaldi. To replace the gang she models fat, tadpole-like figures with features which resemble them. Linda's head is mostly mouth. The twins are a single body with two heads. Hjordis is biggest, with distinct breasts and a sting in her tail. The headmistress enters, watches the progress of the work for a while then says, "Since Violet Stringham and the Sickert-Newtons left I have three vacant bedrooms wha the otha gels sleep, Harriet. Shall we go and see if tha is one you would like to occupy?"

"Oh no."

"I do not wish to deprive you of a bedroom wha you have slept fo nialy faw yias, Harriet, but by sleeping so close to me you exclude yawself from many pleasant romps and pyjama parties. Is tha nobody you would like to be nia? Nobody you would like to tap to through the wall if you felt lonely at night? Most of the gels would gladly be yaw chum if you allowed them an opening. Linda and you wa once so fond of each otha."

"Oh no."

"But if you neva communicate with othas how will you learn to communicate with *yawself,* Harriet? I realize that yaw art is a way of doing that, but the highest art is made through intacoss with all humanity, Harriet. At least study yaw contemporaries in the relevant publications, Harriet."

Harry nods thoughtfully and the headmistress sighs. She

knows that if she orders Harry to sleep in a room beside the others Harry will do so without complaint and revert to bed-wetting and peeing her knickers. The headmistress says, "I cannot let you stay lonely fo eva, Harriet. In a few weeks I will enroll three new little gels. On wet weekends they will play hia. If you awganize some games fo them, well and good. If you cannot do that, please stop them bullying each otha. If I learn that you fail to do even that I will lock this place up and you will return to pigging along with the otha gels in the sculptcha studio."

Harry prepares for the invasion by surrounding the bum garden with a wall of furniture, but also takes the headmistress's advice and studies the work of her contemporaries in international art magazines. She finds that most of her work has so far been well within the modern Euro-American art tradition and that her recent tadpole figurines are distinctly avant-garde. The magazines also stimulate new ideas. When the little girls arrive she has a use for them. On rainy days they put on waterproof boots, coats and hoods and follow her on exciting expeditions to derelict farms and factories, disused railway sidings and old overgrown quarries. Harry strides in front wearing a knapsack holding sandwiches, thermos flask, a kit of spanners, hammer, hacksaw and electric torch. She carries a spade over her shoulder. One of her followers is allowed to carry a coil of rope, the other two a crowbar. They are in search of anything Harry regards as queer and interesting. They discover, dig up or dismantle into handleable sections boulders, knotted roots and branches, balks of timber, rusted implements and machinery. In shifting these to the loft Harry provides most of the phsyical leverage but the united ant-like force of the smaller girls has nearly equal traction power. Hjordis in her Fortress days ruled her people through bribes and terrorism. Harry is no democrat either but rules by example. She drives her people hard but herself hardest. They have no time to bully each other. They help Harry accumulate heaps of things which give her ideas for new sculpture.

One evening after a strenuous excursion Harry is soaking in a warm bath when the headmistress enters. This she can easily do because the bathroom is between their bedrooms and has a door into each, a useful arrangement in years when Harry still needed prompting in the everyday uses of a lavatory. Ethel's manner reminds Harry of these years so she has no sense of intrusion. A more intimate intrusion follows, but Harry's formative experiences were all intrusions. When this one begins she feels she has waited a long time for it.

The headmistress says, "I am going to teach you something enjoyable. I had hoped you would learn it from one of the otha gels, because it is most fun if learned from a chum of yaw own age or slightly olda. Still, a stale old loaf is betta than malnutrition. Half the madhouses in Britain are full of people who neva learned to do this propaly. Lie comfatably back while I pop this rubba cushion unda this bit of you. Part yaw legs a little. I am now . . . very gently . . . poking about fo a little spot which feels enjoyably tickly when gently stroked . . . Have I found it?"

After a while Harry says, "Mm."

"Does mm mean yes?"

"Mm," says Harry dreamily. She would not complain if the headmistress were much rougher.

"In a few minutes I will stop doing this and you can continue doing it for yawself. You have a very nice body, Harriet, it is beginning to bloom. Yaw body will not only look nice, it will feel nice if you stroke it in otha places. Hia . . . and hia . . . hia also . . . Do you eva think of things which make you tingle?"

Harry frowns more deeply than usual.

"Everybody, Harriet, has ideas which make them tingle, ideas which make stroking themselves and even stroking otha people moa fun. These ideas a to be found in litritcha, art, films, advertisements and the games we play. Some of these ideas would be harmful if taken seriously, but only stupid people take ideas seriously. The French—Germans—Russians—Irish sometimes take ideas seriously, but in England we a all liberals at heart, as wise as serpents and harmless as doves. We know that the wildest ideas a just ways of adding funny tingly feelings to a world managed by old-fashioned business methods, those methods no serious person questions. Is this kind of talk boring you, Harriet?"

"A bit."

"Then concentrate on yaw own tingly little dream world and let this talkative old lady stroke you a little longa fo I too am lonely sometimes. Sex is the root of it. Miss Harmenbeck has told you in biology how babies a made, but babies a expensive! Unless you want one the wisest sort of sex is little tingly stroking games with yawself or anotha gel. Do you eva think about boys—about men, Harriet?"

"No."

"I neitha, but we should not despise, we should pity them. Naytcha created them to help women have babies, but they do that in less than a minute. By tha late teens they have passed tha sexual peak and it is downhill all the way fo them. They cannot enjoy sex as much as women, eitha. They stay fertile longa, but it does not console them. They turn jealous and destructive, hence wife-battering, wawfare and most of what is taught as history. Some truly great men try to refawm themselves but usually make a hash of it. Paw Tolstoy. But Leonard Woolf was all right. Leonard was a good old stick."

The daydreams which make Harry tingle are about Hjordis spanking people, but are unlike what happened in the shrubbery. That event was so unexpected and so quickly over that she hardly noticed it at the time. Gradually her imagination has falsified it into something splendid with Hjordis an enthroned witch-queen ordering the twins to spank Harry in terrible ways; sometimes ordering her to spank them back. These daydreams are not satisfactory. The voices sound wrong.

Harry's mother visits the school for the second time on the day her daughter finally leaves it. She asks, "So what has my daughta learned hia, apart from keeping clean and getting out of a sports car without showing ha knickas?"

"She has learned what she wants to do with ha life. She will be a sculptress. She will achieve fame."

"Everybody's daughtas a into art, or drama, or fashion nowadays," says Harry's mother carelessly, "I rather hoped you would make a nun of ha, as you almost promised me the last time we met. Will art be the only love of ha life? Will she be capable of a husband, kids, etcetera?"

"No," says the headmistress serenely, "She will neva be a family woman. She had no propa home life befoa you brought ha hia so I had nothing to build upon. The best I could do was help ha to self-respecting self-sufficiency. She will always be eccentric and lonely, but will not turn to drink, drugs or shoplifting."

"I'm glad you've straightened ha out a bit but I cannot feel grateful," says Harry's mother, "You've extracted a small fortune from ha fatha—thank God I manage my own money. Did she *need* ha own welding equipment? Ha own pneumatic drill and rivet gun? What *use* to ha wa lessons in glass blowing?"

"Ha genius requiad them. True genius grasps in its teens the

implements which mia talent acquias in its twenties. James
Watt and Mozart a cases in point. Harriet will soon be very
famous."

"Yes indeed!" says Harry's mother bitterly, "Ha happy and
glorious in-laws will ensure that. The prospect of a sale to a
national collection is bound to bring dealas flocking."

The headmistress and Harry's mother are both correct. In
her first year at a great London art school the staff find they can
teach Harry nothing. In the second an international art dealer
says, "Let me take you unda my wing."

Harry can build austere, grotesque or threatening forms out
of fiberglass, cement, metal, wood, bricks, plastic and combina-
tions of these. She can mould a five-foot-high tooth or big toe
in clay and have it carved in granite or cast in brass or stainless
steel. She can cover a floor with a lattice of rusty iron rods
mysteriously reminiscent of fallen branches, or with a lattice of
fallen branches mysteriously reminiscent of themselves. She can
fill a room with suspended tubes and aluminium sheets which
tinkle and thunder at the faintest human vibration. There is no
shape or assembly of shapes she cannot create or represent,
apart from a life-like head or torso. The only human forms she
creates are sexless, featureless dummies hanging from real
pieces of gymnasium equipment. The Tate Gallery buys one of
these. She sells well in the USA too, though her entries in the
Venice Biennale, her retrospective in the Pompidou Centre are
ignored or disdained by Italian and French art critics. Her
dealer says this is because the European mainland is so bloody
insular. Harry shrugs. She really does not care what people
think of her work. The excitement of imagining and making it,
the satisfaction of setting it up somewhere are what she lives for.
She likes it to be sold, because then she need not see it again.
Anything returned to her is eventually broken up to make

something else, so her dealer stores everything he thinks saleable and leaves the rest in her studio until it coheres in a marketable form. Harry's indifference to her completed work, indifference to criticism, refusal to attend the openings of fashionable art shows including her own, make many intelligent folk think she too is intelligent. Only her old headmistress knows she cannot write more than her name without a lot of concentrated thought and a severe headache; that ordering a meal in a restaurant or making a snack in her studio are equally beyond her powers, though she handles dangerous industrial equipment with ease and safety. The married couple who feed her and buy for her, the secretary, accountant and dealer who handle her correspondence, money and work often tell each other, "The woman's an idiot!" yet do not mean she is foolish. They are mocking, but also acknowledging, an intelligence they think greater than their own because it is alien.

Since Harry is splendidly gaunt, related to royalty and makes weirdly fashionable objects she is photographed for glossy publications financed by art and property manipulators. Writers hired to embellish the photographs with amusing comments find the job difficult. It is hard to be entertaining about someone with no apparent sex life, social life or conversation. Harry's publicity falls into four divisions:

1. Her family connections.
2. Her studios. (In London and San Francisco she has a vast skylit loft in a converted dockland warehouse, where she lives among her constructions and equipment. Next door to each is a small luxury flat for the married couple who look after her.)
3. Her range of techniques. (This is best conveyed by camera. Harry welding, sand-blasting or casting something has been described as Wagnerian by Bernard Levin.)

4. Theoretical twaddle about her place in the history of British art.

"Aren't you sick of being a Post-Modernist?" asks a man from the colour supplement of a Sunday newspaper. He is famous for his articles on artistic topics because he refers knowingly to famous foreigners in a way suggesting that no intelligent Briton need bother with them. He wants to annoy Harry into saying something interesting for an article to be called THE SHETLAND ENIGMA. Harry replies with a vague nod. He says, "Listen! The last truly great artists had reached maturity when you wa still a kid. They wa trained in a tradition which started with the Greeks, was revived by the Italians, was passed by Michelangelo to Rodin and brought to a conclusion by Moore, Hepworth, Brancusi, etcetera. Do you neva envy these *truly* creative artists?"

"No."

"But to most people nowadays the new things in the galleries look like doodling! They add very little beauty or intelligence to the places wha they appia, none at all to those who see them. Does it occur to you that yaw art may be a game played for nobody's plesha but yaw own? Like mastabation."

"Yes."

"Does it occur to you often, or only when yaw depressed?"

Harry says slowly, "It occurred to me when you asked me about it."

"But it still strikes you as true?"

"I don't know. Ask Harvey about that." Harvey is her dealer. He arranges all her interviews and censors the resulting articles. The journalist sighs and glances down at a list of questions unlikely to produce exciting answers, but better than nothing.

"What was yaw first major commission?"

"The bum garden."

"Eh?"

Harry explains about the bum garden.

"What became of it?"

"It's probly in the loft wha we left it."

"And could I . . . could you . . . could we go down with a photographa and have a look? This is impawtant! Really exciting! You say you wa seven when you made it?" He stares hard at a space inside his head where THE SHETLAND ENIGMA has been replaced by HARRY'S BUM GARDEN.

The Georgian mansion near Bath is no longer a school, but on this warm mild May afternoon the former headmistress is delighted to take tea on the terrace with a photographer, a journalist, and the most famous of her former pupils.

"Who would have thought that a staunch old liberal like me would turn Tory in her declining yias?" she asks, gazing contentedly across the pupil-less lawn, "What strange alterations I have seen! When I was a little gel England ruled a quarta of the globe, Harriet. Only a bit of Eye-a-land had got away. The Em-pie-a now has all gone, all gone, except fo a little bit of Eye-a-land, yet the golden days of my childhood in the twenties and thirties have at last returned. I neva expected that. When I made a school of the dia old place in the forties I thought I would eventually have to grapple with daughtas of coal minas and powa-loom weavas befoa hobbling down at last to the village post office to collect my old-age pension. What a pessimist I was! Not that I resent my yias of service to the young. I think I did you a lot of good, Harriet. I wish I had taught Hjordis the same self-sufficiency, but I dared not attempt it. She would have blabbed."

"How is Hjordis?"

"Dead. Dia me, how shocked you look! I thought everyone knew that, she hit the headlines fo six and no mistake. She was

addicted to *men,* and popula ones—the most dangerous kind
of man. She married a popula young brutalist stock-broka, then
a student politician with terrorist connections, then popula
singas who excited themselves by eating dangerous chemicals.
Hjordis ate them too and died in 1978. The twins also came to
a sad end. They returned to tha people in New Zealand, one got
married and the otha tried to kill ha. Fortunately they a friends
again, but confined to an institution. They send me Christmas
cards. And Linda writes to me. Afta two bad marriages and a
publicity job and an arts degree she now lives in *Glasgow.* She
and a few otha heroic souls a toiling to make the place suitable
fo . . . something. She and ha ilk, most of them English, work
fo . . . money of course, but also fo the good of the community.
Linda is a very, very special sort of social worka: an exhibition
offica, or fine arts advie-za, or arts administrata or all three.
And she has two lovely little gels in Dartington Hall, which is
not quite as liberal a school as mine was but a lot cheapa. I'm
surprised Linda has not contacted you, Harriet. She must still
hold you in awe."

"Could we, er—?" asks the journalist, looking at his wristwatch.

"Off you go. Harriet will escawt you to ha old haunt. You
will see a difference Harriet. No jumble now to distract the eye
from the starkness of yaw formations! In the seventies I per-
ceived that the family lumba was steadily gaining value, so I
waited till I retie-ad and had it auctioned by Sotheby's. The
Victoria and Albert Museum wanted the old clothes, three
museums of childhood wa afta the toys, but I had written to
forma pupils in the States asking if they knew American collec-
tas who might be interested. Indeed they did! A Yank took the
lot, even the furnitcha and knick-knacks. I laughed and laughed
and laughed. And a terribly dull pictcha I had loathed since

childhood turned out to be by Corot. I do not owe my present affluence *wholly* to Mrs Thatcha's tax reliefs."

The photographer takes one look at the loft and quickly makes a phone call. Two hours later a big van arrives bringing a theatre electrician and lighting equipment. Another hour is needed to position the lights accurately; then the photographer scrambles about on the rafter beams until he achieves a wide-angle downward shot of Harry squatting cross-legged and pensive in the midst of two hundred and thirty-four bums. Each bum casts a distinct shadow on the bare planks of the floor. So does Harry, but her upturned face, hopelessly resigned to an ancient and terrible wrong, is the small tragic centre of the composition. This picture is given a double-page spread in the centre of the supplement. Part appears on the cover with the title HARRY'S BUM GARDEN.

Two days later someone at the far end of a telephone wire says, "Guess who this is."

"Linda," says Harry.

"Yaw amazing, Harry! Fancy you remembering my voice straight off like that afta nialy twenty yias! Listen, tha's so *much* I want to say to you and ask of you . . . I'm so afraid of getting emotional and being a dreadful boa . . . Can you put up with me fo foa or five minutes maybe?"

"Yes."

"Well, first, congrats on the splendid coverage the *Sunday Times* gave you. I nialy fainted when I saw the dia old bum garden all ova the supplement. I'm in *Scotland,* Harry. I know yaw too unworldly to have television or read the newspapas but shoe-aly you've heard that Glasgow will be the official European cultcha capital for 1990?"

"No."

"Well it is! So a lot of us have come hia to make the thing

possible and take the curse off the place. You see, many intelligent people still think Glasgow is a bolshie slum full of drunks who slash each otha with ray-zas because nobody wants the ships they used to build. Well we *a* taking the curse off the place. Wia employing Saatchi and Saatchi! Yes, the firm that handles public relations fo Margaret Thatcha and the Conservative Party! How can we fail? We've also discovad a magnificent old neglected Victorian art gallery in the middle of Sauchiehall Street. The town council have owned it fo a century so nothing has apiad in it but local stuff, so now it's being splendidly renovated and wia arranging a programme of shows with a truly intanational appeal. This morning thea was a big committee meeting, and yaw name came up, and because of the *Times* thing even our pet councilla knew you wa Britain's most famous sculpta and a distant cousin of the thingmis. I was very cunning—I said not a word until they started to discuss *Can we get ha?* and at last one of them turned to me and asked (as they all have to eventually) *What do you think?* and I said very quietly, *She and I a quite good friends. We wa at school togetha. In fact I put the finishing touches to most of these smalla bums.* My dia, you should have seen tha faces! My standing soared like a fast lift up the Telecom towa! So they've asked me to beg and imploa you to *let them bring the bums to Glasgow.* We want to give you a whacking great retrospective hia, much bigga than the one in that ghastly Pompidou Centa (the French a so insula). Imagine this lovely curving white marble staircase, a double staircase with black marble balustas. It brings you to a vestibule whose floa is checkad marble with the bum garden spread all ova it! What otha artist has had a retrospective which starts with an installation of nialy three hundred pieces she conceived when she was seven?"

"Hjordis conceived it," says Harry and notices tears on her

cheeks. Perhaps her breathing betrays this because Linda begins talking in a voice both vibrant and solemn.

"I loved Hjordis too, Harry. I loved ha as passionately as you did, though she despised me fo it. The bum garden is ha monument, Harry! You must not keep it from the world. You and I a the last of the gang, Harry, the twins don't matta now. It can't be mia coincidence that you and I a coming togetha on this thing. If I was religious I would say God wants us to do it. I'm not, so I say *fate* wants us to do it. You and I wa once very good friends, Harry. Oh what went wrong?"

"Don't know," whispers Harry, surprised by how wet her face is getting, "What does Harvey say?"

All phone calls to Harry pass through her agent's office to stop her being pestered by unprofitable business.

"He says he's enthusiastic about it if you a, Harry! The Scottish Museum of Modern Art in Edinburgh has nothing of yaws, Harry, which is ridiculous! Glasgow and Abadeen are equally forlorn. If you do this fo Scotland yaw bound to sell at least one may-ja piece. We provide the venue and will pay fo transpawt and publicity, and aftawad the show can return to London and appia in a really impoatant gallery like the Warwick or the Serpentine. Please say yes!"

"Yes, excuse me headache," whispers Harry putting the phone down.

Since the separation from her nursemaid nothing shocks Harry as much as news that Hjordis is dead. Hjordis is the centre of Harry's love life. Basking drowsily in a deep bath of warm water after a hard day's work, Harry imagines erotic adventures with Hjordis in a shrubbery as big as a jungle at first, but in later years it enlarges to a planet. Harry is queen of this world, the most adored and desired person on it and also the weakest. Hjordis is the strongest and most feared. Hjordis is a wicked prime minister who has organized all the men into a cruel army and used it to seize power; but among wild scenery dwell bands of outlaws—cow girls and swamp women and pirate whores who rescue Harry from Hjordis or capture her for reasons of their own. The politics of this world appears in *Four Sisters,* the smallest but most popular of Harry's works.* Four women's shoes stand toe to heel in a square, each one cast or cut in a different almost colourless material: glass, maplewood, stainless steel and white leather. The leather shoe is real, the others modelled on it. Each stiletto heel pierces the toecap of the shoe behind it. Every work of art Harry made shows part of her imaginary world's furniture, scenery or architecture. It is a world where imaginary pains produce some real ecstasy. Everyone recovers immediately from injuries, everyone is ravishingly beautiful, nobody grows old or sick or dies, and certainly not Hjordis. Always glorious and cruel, always plotting to satisfy herself but forever incapable of satisfaction, it is Hjordis who keeps this dream world working. Harry has not seen or heard of Hjordis for over twenty years. There is no obvious reason for imaginary Hjordis to vanish because the real one dies, but it happens. The dream world becomes a reminder of death and of absence, then vanishes also. Harry cannot now imagine anyone who adores or desires her, cannot imagine anything at all.

She locks the studio door and squats on a stool, hugging her body and rocking it to and fro. Sometimes she masturbates, but

---

*The title was chosen by her dealer, who names all Harry's work. Most illustrated histories of modern British art show a photograph of *Four Sisters,* ascribing it to the Pop or Neo-Realist or Surrealist school. Ms Paulina Cameron, topiary adviser to the National Trust, is supervising the cultivation of a hedge shaped like *Four Sisters* for the Melcombe Priory National Heritage Museum. Visitors will be able to walk under the arches of the insteps.

it is joyless exercise. She listens to a clear childish voice chant-
ing *Give me somebody. Give me somebody.* It is her own voice.
It is not praying to anyone, but is certainly praying. She feels
nothing in the world can be done but rock and pray till she dies
of exhaustion. Sleep is impossible. After several hours she hears
voices mingling with her own. A muffled man's voice says her
art is a childish game, like doodling or masturbation. Another
slightly louder voice argues that the bum garden is a monument
to Hjordis which must not be kept from the world.

Shortly after midnight she hears a voice calling faintly from
a great distance. She stops praying to hear better. It falls silent,
but sounds slightly nearer when she prays more quietly. Eventually she can make out the words *Harry Shetland* followed by
a burst of hectic pleading. As the sun starts to rise her prayer
has sunk to a whisper and the pleading is distinct, though as if
shouted upward from a ground far below her:

*Harry Shetland, come down to me please yaw motha and my*
*motha wa friends! Wia the only two in this stinking hell-hole who*
*need each otha! Oh please come down and visit me in my fortress!*
*We'll shut everybody else out—even the twins! I've a lovely tin*
*of delicious biscuits and all sorts of gorgeous things fo you!*
*Chocolate and scent and a silk scarf and a sweet little hampsta*
*in a cage shaped like a doll's house who's called Limpy Dan*
*because one of his feet doesn't work but you can call him any-*
*thing you like please come down! Please I'm so lonely!*

Harry remembers a time when this pleading made her feel
aloof, smug and powerful, but now the pain in it is a pain she
feels through her whole body. She groans, sways dizzily and
nearly faints, but is roused by a loud, commanding voice which
sounds right beside her: *I want a huge bum to go in the middle,*
*a bum as big as me!*

"Yes, I can give you that now," says Harry, suddenly knowing what to do. "Thank you, Hjordis."

She yawns hugely, unlocks her door, phones an order for sandwiches and a glass of milk. She eats, drinks, then sleeps soundly. A day later, before phoning to arrange a meeting with her dealer and Linda, she stares hard into a mirror. Her appearance does not interest her, usually, but today she wants to appear as well as feel like a different woman. Her hair is cut like the fur of a sleek animal, for she hates brushing and combing. Abruptly she summons her hairdresser and tells him to shave her completely bald.

# CHAPTER 9

# A Free Man with a Pipe

Phone rings. Ella patiently lifts the reciever. Most of the calls she answers are for a friend who is seldom in. She says quickly, "Hello."

"Hello, Jean!" says a loud eager voice. "I'm a free man."

"I'm sorry, Jean is out. She won't be back till quite late. Can I give her a message?"

She hears a sigh, then silence, then a sad little voice asks hesitantly, "Is that you, Elaine?"

"I'm Ella Warner, Jean's flatmate."

"Of course you are!" says the voice loudly, "You are Ella Warner, Jean's flatmate. We met at Jean's housewarming party and had an interesting chat. You think modern mothers allow their daughters too much freedom—"

"I don't think I said that."

"You wore a blue trousersuit—"

"A blue dress."

"I got the colour right. I'm Leo Brown and you don't remember a single thing about me." The voice is triumphant and accusing.

She says defensively, "I remember hardly anyone from that party. Why should I? It wasn't my party."

"You'll remember me when you see me, Ella. I'm coming round."

"Don't be stupid."

"I'm taking you out for a meal."

"I've just eaten."

"I'm taking you out for a drink."

"I don't like drinking, usually, and just now I'm studying. I've an exam on Monday. I don't know you and I don't think you know me."

The voice turns hard and ugly. "All work and no play makes Jill a very dull girl indeed, Ella! What you need is a break from your routines, Ella! It will help your studies so I'll knock your door half an hour from now, right."

"I won't open it if you do." Ella is firm about this but does not put the receiver down. She hears another sigh, and silence, and once again the sad little hesitant voice.

"Do you . . . know the lounge bar of The Lorne?"

"Well?"

"In half an hour I'll be having a drink there. I'll be smoking a rather unusual pipe. The bowl is carved to look like the head of a bull—"

"Oh!"

"*Now* you remember me?"

"No, but I remember your pipe."

After four seconds the voice says dully, "If you want a drink you know where to come," and the line goes dead.

Ella returns to her books but cannot concentrate on them. Why should the voice of a lonely, foolish man who wants company upset her so much? She too is lonely but likes loneliness, usually. Most people, she thinks, pay too high a price for company, married people especially. That is why she admires Jean, who for two or three years has avoided matrimony by something like promiscuity, and now talks of having a single-parent family. But Ella, who likes children, knows they are usually happier with a couple of married parents. These thoughts interfere with her studies. It is a warm evening, she needs a breath of open air, maybe a walk will freshen her. The way to the park passes the Lorne Hotel. Curiosity leads her into the lounge bar, which at that hour is almost empty. She buys a half-pint glass of cider and looks cautiously round. The only single man sits in a corner, seemingly lost in thought. Ella is long-sighted. Removing her spectacles she sees on the table before him the unusual pipe beside an untouched half-pint glass of light ale. Though not young he is not elderly. His well-cut tweed suit is neither shabby nor ostentatiously fashionable. None of his features is notably strong or weak, but they and the whole slump of his body suggest a sad perplexity she finds attractive. His lips move slightly as if repeating past conversations.

She replaces the spectacles, takes her glass to his table and sits quietly opposite. He stares at her in a confused way, then says without enthusiasm, "Oh, hullo. You made it," and adds reproachfully, "you should not have bought that drink. The treat must be on me. Waiter!" With a sweep of the arm he summons one of the bar staff and orders two whisky liqueurs.

"But—" says Ella, who dislikes whisky in any form.

"No buts tonight! This calls for a celebration. You must be wondering why I asked you here."

"No."

"Surely almost total strangers don't ask you out every night of the week?"

"On the phone you sounded as if you needed to talk to someone. I thought you were lonely."

"Ella! How can you think so little of yourself? Ella, we hardly exchanged two words at that party but you have qualities men—some men—find unforgettable."

"What qualities?" asks Ella, interested but not overwhelmed. She knows most men see her as a nice young aunt.

"Oh, your hair, your voice, your . . . the bits matter less than the way they fit together."

The waiter brings two glasses of liqueur. Leo pays him, lifts one then frowns into it as though it is far too deep. After a moment he puts it down and drinks the beer instead. It occurs to Ella that he too dislikes whisky liqueur. She says, "Is something wrong?"

"What do you mean?"

"One moment you're excited, the next you're flat and dull."

"I keep remembering a dream I had last night."

Ella, highly excited, cries, "I had a dream last night! Can I tell you about it?"

"Go ahead."

As Ella talks her mild face grows vivacious. He watches it closely, without pleasure. "I was walking along a road in the country, it was a dull ordinary day and I was worrying about my exams when I suddenly felt this warm golden light shining down on me from behind. I didn't dare turn and look but I knew, I *knew* that a huge golden aeroplane was sweeping after me in the sky and the warm happy feeling came from that. I knew the aeroplane was the Concorde."

Leo drinks the last of his beer and says, "Well?"

"That's all, but it left me feeling happy all day. What did you dream?"

"There was a stone head on my sitting-room floor, about six feet high, a piece of a statue of an Egyptian king. It should have been hollow but it was stuffed full of dirty rags and I was trying to pull them out through the mouth with my hands and then I realized there was . . . the corpse of some animal in the middle. I couldn't go on. I tried to cram the rest of the dirt back in but it wouldn't go in." He pauses then says with vast indignation, "The whole room was an *utter mess!*"

She shudders and says, "No wonder you're depressed."

There is a change of feeling between them. Her sympathy has cheered him and she, seeing this, relaxes and murmurs, "I wonder if it means I'll pass the exams."

"What are you talking about?"

"My dream."

"Your dream means sex."

"Oh no!"

"Wait a bit!" he says, raising a forefinger. "You're walking along a dismal ordinary road worrying about exams. That's ordinary life, right? Then you feel something warm and beautiful coming after you, something you're afraid to face. It's called the Concorde and you know what Concorde is French for, don't you?"

"Concorde is a place in America," says Ella, seeing a way out, but he smiles and talks over her like a firm but patient teacher: "Concorde is the French for *togetherness,* Ella. That dream is prophetic, Ella. It tells what the future holds if you

have the courage to face it. I think that coming here tonight
shows you *have* the courage to face it."

She is unwilling to be impressed by this and says, "What does
your dream mean? Is it about sex too?"

"Let's change the subject," he suggests briskly. "What do
you do? Are you a student?"

"A nurse. But I'm studying to be a physiotherapist."

"I know about that. Deep breathing. Physical jerks."

"The main thing is relaxation," says Ella, and adds dreamily,
"deep, controlled relaxation . . . I think I may be good at it."

"Why?"

"Well, we have a little boy with really bad asthma. It's so bad
he's afraid to sleep at night. The doctors put him on steroids,
but of course they couldn't keep him on these for ever—they
destroy certain glands if you do—and now he's as bad as he was
before. Do you know, even in his worst panics I can almost get
him to breath perfectly easily? I make him lie down flat—it's
almost impossible to get asthmatics to do that—and with a little
light massage I get him breathing slowly and evenly and deeply,
and in ten minutes he's in a perfectly normal sleep. I've tried
to teach the boy's mother to do this for him but she can't. She
loves him, she'd do anything to make him well, but when she
talks to him or touches him his muscles tighten. He doesn't
trust her—doesn't trust her physically."

After a moment Leo says defensively, "I'm quite good at my
job too."

"Yes?"

"Sales representative for Quality Fabrics. I realize that
means nothing to you. I suppose you think travelling salesmen
are a dying breed."

"No! Why should they be?"

"Because of chainstores, supermarkets, new shopping centres. Well let me tell you, we are NOT a dying breed. That sort of competition has done nothing but weed out weaklings. Survivors like me are travelling further and earning more than ever. When I took on this job Quality Fabrics gave me the central lowlands. Now all Scotland is my province." He stares at her challengingly.

She responds with a small smile which becomes bright when she thinks of something to say. "You must pass through some lovely scenery."

"So I am told."

"But surely—"

"Ella, I am the best driver I know. In ten years I have not once had an accident that could be traced to my negligence. While driving I keep my eyes on the road and my mind on—not just the car ahead of me—but the car *in front* of the car ahead of me. I travel north to Thurso, east to St Andrews, south to Berwick, and for all the scenery I see I might be driving backwards and forwards through the Clyde Tunnel."

"That's terrible!"

"It never struck you that driving should be enjoyed for its own sake?"

"Never."

"Well, I enjoy driving for its own sake. That's why I'm good at it. Using a highly sophisticated implement which every year slaughters thousands, I am constantly achieving and reconciling two different things, maximum safety and maximum speed. This achievement absorbs my whole personality, I am glad to say. Too many folk nowadays do nothing with their personalities but flaunt them."

After a pause she says, "I agree."

Again they notice he has impressed her and again he grows more cheerful, clinking his glass against hers and saying, "Skol!"

She smiles and sips as little as possible to avoid grimacing. He gulps his fast, perhaps for the same reason, and she feels inside her a definite tickle of amusement. She finds him entertaining, though perhaps not in the way he wants to be.

"You see," he says, with an air of reckless expansion, "I'm a free man. I choose my own hours and my own itineraries, nobody sets me a routine. A routine job must be hell on earth. You must know that, working where you do."

"But I like my work. Hospitals are the best places in the world."

"They're terrible places!"

"They are not!" says Ella, angered into boldness, "If anyone throws paper on a hospital floor a cleaner picks it up. If an old man wets his bed there's somebody to wash him and change the sheets. If somebody is in pain and dying we have drugs to make them comfortable. Outside hospitals the only safe people are the rich people, but in hospitals nobody is neglected or starved or made to do work they're not fit for. There's always someone on duty, someone responsible in charge."

"How old do you think I am?"

". . . Forty?"

"Thirty-five," says Leo in an injured voice, "and I have never once set foot in a hospital or visited a doctor. Yes, I'm fit."

"But not relaxed."

"Of course I'm relaxed."

"Why do you breathe like that?"

"Like what?"

"Quick and shallow instead of deep and slow."

He looks at her in a haunted way and does not reply. She says conversationally, "You've gone dull and flat again."

"Do you talk like this to everybody?" he asks in his ugliest voice.

"I'm afraid so."

"You must find it hard to keep a boyfriend."

"I do. Yes."

"I'm trying to help you, Ella, but my God you're making it hard for me . . . My divorce came through today."

After a moment she pushes her glass towards him saying gently, "Would you mind finishing this drink?"

"Don't you like it?"

"I'm sorry. I've tried to. I'm sure it will do you more good."

He looks at it, drains it like medicine, coughs a little then says, "Ask me anything you like."

"But—"

"Don't worry, you won't be probing a wound. We've been separated for years."

"I see. Did you—"

"If you want to know if I was unfaithful to her or she to me the answer is no. In both cases. As far as I am aware. But we were incompatible. She kept telling me I got on her nerves and after a while this got on my nerves."

"How did you get on her nerves?"

"Well, when I got home from work in the evening I was exhausted. I've told you why. I was holding down more and more of Scotland for Quality Fabrics. I drove an average of 350 miles per day. Her office job must have left her with plenty energy for as soon as she saw me she started to *talk*. Telling me things. Asking questions. And she insisted on being answered. A simple 'yes' or 'no' or 'that's nice' wasn't good enough. She wanted detailed discussions when all I wanted was a quiet meal then an hour by the fire with the newspaper followed by a spot of television. What did I know about hats, shoes and the neighbour's dog? Why should I care about whether new wallpaper should be pink to harmonize with the carpet or green to contrast with it? Life is too short."

"She sounds as if she loved you. Or wanted to."

"If she'd shut her mouth for a couple of hours I could have loved her back, or sounded as if I did. But she kept driving me out of the house. To pubs like this, as a matter of fact, though I am definitely not a drinking man. A half-pint of lager is *my* normal limit."

"Did you talk to people in the pubs you visited?"

"Yes, of course. Talk is easy in a pub, it happens without thinking. Before I married I talked to the wife all the time in pubs. But home should be different, it should let a couple enjoy silence for a change. I once read an article on how to make a success of your marriage, and one thing it said was *never let your wife feel you take her for granted.* That made me laugh. If you can't take your wife for granted who can you take for granted? Everybody else you meet—especially the women— you've got to be polite and entertaining to, you've got to show yourself and sell yourself to them like I show fabrics to a potential buyer. Like I'm showing myself to you just now. But surely a *wife* should grow out of needing that treatment."

Ella frowns, purses her lips like a doctor considering a case then says, "No children?"

"None."

"You should have adopted one."

"Ella, I notice you are keen in the mercy and kindness approach to existence which makes you hard and insensitive at times. I know there are many helpless, unloved children in the world but would it be fair to get one in like a paperweight to stop an unlucky marriage blowing away?"

Ella says stubbornly, "Children are dying from lack of love and your wife had more of it than you could take."

"You're a hard woman, Ella," he says sadly, "a hard, hard woman."

"I'm sorry, Leo," she says with real regret, "I don't mean to be."

"That is the first time you've spoken my name."

"Oh?" Her hand rests on the table.

He places his own on it, saying softly, "Come home with me, Ella. We're on the verge of saying important things to each other. A hotel is no place for genuine . . . concord."

"Oh. Well . . . all right, just for an hour, but it mustn't be any longer, Leo." Her voice has the comradely sound of one private soldier in the great sex war talking to another. Unluckily Leo, being a man, thinks he belongs to the officer class.

He stands, waves to the bar and shouts, "Waiter! Two more whisky liqueurs!"

She stares at him. He snarls, "You pity me, don't you? That's why you're ready to come back with me. I'm one of your orphans."

She whispers fiercely, "Sit down! People are looking at us and I don't want a whisky liqueur."

"Then give it to me out of the kindness of your heart like you gave the last one."

"Why do you sneer at kindness?"

"It is insulting to man's essential nature."

"What is man's essential nature?"

"I don't know."

"You want me to be nice to you as if you were doing me a favour."

"I want to be admired!" cries Leo wildly. "Is that too much to ask?"

"Admired for what?"

"If you see nothing else in me you might at least notice I am made in the image of God!" After this outcry he slumps into gloom again, adding lamely, "If you had a religion you might."

"Have you a religion?" asks Ella, who now has no idea of what they are discussing.

"No."

"Excuse me, sir, you have to leave," says the waiter. Leo is astonished.

"Why?"

"You're making too much noise. And swearing upsets the ladies."

"I didn't swear! We were discussing religion."

"That can lead to trouble sir. You'd better leave."

With quiet dignity Leo takes his pipe from the ashtray and rises saying, "Goodnight. You are not losing a regular customer, but you *may* be losing someone who might have *become* a regular customer."

Ella, beside him, has a fit of the giggles which her strongest efforts cannot quell before they stand on the pavement outside. He says, "You thought that funny."

"I'm sorry."

"Goodnight."

"Don't you want me to come with you?" she asks. He stares amazed into her calm friendly face, then smiles gratefully and seizes her hand.

He leads her to a terrace overlooking the park, a terrace built for the rich of the previous century. Wealth still resides there. They come to a building like a church with broad steps to a high door. The door is glass. Ella sees through it a refreshingly antiseptic floor of big black-and-white chequered tiles, a brown clay urn with huge spiky leaves sprouting from it, the door of a lift. Leo takes her in to the lift. Leo's apartment is a large sitting-room with a glossy lavatory and small, well-equipped kitchen. The furnishings are the sort found in expensive modern hotels and fill Ella with a sense of desolation almost greater than poverty would. She thinks a huge stone head on the floor could only improve the place. However, she says, "How clean and tidy everything is."

"I can't stand mess," says Leo complacently and busies himself in the kitchen. Ella looks round in a puzzled way, seeking (though she may not be aware of this) a clue to his childhood or to a previous loving connection. A bookstand holds nothing but car manuals and trade journals. The only wall decoration is a large map of Scotland mounted on a board and stuck full of red-headed pins, so she studies that.

"My territory!" he calls from the kitchen. There are hardly any pins inside the boundaries of the four cities. Most are stuck in obscure little towns a few miles from these, towns which in recent years have been occupied by prosperous commuters and retired people. In the highlands some pins pierce the main tourist resorts, and there is a denser sprinkling through townships near the English border. One yellow-headed pin occupies a southern patch of brown moorland. She peers closely to discover the reason for its uniqueness.

"That marks the spot where mother nature once seduced me," says Leo, bringing in a tray of tea things and placing it on a low table. "I suppose you want to hear all about that."

"Oh, yes please!" says Ella. For her own amusement as much as his she acts like an eager little girl, sitting on a chair with legs tucked under her, chin on fist and mouth and eyes expectantly open. Leo switches the table light on and the ceiling light off to give the room an intimate atmosphere. He sits on the sofa, pours two cups of tea, hands her one and says, "You see—"

He finds he cannot talk without referring to the map so rises and goes to it, switching on the ceiling light again. "I was driving along the coast from Stranraer one Saturday, just about here. In those days I got bonuses for weekend work. The day was hot, the road busy, I'd had an exceptionally hard week so instead of driving up to Ayr I turned inland north of Ballantrae. This line marks a third-class road. You can see why I thought it might be a shortcut. Anyway, I ran up this twisting valley, and passed some old farms and came up onto these moors. There was a gate across the road (it's not marked)—I suppose to keep sheep from wandering. So I had to leave the car to open it. Otherwise nothing would have happened because the air was not just warm, it had little fresh breezes blowing through it and I could hear two or three of those birds going poo-ee poo-ee in the distance . . . What do you call them?"

"Lapwings," says Ella.

"No. Curlews," says Leo, "That's the name. Curlews. Anyway, I shut the gate behind me and drove on for a mile or two and reached a second gate, where the yellow pin is. But instead of just opening it and driving through I lay back on a bank of heather for a puff at the old pipe. There was not a human being, or a telegraph pole, or another car than my own in sight, only heather and ferns and this hill opposite, with an old house among some trees at the foot of it. Everything was warm and . . . brilliant, and calm. I could hear a cricket near by, in the grass. Do you know what I did?" He stares at her accusingly. She shakes her head. He speaks on a note of astonished indignation.

"I fell asleep! I fell asleep and woke up ninety minutes later with a splitting headache and a fit of the shivers! I was totally behind schedule. I got to Dalmellington all right but I was too late for Kilmarnock and Strathaven. That little nap of mine cost Quality Fabrics two hundred pounds' worth of business. It was a lesson to me."

"Were they angry?" asks Ella softly.

"Who?"

"Quality Fabrics."

"Certainly not! That loss is my estimate, not theirs. And it would need more than one accident of that kind to damage a man with a record like mine. But it showed I was human, like the rest. If I hadn't pulled myself together I could have gone to pieces entirely. Men do, in my business. Usually through drink. This yellow pin is a warning to me."

He sits beside her and sips tea. She murmurs sympathetically, "No wonder you can't relax."

He puts down the cup with a touch of exasperation. "Ella, you haven't understood a word of what I've told you. I *can* relax, but I've chosen not to. You like routine but I'm an individualist, a *free man,* Ella. The price of freedom is eternal vigilance. June never understood this. In our three and a half years of married life she never once sympathized with what I was doing for her."

"Were you doing it for her?"

He sighs and does not answer.

After a while, mainly to fill the silence, she says, "I'm surprised you haven't an ulcer."

"Perhaps I have. I get stomach pains after meals nowadays and . . . there's a swelling." He puts a hand to his stomach. She sits up and says seriously, "You must see a doctor."

"I told you. I don't go to doctors."

"Let me look."

"There's nothing to see, but you can feel it I suppose." He

unfastens the waistband of his trousers and leans back. She sits beside him, slips her hand in and palpates his stomach, frowning thoughtfully. She says, "I can't feel a thing."

"Lower down, in the middle."

Her fingers touch the swelling and rest on it. He murmurs, "What soft smooth fingers you have, Ella."

She murmurs, "Aren't you cunning?"

He draws her to him. She takes her hand from his trousers and removes her spectacles. They clasp and kiss. He is surprised by how easy this is. He says, "You aren't tense."

"Why should I be?"

"That talk about the suffering masses made me think you were more . . . rigid."

She smiles. Men are always surprised to find she isn't rigid. They undress and move to the bed. There is a lack of urgency and embarrassment which amazes him. He says, "You're special."

"I'm not."

They clasp and kiss again. He murmurs, "Woman . . . is the downfall of the weak man but the relaxation of the warrior."

"What a silly thing to say."

"Napoleon said it."

"Then he was silly."

"Can I see you tomorrow?"

"Yes. I might wake up here."

"But tomorrow night?" he pleads.

"I think . . . maybe."

"And the day after?"

"I've examinations then."

A little later he is so delighted that he cries, "June, you're beautiful. You're so beautiful, June."

She hits him hard on the side of the head.

She gets up and starts dressing. He crouches on the bedside, sucking the knuckles of a clenched hand. Her indignation is less when she has fastened her skirt—what moves her most in this world is pity. She says, "I'm sorry I hit you, Leo, but you've been thinking about another woman all evening."

He does not move. She looks at him and says, "I'd better go now, hadn't I? It's quite late."

He does not move. She finishes dressing and says, "I really am sorry I hit you, Leo, but I'd better get back to my studies."

He does not move. She goes to the door, opens it and hesitates, trying to think of a more encouraging farewell. At last she says, "I admire you, Leo. Really I do . . ."

He does not move. Truth and the silence compel her to add, ". . . in some ways, just a little. Goodnight."

She leaves.

He huddles a long time on the bedside then starts glancing toward the telephone in a furtive way, as if it is an enticing drug with vile after-effects. He stands, pulls his trousers on, sits beside the phone and dials. A little later he hears a woman say, "Hello?"

He answers in his small, hesitant voice.

"Hullo, June . . . I wondered if . . . I thought that after the legal business this afternoon perhaps you felt a bit . . . lonely?"

"I can't help you any more, Leo," says June sensibly, "It's too late. I'm sorry you feel lonely but it's too late to talk to me about it. Goodnight, Leo."

She does not at once put the receiver down. Several seconds pass before he hears the deadening click. He keeps his own receiver pressed to his ear for another minute, slowly replaces it, lifts tobacco tin from mantelpiece, opens it and slowly fills from it the bowl of his rather unusual pipe. Six years have passed since he last saw June.

# CHAPTER 10

# Culture Capitalism

arry meets her dealer and Linda, who has come south to discuss Harry's 1990 exhibition in Glasgow.

"First tell me about the European Cultcha Capital thing," says the dealer, "Why Glasgow? How has a notoriously filthy hole become a shining light? Is it an advatising stunt?"

"Certainly, but we have something to advertise!" says Linda, "It all began when John Betjeman discovad Glasgow in the sixties and found what nobody had eva suspected. The city centa is a mastapiece of Victorian and Edwardian architectcha. But in those days it was unda such a thick coating of soot and grime that only the eye of a masta could penetrate it. Even moa off-putting wa the people. In those days most Scottish impoats and expoats passed through Glasgow, and the good middle bit

was squashed up tight against docks and warehouses and the
tenements of those who worked in them. What would visitas
think of London if Trafalga Squaya was on the Isle of Dogs?
If every day hordes of horny-handed men in filthy overalls
percolated up and down Regent Street and half filled the Fleet
Street pubs? But London is vast, so the classes segregate themselves easily and naturally. They couldn't do that in Glasgow
so respectable Londonas passed through it in fia of thea lives.
It is perhaps not logical fo well dressed British people to dread
the working classes, but when they flagrantly outnumba us the
recoil is instinctive.

"Anyway, nothing could improve Glasgow befoa all its old
industries got taken out, but they have been! And befoa that
happened all the people who worked in them got decanted into
big housing schemes on the verge of things. So the middle of
Glasgow is clean now and will neva be filthy again! The old
warehouses and markets and tenements and churches are being
turned into luxury flats and shopping malls and a surprising
variety of very decent foreign restaurants. Which is wha we
come in—I mean the English.

"You see Glasgow is in Scotland and from oua point of view
Scotland is slightly like Rhodesia in the early yias of this century. Most British industry and money is in the south of England now, so it's crowded! But we English detest crowds. At
heart each of us wants to be a country squia, with wide-open
spaces nia oua house and grounds, and if possible a village
atmosphia wha we can relax with a few like-minded friends. But
a place like that costs a fawtune in England and the neara
London you go the moa astronomical the fawtune gets. All the
nice English villages have been bought. But by selling quite a
small propaty in London you can get enough to buy—"

"Yes yes yes!" says the dealer impatiently, "I know about

propaty development in the north, I own a small tax-avoidance forest near Invaness, but wha does the *cultcha* come from?"

"From the Thatcha govament," says Linda promptly, "and from Glasgow District Council. Glasgow used to have the strongest local govament tha was, outside London. It owned a huge public transport system, housing schemes, docklands and lots of otha things Thatcha is allowing it to sell. Like local govaments everywha it is being steadily abolished, but since the people's elected representatives usually draw salaries until they die and get all sawts of perks *they* don't complain. Maybe they don't notice! Howeva, they want to show they can do moa than just sell public propaty to private speculatas, so they have gone in fo Cultcha with a capital C—and tourism. Commercially speaking cultcha and tourism a the same thing.

"The European Cultcha Capital notion was started by Melina Mercouri, the Greek minista fo aats. Athens had been stone-cleaned, she wanted tourists to know it, she suggested to Brussels that Athens be the first Cultcha Capital, then otha countries could have a shot. Nobody objected. So Italy chose Florence; the Nethalands, Amstadam; Germany, Berlin. France predictably chose Paris. But being Cultcha Capital is expensive! You must advatise yawself. Put on extra shows and consats. Invite foreign guests. Stage boring receptions. Margaret Thatcha isn't keen on all that crap; anyway London has enough of it. Like a sensible monetarist she put the job up fo grabs and offad it to the lowest bidda. Bath and Edinburgh put in fo it, Cardiff, Birmingham and Glasgow: but only Glasgow gave a quiet little promise that if it got the job it would *not* ask the central govament fo cash. So Glasgow, which the Lay-ba Party has ruled fo ova half a century, was given the job by the Tory arts minista who announced that Glasgow had set an example of independent action which should be followed by

every local authority in the United Kingdom. Wia funding the
entaprise out of the rates and public propaty sales and sponsaship from banks, oil companies, building societies and whateva
we can screw out of Europe.

"And Glasgow deserves the job! It's the headquartas of the
Scottish Opera, Scottish Ballet, Scottish National Orchestra,
the Burrell Collection, the Citizen's Theata, the Third Eye
Centa and an intanational drama festival: all of them directed
and mostly administaed by the English, of course. Sometimes
the natives get a bit bolshie about that but I'm very firm with
them. I say very quietly, 'Listen! You Scots have been expoating
yaw own people to England and everywha else fo centuries, and
nobody has complained much about you! Why start howling
just because wia giving you a taste of yaw own medicine?' They
can't think of an ansa to that one."

"But shooali the natives have some local cultcha of tha
own?" says the dealer, "What about these young paintas
who've emerged? Campbell and Currie, etcetera."

"The ones who did well in New Yawk? Yes, we'll let them
have a show or two."

"Has Glasgow nothing else apart from Billy Connolly?"

"Some novels by Glasgow writas have had rave reviews in the
*Times Lit. Sup.,* but I'm afraid they leave me cold. Half seem
to be written in phonetic Scotch about people with names like
*Auld Shug.* Every second word seems to be fuck, though hardly
any fucking happens. The otha half have complicated plots like
SM obstacle races in which I entie-aly lose my way and give up.
As a matta of fact, Harry, I have one of these books hia to give
to you! Some of it reminded me of games we once played with
Hjordis."

"I'm sorry, what did you say?" Harry, though scrupulously
clean when not working, still finds dirt interesting. She stopped

listening to Linda when she heard Glasgow is now a clean place; she retired mentally into the old play-loft, making occasional trips to the shrubbery. The name of Hjordis restores her wholly to the present. Linda repeats her last sentence and hands Harry a book entitled *Another Part of the Forest.* Harry stares longer at the cover design than Linda and dealer think it deserves. It shows what first seems a moonlit tropical jungle where eyes glow in the dark between vast blue-green leaves. Then Harry sees the leaves are not tropical but are hawthorn and elder and bramble leaves painted big. Deep among these leaves Harry hears her dealer ask if she wants her next retrospective to open in Glasgow?

She looks up and says, "No, I'm done with retrospectives. Apart from the bum garden everything I've eva made has been shit—a waste of time—a silly game I played with myself. I don't know why others liked it, apart from you. You live by selling that sort of shit." She is looking at her dealer and her clear distant voice suggests neither blame nor regret.

Aghast, Linda is going to shout "But!" so the dealer says "Sh!"

Harry seldom talks at length and if interrupted stays silent for days. Harry says, "The bum garden was good because someone else wanted it. It was wanted by the only person who eva wanted me, too, once." Tears stream from Harry's eyes though her face and voice stay calm and unmoved. Linda weeps in sympathy.

"But technically the old bum garden is kids' stuff. I will make it betta and bigga in polished steel and white glazed ceramic spreading through several spaces—large ones. How spacious is yaw Sauchiehall Street venue, Linda?"

"Huge. Hia's a plan of it. This immense gallery opens into three equally big ones. We have two awdinri big galleries and two small ones in the cornas. Hia is the vestibule: a landing approached by the magnificent double staircase. Skylighting throughout in ceilings ova twenty feet high."

"It'll do. I'll put the shrubbery into the cornas. I've just seen how to tackle the leaves. Enamelled tin. The big middle gallery will be shrubbery too with birds everywha, birds of glass and polished wood among leaves, birds pecking broken ceramic cake from the green matting floa. Little gels stand in odd places nobody sees at first, little terracotta gels wearing real frocks of the period. One of them in overalls sits high up on a leafy trapeze. The olda gels will be glazed ceramic, the clothes ceramic too, all bright white except fo some culla whea they feel proud of it, red on lips, pink on cheeks, polka dots on a dress, candy stripes on a blouse. Anotha breed from us, the olda gels. We squawk, they murma and coo. I will record and play these sounds along with birdsong and the song from The Fortress, *I met an old woman* no *I met a young woman who gave me a rainbow.* But the huge dark bum-shaped Fortress is the middle of everything. Barbed wya brambles stop the adults getting nia but the light and music leak from chinks in the black walls made of tarry black wooden railway sleepas and tarpaulin, how they flamed when Ethel drenched them in paraffin and applied that match. But what happened to Limpy Dan the hampsta, Linda? Did you see him inside The Fortress?"

"Thigh neva let me in!" sobs Linda, "I was nuffin but a applicant—allwise allwise allwise!"

"I feel excluded from something," says the dealer brightly, "Would you two ladies tell me what it is?"

They explain. He becomes furiously thoughtful. Nostalgia and grotesque infantilism are booming in many places, but especially Britain. From Christmas pantomimes and revivals of *Peter Pan* he has seen it expand through books, films, computer games, fashion design, interior decoration and architecture. Harry's work has so far been no more infantile than most contemporary work, but more noticed because of the surprising range of materials she uses, and because of her royal relations. These royals have no interest in her, have never said a word to promote her career, but important members of some purchasing committees do not know this, and one who wants a knighthood has boosted the sales-price of Harry's work to a height which knowing heads of the London art market think cannot last. Harry's dealer is one of these heads. He sees that if Harry now makes a lavish indoor sculpture park representing her eerily horrid schooldays (and with the right help Harry can make anything) then Harry's work will be profitably sold by the London art market to the end of the century. So much can be said about it!—this tragically feminist remake of Pooh Corner, Never Never Land, the Secret Garden; this shrine to a dead millionairess who was loved by Marc Bolan, Jimi Hendrix and Sid Vicious, if only for a few minutes. Get the show an explanatory catalogue written by a brainier than usual popular writer (William Golding too old and grand perhaps but try him and Muriel Spark Iris Murdoch Fay Weldon Germaine Greer George Melly Angela Carter David Lodge or whoever wrote *The History Man* Adam Mars-Jones or whoever wrote *The Cement Garden* Roald Dahl Martin Amis *Tom Stoppard? Harold Pinter?* Whoever springs to mind seems suitable) it could be a small bestseller, a cult book if televised why not a feature film? Bill Forsyth directing? But first, the exhibition.

Dealer's flattened hand whacks arm of chair. "Funding!" he announces. "Funding! Harry I'm glad yaw think all yaw previous work is shit. Yaw wrong, but it means yaw going to astonish us with wildly exciting new things. But rooms full of steel, ceramic, polished wood, etcetera need heavy funding. So do assistants. We need at least six: three high-tech boys and three gophas.* Linda! Let's see if you and I can crack the sponsaship problem from the Scottish end. Has Scotland a steel industry?"

"Yes, the remains of one. It limps from crisis to crisis, begging money from the govament and getting smalla all the time. It might welcome a bit of publicity."

Money talk bores Harry. She opens *Another Part of the Forest* at random and enters a room where a white American woman is questioning a young black American woman sent by an agency that supplies rich folk with domestic servants. Harry, reading, begins to tingle. The questioning shows the older woman is selfish, bossy, cares for nothing but the comfort and appearance of her body, spends most of her life having it pampered and groomed for frivolous social appointments. She is fascinated by her potential servant and seeks to hide this under condescending insolence. The young black woman's answers show she is intelligent, can provide the sort of body care the other wants, but is not at all servile. She too is insolent, but her insolence is put in words which could be interpreted as compliance, and this is partly what fascinates her potential employer. All has been discussed, when suddenly, after a long silence, the white woman says in a low rapid voice, *"Can you take shit?"*

*"What does that mean?"*

*The white woman licks her upper lip, sucks her lower one then says, "Well. I'll tell you this. My momma once married a man who was a real gentleman, the finest gent you ever did see. She truly loved him, and so did I, except when he came home drunk*

*A "gofer" is a fetcher and carrier in the film and other entertainment industries. It is unconnected with gopher, a burrowing pouched rodent or ground squirrel of the spermophil genus: unconnected with gopher, a miner who digs without hope of lasting achievement. (See *Shorter O.E.D.*)

*and said things so filthy you couldn't believe. But we put up with it. Had to. He left after a while. I never knew my real daddy so this guy was . . . influential, I guess. And when I get low, which feels like half the month, I've a mouth like Satan's ass-hole. This shitty language pours out of me over anybody near, especially if they're—you know—subordinate. That's why I lost two husbands and why my maids keep checking out. So?"*

*The two women watch each other then the black woman says,* "What kinda shit do you give? I need a sample."

"Well, like . . . nigger bitch?"

"Oh that! I heard that one before. I slapped the face of the last white bitch who called me that."

"But she wasn't paying you twice what you earn in a high-class hair salon."

*The black woman lights a cigarette, inhales and after a while says,* "For shit like that I want four times what they pay me in the salon."

"You mean it?" *asks the white woman, staring.*

"Yeah. I mean it."

"O.K."

"You mean it?" *asks the black woman, staring. The white woman lights a cigarette, inhales and says,* "Yeah."

"You're rich!"

"Rich but no fool! I get value for money. I'll be mean as hell if I'm paying you that much."

"Just words?"

"What else could it be?" *asks the white woman, smiling,* "Tell me! I'm truly interested."

"It could be nothing but words," *says the black woman firmly.*

"All right, that's the deal. Start tomorrow."

"The hair salon needs a week's notice—I promised that."

"For my money you start tomorrow."

*After a pause the black woman says, "Give me my first pay cheque here and now—a month's pay in advance. I'll start when my bank clears it."*

*"Why you—!" cries the white woman and chokes back a word. Her face whitens but she calms herself and says, "What guarantee have I you won't walk out of here and not come back?"*

*"None at all, but you're rich enough to risk it. And would I lose the chance of another cheque like that just because you shit through your mouth?"*

*"I don't think you will!" says the white woman quietly after a pause. "But I'm sure you won't mind signing a receipt just to put my mind at rest." She writes a cheque and a receipt, signs the first as the black woman signs the second, then the bits of paper are exchanged. As the white woman hands over the cheque she says, "Take it! Nigger bitch."*

*"Why* thank *you, Ma'am!" says the black woman with a sarcastic drawl, grinning triumphantly at the white woman who grins triumphantly back.* End of chapter.

End of chapter, so Harry turns a page and encounters two wholly different women talking in a completely different land and century. Harry hunts forward and backward through the book but the two who made her tingle appear nowhere else. Each chapter contains a dialogue between women trying to trap each other but seem otherwise self-contained, with no male characters, no plot, no climaxes: nothing but furtive movements toward something sexy and sinister which never happens. *Is this supposed to be funny?* thinks Harry, exasperated.

"Stop filleting that book, Harry!" says her dealer. "We want to ask you something. You know how we got you that place in San Francisco so you could work and sell in America without a lot of dreary hassle over customs and impoat licences. Well there are equally good financial reasons fo you working in

Glasgow while preparing the exhibition thea. I won't boa you with the details—they involve development grants, youth opportunity schemes, local govament politics and publicity of the dreariest kind. They also involve screwing a lot of money out of Scotland and some out of Europe. Linda says we can rent studio space beside a decent apartment wha the Hopcrafts can live and look afta you."

"Right in the heart of Glasgow!" cries Linda, "Not five minutes' walk from my office. I'll love being yaw Scottish business manayja! I'll help you higha and figha all the local assistance you need. I'll handle yaw publicity, and show you around. I'll even introduce you to the native chiefs, which is not essential, but ratha fun."

Harry hates restaurants, cannot face parties of more than four people, so on her first evening in Glasgow Linda takes her to dine at the home of a native chief. He is a former Lord Provost who now runs his own housing association consultancy and Harry is enchanted by him, listens open-mouthed to every word he says, brings to his occasional silences a hungrily expectant attention that compels him to say much more. Linda and the man's wife are astonished. He is three inches shorter than Harry, has the appearance, manners and conversation of many other British businessmen, and a voice with the tones and accents of Harry's long-lost, best-beloved nursemaid. It fills her with warm feelings of perfect safety and helpless anticipation. If he told her to climb on to the dining table and undress she would unthinkingly obey. He notices his effect on her and thinks it natural. When Linda and his wife leave the room for a moment he suggests a meeting two days later in a private lounge of the Central Station Hotel. Harry nods and would faithfully keep that appointment but next day something makes her forget him forever.

Harry spends the night where she will live for at least another year, in a block of converted offices and warehouses filling the north-west angle of Glasgow Cross. Next morning Linda calls to escort her to her new studio in a converted warehouse on the other side of the High Street. While waiting for the traffic lights to signal a crossing they are passed by many clusters of people talking with the tones and accents of Harry's long-lost nurse-maid.

"I'm afraid this always happens at weekends," says Linda apologetically. "Crowds of people from the housing schemes—employed ones who can afford to take a bus—use Argyle Street as a shopping senta. Also the Barrows."

"Barrows?"

"A district nia hia full of little stalls, the sort you see in street markets all ova London. Glasgow has most of them in one place . . . Do you want to wanda a bit?" asks Linda, seeing that Harry inclines to go with the crowd.

"Please."

They wander along the Gallowgate, through Barrowland and across a corner of Glasgow Green. In London and San Francisco Harry hardly ever walks, travelling between the few buildings she knows in a car driven by one of the Hopcrafts. This is her first experience of crowds where shabby and smart folk mix. Turning west along Clydeside they pass the old court house and are about to go under a castellated Victorian railway bridge when Harry stops at the entrance to a narrow but busy lane.

"Don't go in tha," says Linda, "It's too squalid."

"Dangerous?"

"Oh no! It's just a miserably pooa market—a losers' market. You won't find bargains in it. Do come away."

"Mm," says Harry, and walks in.

Most of the market is in arched vaults under a disused railway viaduct, each vault lined with trestle tables spread with what seems the salvage of rubbish dumps. Everything still usable or wearable was of the worst quality when new and has since passed through several owners; everything once good-looking is hideously damaged. Yet a stream of people seem interested in buying. The queerest sights, however, are not in the vaults but on the cobbles of the lane outside. A woman with a twisted smile on her newly bruised face squats over a spreading pool of urine. Is she really trying to sell the last year's calendar, rusty forks and baby's plastic rattle on the stones before her? Is that barefoot man with the head of a broken-nosed, slack-lipped Einstein really trying to sell the cracked shoes in his hands?

"Hawf deid flooers tenpence!" screams someone, blocking Harry's vision with a huge bunch of half-dead flowers. "Split the stalks, pit them in waater wi an asprin an thull revive! Thull revive!"

Harry giggles and walks on. Linda at Harry's elbow mutters vehemently, "I hate this. Hate it. I am not a socialist, but these people should not be allowed to flaunt themselves in this way. They should be put somewha wha we can't see them. The city plannas will pull this place down eventually, oh *God* make it soon!"

"I like it," murmurs Harry drowsily. "I think these people have as much right to exist as you or me. I will come hia often."

The lane ends in a small doorway. They go through it toward a car park and the glass and aluminium ziggurat of a vast shopping mall.

"It's easy fo you to be cold-blooded: yaw an aristocrat," says Linda sharply. "My daddy topped the hit parade in 1963, so

I'm working class by breeding and bourgeois by education. Some sights I just cannot stomach."

"Has Glasgow an agency which will supply domestic servants?" asks Harry, still speaking drowsily.

"Probably. Why do you ask? Do you find the faithful Hopcrafts inadequate?"

"No, but I may need a lady's maid."

"*A lady's maid?*" Linda stares at Harry who is dressed, as usual, in crumpled army combat trousers, shirt, tunic and boots. Several women of Harry's class sometimes wear neatly laundered forms of such clothes nowadays. Harry has always dressed this way because it suits her work. With the addition of a machine-gun and facial hair she would look like a mercenary soldier in a tropical campaign.

"My motha had a lady's maid," murmurs Harry in an absentminded way. "Throughout the Second World Waw, when everybody else's lady's maids went to work in munition factories, my motha somehow contrived to keep her lady's maid."

Harry finds an employment agency and pays it to send her applicants for the post of lady's maid. Each evening after work she waits for them in her flat, tingling with a hopefulness which dies when Mr or Mrs Hopcraft admits the applicant to her sitting-room. Most are so alarmed by her appearance that they can only look at her sideways. She murmurs, "What can you do fo me?" and after they've told her says, "Well, I may be in touch."

That means *no*. Those who act more suitably have the wrong sort of voice because they are English (she forgot to tell the agency she didn't want that sort) or because they are Scots whose accents have an English sound. After a fortnight a small full-bodied woman is shown in who looks at Harry with a curiosity which is neither challenging or amused. Harry says, "I need a maid. What can you do for me?"

"I honestly don't know," says Senga, "What do you want me to do? I'm good at hair—I'm a trained hairdresser—but you don't have any hair. So what do you want?"

Harry sighs with relief because this woman is exactly right. "I want anything you want," Harry starts to say, but changes it to, "I want . . . can I give you a drink?"

"Aye. Yes. Sure. I'll take anything but kicks and slaps. I've had too many of those."

Harry opens a well-stocked drinks cabinet: one installed by Linda and the Hopcrafts for the entertainment of her dealer and his associates. Harry last tasted alcohol when she was seventeen, hated it, and has since drunk nothing but lemonade and orange juice—even coffee and tea disgust her. She stares at the bafflingly labelled bottles and at last says, "I hate to be awkward but will you poa it for yawself? I'm hopeless at most things."

Senga, frowning thoughtfully, nods quickly several times, pours herself a large Bacardi and soda and asks, "What will you have?"

"The same," says Harry automatically. Senga hands her a nearly full cut-glass tumbler and says, "Since we're drinking together could we mibby sit down?"

They sit primly at opposite ends of a long sofa. Senga says, "Cheers."

Harry sips her drink like an obedient child taking medicine. It tastes less poisonous than she expects. *I am growing up!* she thinks. Happy tinglings in her body make her so passively content that when Senga says cheerily, "Now then, out with it! What do you want me for?" Harry cannot answer.

So Senga asks once more. Speaking at first with difficulty but growing more fluent Harry says, "When I was tiny I was always dressed by somebody else. They got very cross if I did not sit very still in my nice frocks and be very good all the time. But you see I wanted to be wicked. And now I cannot CAN NOT buy nice beautiful clothes or care a damn how I look. I order hard-wearing useful clothes from illustrated catalogues and fling them on anyhow so I look like something the cat dragged in, usually. A fright. A tramp. But I had this very nia friend once," says Harry, laying down her glass and rocking her body forward and back, "I had this close friend who sometimes got very strange lovely clothes made fo me. I didn't always want to put them on because she enjoyed how I looked moa than I did, but when I submitted (and I always submitted, nobody was ever strong enough to disobey Hjordis) when I submitted and dressed up and did as she wanted—not how I wanted—I was entie-ally happy. Entie-ally happy, in those days, sometimes. But she died long ago and now I've nobody. Nobody. Nobody. Please. Help. Me."

Forgetting that the Hjordis she has lost is imaginary Harry clasps her hands behind her head, drags it down between her knees and in that position wails as loudly as she can, which is not very loud. Senga puts her own glass down, goes behind the sofa and gently and firmly massages Harry's neck and shoulders, saying, "Don't worry. Calm down. Everything's going to be fine. You've found your wee Scotch auntie so your troubles are at an end."

After a while Harry comes to feel so safe and calm that they are able to talk about arrangements, though Senga suggests most of them.

"You don't need a living-in maid," she points out, "You work most of the day and don't wear special togs for that. I'm just a pal you want to relax with sometimes, a pal who'll overhaul your wardrobe and dress you up special for special occasions, or just for fun. I don't think the people who feed and clean up for you need know very much about us two. Now, I've a small business which doesnae pay very well. I make clothes for people, working from the house. What I need is a wee workshop, a room where you can see me when you need something or just want to relax a bit. The initial financial outlay need be nothing great, and will be well worth it in the long run. I'm full of ideas."

# CHAPTER 11

# Dad's Story

I f a man is middle-aged between thirty-five years and fifty-five I have been old for several years. When I stopped being young I did not expect life to go so quickly but I have no other complaint. I will likely take twenty or thirty more years to die and it will be the smooth comfortable dying of someone protected by money. My ceiling admits no rain so I enjoy the movement of clouds over the rooftops. Every weather, every season has its unique beauty and this large window allows a good view of it. My flat is at the top of a building on a hill so I see far across the roofs of the other tenements and terraced houses. A tree-filled groove zigzagging among these roofs shows the course of a small river. It flows into a fine park in the middle distance, a park between two hills. One is crowned by the pinnacles of our mock-gothic university, one by the towers of an old theological college converted into luxury flats where my friend Leo lives. I see all this distinctly, and much of the city beyond, and on a clear day many fields and tree clumps on the hills beyond that. I am in the west end where most of the prosperous residential districts are in cities where the wind usually blows from the west. Even so, smoke from the east and other industrial districts so stained our finest buildings that a few years ago they made a very poor impression on visitors. Since the industries closed the richest districts have been extensively cleaned, partly with public money and partly through tax concessions to property owners. We now advertise our city as a splendid one and a lot of foreigners are buying places in the posh parts. I am lucky to have moved here from the east (where I was born and educated) before the prices went up. Like all poor parts of Britain the east end has got poorer in the last twenty years and will be poorer still when the poll tax is in full working order.

My job is making folk laugh, but I started my working life in another ancient profession which never escapes from childhood. My school qualified me for a university which qualified me for a college which qualified me for a school, but as a teacher. Many teachers marry each other. I was never sexually attracted by my own kind, but used to like their company. My social life after four o'clock on weekdays was going to Brown's tearooms in Sauchiehall Street and sitting round a table with colleagues of the same age. For the first half hour we never spoke. Our voices were hoarse, our brains wasted by seven hours of deliberately depressing children of the ignorant working class. (Our school served a poor district. Had it served a prosperous one we would have been equally shattered by seven hours of pushing middle-class children up to the level of their happy parents. Irony.) Slowly our brains would recover and *words* start to enter these silent conversations, then gossip, light badinage and facetious social and political commentary, all excellent training for me. I listened more than I talked. Professional humorists are never at the centre of happy groups, talking briskly and keeping everyone cheerful. We stay on the edge, listening carefully and trying to think of something better to say. And when we think of it we say it too late, or in the wrong tone of voice, so others don't hear it, or ask us to repeat it, and when we do there is a definite pause. The others may smile, but it can take them as much as a minute to start the conversation going again.

One or two who sat with us in the tearoom had gone into the Scottish BBC instead of the ordinary education system. One day the talk turned to religious prejudice and someone remarked that, despite the fact that our city had a very large Catholic population—certainly as many practising Catholics as there were church-going Presbyterians—there were many anti-Catholic slogans scribbled in the lavatories and on walls, but nobody could remember an anti-Protestant one. I suggested it was easier to write *FUCK THE POPE* than *FUCK THE MODERATOR OF THE GENERAL ASSEMBLY OF THE CHURCH OF SCOTLAND.* Someone chuckled and the conversation turned to other things. But a fortnight after I heard my joke on a Scottish Home Service comedy show. *Fuck* had been replaced by *To hell with,* because it was illegal to say fuck on the wireless then but the joke was essentially mine. One of our BBC friends had passed it on to a professional mouthpiece. After that I no longer spoke my witticisms aloud. I saved them up, wrote them down and posted them to Jimmy Logan, Stanley Baxter, Rikki Fulton, Lex Maclean and Johnny Victory. Yes, all these immortals have owed the laughs they pulled to me. Not to me only. I know four other humorists in this city whose jokes are far more brilliant than anything I've written. I don't envy them. Though brilliant they are erratic, and professional comics need predictable streams of second-rate jokes more than brilliant gags that stop the show. Which is why I earn enough by my jokes to have left the teaching profession, and these brilliant boys have not. But I am too intelligent to feel smug.

For I am not a satisfactory man. I drink when not thirsty and hardly ever climb to the top of a high hill, though I used to enjoy reaching the top of hills and felt better, slept better when I came down. No wonder I am flabby in body and mind. My jokes are not radical criticism, they confirm what most of us feel: that black, brown, yellow people, all Irish and foreigners, drunk men, the working classes, very fashionable folk, highly educated folk, all clergymen, homosexuals, wives and attractive women are essentially daft. Which may seem fair enough, but I never make fun of royalty, financial institutions, the police, higher clergy and politicians. Most professional comics won't buy jokes against these people. I do nothing about how my city and nation is governed, except occasionally vote for a party too small to change things. In the Athenian sense of the word I am an *idiot*. The old Athenians invented that word for people who take no effective hand in making the laws which control them. Let's drop the topic, it embarrasses me. I will describe exactly what happened last night with enough fanciful changes and additions to make the description interesting and believable. I met a woman who calls me Dad (though I am nobody's dad) and it felt like a turning point.

But that was not the first thing to happen. The first thing was feeling happy all day because Donalda was happy at breakfast-time. We had made love a few hours earlier, so, "I don't need you tonight," she said on a note of cheerful self-mockery, "Do what you like tonight."

I was careful not to look pleased as that would alarm her, but I was very pleased, though I said, "I'll probably work late, or play chess with Q. And maybe I'll call on you afterwards, but of course I'll phone first."

This was a dangerous thing to say. If I failed to phone she might tell me later that she'd been unable to sleep for half the night. It would be no defence for me to say, "I did not promise to phone you, I said I *might* phone you. I said it to make you feel safer, and out of gratitude. I was grateful to you for saying I could do what I liked."

Why does Donalda seem like my jailor sometimes? Donalda is not a jailor, not a harsh schoolteacher. She is gentle. When busy and happy she has a shining quality, that quality of bright directness most people lose with childhood. Her lips do not shut in the firm line of those who want to control people. When working with her hands (she is a dressmaker) her lips stay slightly apart in a small, expectant smile. She has an emotional age of twelve or thirteen. This does not annoy me because my own emotional age is about that. Donalda shouts when angry, weeps when miserable, tells people when she is happy. But the longer I know her the less she turns her shining qualities on me, or perhaps the less I notice them. Nowadays most of her words seem to say how nasty and unsuitable I am. Certainly I drink too much. Why does she not get rid of me like other women who once loved me? I am good at being rejected. I don't rave, plead or quarrel, I stay polite and friendly. I am hurt enough for the rejecters to know they have shut me out of something wonderful and precious, not so hurt they need feel guilty about it. Why is Donalda FAITHFUL to me? I never expected faithfulness, or asked for it, or promised it. When we first dined together she told me she wasn't that sort at all. Which reminds

me of the dream I had the first time we slept together. My book
had just been published.

My book was published and I got very depressed. A few years
earlier *Punch* had published a funny wee story of mine. That
had made me ambitious. I wanted to be as famous as Q, so I
started writing a whole book of funny stories. Unluckily I have
only one basic joke. Conan Doyle, O'Henry and Thurber were
like that, but my joke is about sex which makes it painfully
obvious. So I carefully set each story in a different time and
place with characters whose voices, faces and jobs were different too. I hoped this would fool readers into thinking the joke
was also different, and that readers who weren't fooled would
read on to see how I disguised it next time.

Well, I sent the book to a London publishing firm and six
months later it was returned with a letter saying they regretted
not returning it sooner, since publication of it would reflect no
credit whatsoever on themselves or on me. That shattered me.
Nine months passed before I was strong enough to post it to
another London publishing firm, nine more before I had the
courage to phone and ask if they liked it. A man said to me,
"Haven't you heard yet? Yes, we're doing your book. I'm no
judge of humour myself but two of our readers think you hit
a contemporary nerve."

I lived in dread and anxiety another six months because I
feared that when my book appeared nobody would laugh at it.
I needn't have worried. The *Times Literary Supplement* called
me "a major name in British humour" and only the *Sunday
Post* complained about the sex. For a whole fortnight reviews
appeared in periodicals which notice such things. For a fortnight every critic in Britain seemed to find my book as funny
as I did, and then, suddenly, silence! They stopped laughing at
it and went on reviewing books by other authors as calmly and

approvingly as if I had never published a word. I realized that before they noticed me again I would have to get ANOTHER book written and published, and I am not a demonically industrious writer of the Enid Blyton, Iris Murdoch and Dickens sort. I enjoy writing, I forget myself when doing it as much as Leo forgot himself when driving a fast car, but unlike Leo I am easily distracted.

Anyway, I felt like a husband whose wife, after a deliriously happy honeymoon, elopes with a lot of other men. I got drunk and dimly remember a big gallery with paintings on whitewashed brick walls, a crowd which chattered and sipped wine with its backs to the paintings, a small, plump attractive girl with very black hair who seemed amused when I picked her up and whirled her about a bit. I don't often act so daft. A month later I met her at a party when I was sober and saw lines on her face which showed she was nearly forty. She still looked girlish. That deep anxiety all adults feel was half-hidden in her by unusual willingness to be pleased. When I asked her out for a meal she said, "Aye. Sure. Great, but don't tell anybody. If Senga finds out she'll murder me. Senga hates men."

She explained that Senga was her lover and sometimes her employer. I did not ask for details. My parents taught me it is wrong to ask for details of people's private lives. Had Senga been a man I would have called the affair off because I'm afraid of men. However, I met Donalda in a restaurant and was about to pour wine into her glass when she said sadly, "Better not. After a glass or two I'll go to bed with almost anyone."

I said, "Hooray!" and filled her glass to the brim, and after the meal she came home with me.

Of course I hoped we would make love, but in sexual play no man is more dependent than me on the will of the woman, so I was pleasantly surprised to find we could and did make love. Then I fell asleep and dreamed I was Baron Frankenstein. The monster, looking just like Boris Karloff, lay on the bed-like operating table they show in the films. My hand was on the switch which would pour in the life-giving current, but I had not pulled it yet, for I realized the monster's life would be a sad one and I would be to blame for it. But I did pull the switch, the monster opened its eyes and stared at me, I woke up and so did Donalda. When I told her my dream she burst out laughing. "That was me," she said happily, "that was me! You'll never get away from me now."

I found this amusing. I felt safe because she had Senga and I too had another lover, though Donalda said firmly, "I don't want to know about her. Don't tell me *anything* about her. And never, please, never tell me when you visit her or she visits you."

I promised not to, feeling glad to know such a sensible woman.

How lucky I was then! Donalda usually visited me at lunchtime. I kept the curtains shut and, as the weather was cold, had my mattress on the carpet near the gas fire. I loaded that mattress with pillows, coloured cushions, a tray of fruit, cold meat, savoury cheese, pickles and wine. The lights came from five or six candles on the floor around us. I propped mirrors behind these so they seemed twice as many. The other woman sometimes came in the evening. She and I never fucked together (she had a satisfying husband) but we kissed, roly-polied around, ate, drank and talked a lot. A few days later Donalda made two discoveries, one that pleased, one that angered her. I forget which came first. The pleasant one was that Senga was having an affair with someone called Harry.

"As soon as I heard about it I ran round to the shop," Donalda told me gleefully, "and I said, 'Sit down, Senga. I have something to tell you.' And do you know her face went as white as a sheet!"

Donalda then told Senga that she (Donalda) knew Senga was having it off with Harry, but she (Donalda) did not mind, as she (Donalda) was having it off with me, and from now on each couple should stick with their recentest lover and be nothing but good friends to the old one. Senga gloomily agreed this was probably the best arrangement, but said Donalda was a fool to get entangled with a man: "But she wasnae cross with me or anything daft like that," said Donalda cheerfully, "So me and her are still doing business together."

The discovery that angered her was: when and how often the other woman visited me. She learned this from an observant neighbour of mine and behaved as if I had done what I promised not to do and told her myself. Her anger did not frighten me because I knew I had not been wicked, but the grief which accompanied her anger was terrible. The thought of me cuddling that other woman was a pain as real to her as raging toothache. I must not give pain like that to people and certainly not to a woman who is fond of me because I seduced her. I promised she would never again discover that I had loved someone else. I made that promise without guilt or remorse. I made it gently but firmly, like a doctor binding up a child's broken leg and explaining why the leg would heal and not get broken again. This treatment worked. At the time I did not know my promise was a declaration of marriage.

Yes, I am a married man. Donalda and me live so near together, she is so observant and inquisitive that I can never make love to someone else without her discovering, so I don't do it. This is no great deprivation but it makes me an unsatisfying lover. Lampedusa said once, "Marriage is a year of flames and thirty years of ashes." He was Sicilian. I doubt if Donalda and I flamed together for more than a fortnight. We sleep together four or five nights a week nowadays but lovemaking happens once a month, if I'm lucky. Nobody is to blame. In bed two nights ago she said, "When I first knew you I felt I could-nae have enough of you. Why are we different nowadays? Is it because we're older?"

I said, "Partly. And I think you are the last woman I will ever love, that after you comes nobody but death. The thought does not chill me but it makes excitement difficult."

"What a horrible thing to say! That I remind you of death!" cried Donalda, who is terrified of death. I hate deaths made by governments, business corporations and self-employed crimi-nals, but when in good health the inevitability of death soothes or braces me. Donalda is different, so I tried to put the matter more tactfully. I said, "When we made love in the old days I was livelier because then I felt you were just one in a whole crowd of possible lovers."

"Do you mean that when we made love you were imagining other women too?"

It was worse than that. When we made love I imagined other women *instead* of Donalda, and other men instead of me. I could not ejaculate without imagining my prick belonging to someone more powerful and cruel than I am: a tyrant with a harem of captured brides, a cowboy sheriff with a jail full of deliciously sluttish prostitutes. My book is full of these fancies. I once read it aloud to Donalda, she laughed wildly at bits the *Sunday Post* called facetious chauvinistic pornography, and now she is upset by a reference to notions which make me randy! But we all know facts with part of our brain while using another part to think, talk and act as if facts don't exist. Donalda prefers to forget my sexual fancies and has never told me hers, yet she must think of more than me when we make love. I am an interesting fellow but too fat, wheezy and self-obsessed to fully occupy a woman's mind at these times. If she is not thinking of tomorrow's shopping list she *must* be glamorizing the occasion with something fanciful. I once knew someone who enjoyed hearing my fancies while we made love, but Donalda and me are shy at these times and say nothing aloud but our names. I sighed and turned my back to her feeling lonely and gloomy, though I had no reason to be. I am lucky to sleep beside her so often. Fucking is less important than the publicity for it suggests, but in the old days when Donalda and I did not fuck she at least slept in my arms. Nowadays we sleep back-to-back, and when I press as much of my back against her as possible she moves further away. Sometimes I wake in the morning and find I'm alone. My snoring has driven her into the spare bedroom. Yet she loves me and I like nobody better than her. We will almost certainly stay together until death interferes.

But the night before last, without warning, Donalda turned and embraced me and brought me alive and awake all over. She only does this nowadays when I least expect it, never after a quarrel but always when love seems impossible. At first I move with her in a half-hearted way, then it feels perfectly possible and we swim together with me on top, because she prefers that. My body enjoys the exercise, my mind is nothing but a sad pleased blankness. But when Donalda murmurs that she wants me to ejaculate I can only do it by imagining wicked things. On this night I imagined a beautiful discontented customer walking into a shop like the one where Donalda works, a shop I have never visited. For some reason I cannot imagine wicked glamorous men nowadays or any sort of penis, but only women who seduce each other in sly cruel ways which have no base in my experience—the lesbians I know are rational folk who never seem to humiliate each other. The lesbians I imagine, however, did many things to this lovely discontented woman which made her completely content and helped Donalda and me to a satisfying conclusion. The next morning, which was yesterday, Donalda said, "I don't need you tonight. Tonight you can do what you like."

We got up, washed, had breakfast. She phoned for a taxi, swiftly painted her face, kissed my cheek making a distinct mouth-print on it ("To warn off others," she said) and left for the shop. When we first met she went to work by bus, so the shop must be doing well. The great thing is, I was left feeling happy and guiltless in my own place of work, which is home, thank goodness.

I never pitied my father when he left home for the factory each morning but I knew he drilled bolt holes through engine casings from necessity, not choice, and I had no wish to follow his example. Yesterday Donalda left me in charge of this quiet factory where I am the designer, craftsman, struggling apprentice, unskilled labourer, canteen staff and supplier of raw materials. All of us are equally important and are paid exactly the same. Our machinery is old-fashioned but my friends O and P and Q, who work with word processors, do not think my product inferior to theirs. I siphoned good black ink into the slender rubber well of my steel pen and laid reference books on a convenient table. I clipped sheets of lined paper to a board, sat down in the very comfortable chair I never use when I have visitors, and wrote the Darien Scheme section of my *Grand Caledonian Encyclopaedia of Scandalous Instances.* The *Encyclopaedia* is factual, and normally I cannot write the truth as fast as I write short funny things like this. Yesterday I mastered my material so quickly that whole sentences were conceived before the sentences leading to them. The scurrying this caused was all that disturbed the flow of work, apart from two visits to the kitchen to make and eat instant pizza. (Cover a slice of buttered bread with chopped onion and tomato, cover the whole thing with cheese and toast it.) I worked so well that the sun set and it was ten o'clock before I remembered I had been allowed to do exactly what I wanted that evening. It was too late to play chess, not too late for the pub. I phoned Donalda to tell her I would not visit her that night (she dislikes me when I've been drinking) but there was no reply. She must have been working late. The shop has no telephone so I had done all I could, and I went out with a guiltless conscience. As I entered a pub which cashes my cheques a woman leaving it stopped and said, "Hullo, Dad, I'm reading your book again."

She was in her early thirties, very tall and gaunt but not anorexic. Her neck-tendons were distinct but muscular, her head completely bald. Bald women usually appal me but this one seemed a handsome specimen of a new race: not white, not black, not Semitic, not Asiatic. Her neck and smiling head were the colour of a light brown biscuit. Her chin was strong and sharp, her nose wee and snug, her small delicate pointed ears were pierced through the gristle (not the lobes) by the hoops of huge silver ear-rings. She wore an ankle-length leather coat with very wide lapels and her hoarse little voice seemed to come from a great distance. I did not know her name or profession but had seen her in a pub near Glasgow Cross frequented by the Print Studio crowd and other arty people. She said, "You have an astonishingly dirty mind. You made me feel quite . . . mm mm."

I assumed mm mm meant sexy so I said, "Good."

We continued looking at each other. She did not stare at my face but closely watched it with this gloomy intense smile, her mouth turning down, not up at the corners. I was fascinated but did not know what else to say. Could she possibly desire me? If we became lovers what would Donalda do? She suddenly chuckled, touched my arm and went to the car park. I climbed some stairs to a crowded room where I joined O and P and the famous Q who saluted me smartly and said, "Good evening, Major Name."

We discussed books, human freedom, the uselessness of Scotland's fifty Labour MPs, the Culture Capital of Europe in 1990 and its coincidence with the three-hundredth anniversary of the battle of Boyne Water. A happy heat was spreading through my veins while we spoke: adrenaline, of course. The woman who called me Dad had stimulated my heart.

She stimulated my heart and gave me the freedom of the universe last night. I felt able to swim over, under, inside every woman in the world, able to love and own the whole as completely as well-loved babies own it after a good meal. Outside babyhood hardly anyone feels healthy for long, but viewed in health and without prejudice the universe is an orchard of strange lovely bodies: fruit, stars and people freely grown for us by God (if we're religious) or by the universe itself, if we ain't. Most bodies cannot be visited or grasped without expense or danger or embarrassment—the moon, for example, and the woman who calls me Dad—but through beams of light and air pressure thousands of bodies harmlessly visit and touch every one of us. Donalda should not fear the nourishment I get from light and airy contacts. All such nourishment makes me more fluid—more able to love her. I must tell her so. When I see her tonight (or on Monday night if she has to work the whole weekend) I will say, "Sit down, Donalda, I have something to tell you." No, that would alarm her. I will take her out for a very posh meal, maybe in that new restaurant boat which chuffs up and down the river. She will think I am compensating her for some pleasure I enjoyed without her, but she will not accuse me of it at once. She will ask what I did on Friday, Saturday, Sunday. When I left my house. Who I met. Where I ate and drank. What happened after that. I will give short accurate answers which will make her more suspicious than ever. She will try to annoy me into telling more by saying:

"So you had a real wild night."

"Of course I know you did more than just talk."

"Whose house did you fall asleep in?"

I will not be annoyed. I will say calmly, "It was an ordinary, enjoyable night."

"I talked and drank, that was all."

"I went home to my bed and nobody came with me."

At last Donalda will accuse me of hiding something so I'll tell her about my short talk with the bald woman. She will be furious. I will smile tolerantly and say, "You have nothing to fear. That talk led to a revelation which some folk would call religious. I realized . . ."

I realized something which words will hardly explain, so why try? Like most middle-aged people I have had many revelations which felt like turning points and maybe were. If I am a different man from yesterday my actions, not my words, will show it. I will continue to act as usual but with more courage and firmness, perhaps. If Donalda notices a difference she may even like it. She sometimes says she regrets how bossy I let her be.

# CHAPTER 12

# Class Party

Donalda fastens her mouth on June's mouth in a kiss which is almost a bite and June enjoys a melting delicious weakness like nothing she has known. Her astonishment at this feeling is so great that she does not move when Donalda releases her, stands, touches buttons on the radio phone and says, "Senga? Senga, she's all ready for you, and she's got no arrangements this weekend, nobody's coming, or expects her . . . Yes, bring up the teacher."

Donalda, a little nervously (June thinks) straightens her skirt and tucks her blouse into the waistband without refastening anything. A buzz from entryphone. Donalda presses street-door switch, opens door to landing then stands beside it, listening to the coming of her friends. June has several seconds to think about screaming, a few seconds to do it. She doesn't do it because she is almost certain that most of her neighbours are out on Friday nights, and if some are at home, and come when she screams, and the visitors run away, what will the neighbours find? June nearly naked in an embarrassing skirt with her arms bound behind her. All her life June has dreaded embarrassment more than pain, which she has hardly ever experienced and even now does not expect. She feels part of a surprising play or dream which cannot hurt much—if it does she will walk out of it or wake up. The obvious reason for not screaming—that as soon as she starts Donalda will jump on her and gag her—does not enter her head.

Senga walks into the room like a woman glad to be home after a long holiday. She carries two red nylon hold-all bags and dumps them on the floor. She wears a long waterproof coat and casts it off on to the sofa before waltzing round the room with outspread arms.

"Notice!" she announces to the world in general, "that I am wearing our school uniform, the same sexy skirt and blouse my pal Dona wears, and which so fascinated one of my customers that she ordered it before she knew she was joining the school. She seems to have messed it up a bit but that always happens at playtime." She stands still and looks hard at June who now sits up on the hearthrug, alert and puzzled but not frightened.

"How was she, Dona?" asks Senga.

"Very nice," says Donalda, "lovely at first. She lay down and opened up to me as easy as a wee pet lamb, just like what you said she would. But she soon got bored with me."

Senga puts her hands on her hips and tells June severely, "You are ignorant! I bet you've never made love for more than ten minutes at a time. You're too good looking to be so ignorant. Plain Janes like Dona and me had to learn to enjoy ourselves late in life because nobody else was keen on us, but hundreds must have wanted to teach you. How did you miss them? I bet the only people who taught you to be a woman were a frigid mother and some stupid men. You are very lucky that we caught you before you got too old . . . She's not too old for you, is she Miss Cane?"

Senga asks this of a woman who has entered the room behind her, also wearing a long coat which she has cast off on to the sofa. This is the lean bald lady of the second photograph, she wears the same big overalls with the bulging sidepockets, she now stands with her back to the door, legs astride. But despite her challenging stance and clothes she looks shy and downcast. She keeks at June sideways, her chin pressing hard into her naked shoulder as if trying to submerge in it. She mutters so softly the words are inaudible.

"I must explain about our school," Senga tells June cheerily, "Our headmistress needs discipline because nothing good can be learned without it, but she is an ideas person, not an enforcer, usually. She leaves discipline to the head girl, who is me. Please turn round, Miss Cane."

Obediently the tall woman turns to the door and at once looks perfect. The shyly brooding evasive face is the only thing wrong with her. Senga, Donalda and even June stare entranced at her athletic figure, the broadshouldered naked back tapering to a slim waist under a couple of crossed straps, the fine legs with outstanding calf muscles below the trousers rolled up to her knees. Senga shakes her head, becomes businesslike again and points to a slender pocket between the tall woman's hip and knee. What seems a hook sticks from the top. Senga puts a finger under the hook and raises it far enough to show it is the handle of a flexible cane.

"I'm not showing you this to prepare you for a cruel orgy," Senga tells June. "We'll have a wee bit of one, of course, but our headmistress is too good a teacher to rely mainly on punishment. Usually she relies on me. Turn round again, Miss Cane, please."

The woman faces them and again looks peculiar.

"And now," says Senga, folding her arms and looking like a schoolteacher too, "I must once again ask you, Miss Cane, if you want to take the new girl? Do you like the look of her? Please speak up because we all need to know." The woman whispers yes; she's beautiful in a voice so soft and hoarse that June hardly hears it.

"Then money must change hands," says Senga firmly. "Among many useful items which I packed into your great big pockets, Miss Cane, is a pen and cheque book. Unbutton the pocket on your left leg and produce them."

For the first time the tall woman stares hard at June and seems unable to stop looking. Her hands, as if of their own accord, go to the pocket and take out what Senga ordered. Meanwhile June without conscious effort has risen to her feet. She stares back into the woman's face because it fascinates her. June also tugs at the strap which ties her wrists behind her, it does not yield but this does not distress her. Her body moves without consulting her mind. She hardly notices that Donalda and Senga now stand on each side of her.

"Write down the seventeenth of October, nineteen eighty-nine," says Senga, "and Hideout Leathercraft and your name. I will then mention an exact sum of money. Have you written all that? Are you ready? Three thousand pounds."

The woman stares from June to Senga and whispers you're joking.

"Oh no," says Senga firmly, "you are buying the best weekend of your life and don't pretend you can't afford it. If you sell your holiday home in Greece you can buy a hundred weekends like this. But I'll give you thirty minutes to think about it, thirty minutes to see what you'll get for the price. I need a clock . . . Is this the bedroom?" Senga bustles toward the other room in June's flat and suddenly June awakens from something.

Suddenly June decides this is not a fascinating dream but an embarrassing and silly situation.

"Listen!" she cries, "I'm tired of this! The three of you are posturing all over my room as if I'm nothing but a . . . a . . . an audience and I don't like it. Untie my hands and clear out. At once. Now!"

"Hold her," says Senga firmly, fumbling in the pocket of her skirt. Donalda steps behind and puts an arm round June's waist, a hand over her mouth. The hand stays there by pinching June's nose between forefinger and thumb while June wrenches her head and tries stamping on Donalda's feet but plump wee Donalda is tough and heavy and inexorable. She does not move.

"Mouth," says Senga. June finds her mouth uncovered and draws a breath to scream but something hard enters, crushing her tongue. Across cheeks, ears and nape of neck she feels a strap tighten which no amount of head-wrenching shifts, though her hair is shaken over her face. It blinds her.

"Sit," says Senga. June is dragged backward and down till she sits on Donalda's lap, tied tight to Donalda's body by an arm round her waist and neck. June can do nothing but kick her legs about. Senga steps between them, parts the hair over June's face and says kindly, "The gag you are tasting will turn all your yells to moans and mumbles, but when you get used to it you will be able to say *please* and *thank you.*" She kisses June's brow then walks to the bedroom, goes in and reappears with a small stool and says, "I need some more nice things from your pockets, Miss Cane."

Senga steps up onto the stool and the bald woman hands her

a bradawl, a gimlet with a long thick shank, a ring screw of the sort children's swings are hung from, then a pair of handcuffs. Senga bores an efficient hole in the underside of the lintel, screws the ring into it using the gimlet as a lever, and locks one of the handcuffs into the ring. As these preparations start making sense to June she grunts and kicks more wildly and uselessly than ever.

"Lift her," says Senga.

The lean woman embraces June's legs around the knees, Donalda stands and they carry her to the doorway.

"Higher!" says Senga. June is hoisted to shoulder-height with her face to the floor and stops struggling for fear of being dropped.

"Sensible!" says Senga, doing something to June's arms which frees them. Senga grips a wrist, drags it up, clips the steel cuff round it. Then Senga steps off the stool and says "Stand."

June's feet are dropped onto the stool and she totters there, trying not to fall off, flinging her free arm about to keep balance while the other arm wags above her head with the cold steel round the wrist.

"Steady!" says Senga from behind, putting her hands on June's hips on each side under the waist. This steadies her.

Not blinded by her hair now but by tears of rage and frustration, June only sees that she faces into her bedroom when Donalda, with a tissue, delicately dries her eyes and cheeks and says softly, "You've nothing to worry about—I wish I was you. Being a new girl is the best fun of all and you'll feel great afterward—a new woman!"

June's free hand hits the side of Donalda's face with a sharp crack like a gunshot. Donalda jumps back, her face whitening with shock. She fingers her right cheek on which a bright blush shaped like a palm with five dim fingers starts to develop.

"That hurt!" she complains sadly. "And I was only trying to be nice."

The lean lady chuckles, goes to Donalda, embraces her, smiles down at her mournful face then abruptly kisses her mouth. It is a long kiss. When Donalda is released she looks cheerful again and smirks at June as if saying: Somebody likes me even if you don't. Senga, chuckling also, has grabbed June's free forearm and twisted it behind her back, hard enough to easily hold it there but not hard enough to hurt.

"Oo you wildcat!" coos Senga admiringly, "Oo you spitfire! Does she look wild and glaring and insulted and beautiful, Miss Cane? I can't see from here."

The lean woman sits down on the edge of June's bed with her knees wide apart and hands gripping them. She gazes at June's face, smiling and nodding.

"Good!" says Senga. "But our heroine has studied a photograph from my wicked album hard enough to know that she must stand a lot straighter than this and wear her highest heels. Look in the wardrobe, Donalda, and get me some of those magazines in case the heels aren't high enough."

June chokes with little sobs of fury while Donalda rummages eagerly in her wardrobe until she finds a pair of black open-toed shoes with four-inch stiletto heels and a slingback fastening. She then collects five or six *Vogue* magazines from a pile on the bedside table. June is whimpering now. Senga kneels behind her, embraces June's legs, lifts her off the stool and knees it aside. June clutches with free hand the cuff round her wrist, clings tight to stop herself swinging by one arm. Donalda kneels humbly before her and fits and fastens each foot into its shoe, then Senga lets her legs go. For a sore second both of June's arms are stretched by the weight of her whole body, then her downward-yearning toes touch the pile of magazines slid under them, her heels touch it too, her weight is shared equally by every stretched muscle between her fingers and toes. Senga tests this tautness by rippling her fingers over her hips and bum, lightly caressing June's waist, stomach, breasts; lightly stroking her spine, shoulderblades, arms. Senga is breathing hard from recent efforts and another excitement. When June tries to spit at her she smiles and murmurs, "You wanted this, oh you wanted it!"

Beads of sweat now glisten on the naked parts of June's body. With a small moan Senga embraces her and explores her left armpit with nose, lips, tongue.

stop says the woman on the bed.

"I will not!" cries Senga turning fiercely to that woman. "She belongs to Donalda and me, you havenae bought her yet! Thanks for reminding me."

Senga goes to the bedside table, lifts the clock from it, changes the alarm switch and puts it on the mantelpiece where June can see the dial. "It will ring in thirty minutes," she tells June, "then we'll give you a rest."

"You're being unkind," Donalda tells Senga. "Half an hour is a long time to stand like that."

"You stood like that for forty minutes," says Senga.

"Yes but I'm tough. I've had a hard life. She hasnae."

"She needs the exercise and I need a drink," says Senga, sitting down beside the bald woman.

"I poured drinks for us before I asked you up," says Donalda, "But of course nobody notices what I do."

"What was it?"

"Sherry. *Her* sherry. Harvey's Bristol Cream."

"Ugh," says Senga and the bald woman says bubbly.

"You heard her," Senga tells Donalda, "bring the bags in."

"We may have a new girl now but I still seem to be the skivvy around here," grumbles Donalda, and squeezes sideways past June into the other room muttering, "Excuse me."

i'm signing that cheque says the lean woman, doing so.

"I won't take it till the alarm goes off," says Senga, staring at June. Senga's expression is not gloating or triumphant, she has the lost look of a child watching something wonderful which she is too poor to possess. Suffering makes most folk uglier but though June's face and breasts are glazed with a mingling of tears and sweat her distress makes her more beautiful than ever. She moves her head slowly from side to side, trying not to think, not to feel the strain in every part of her body. It is not a very great pain—she would faint if it was. It seems bad because it is continual, she cannot escape it, it is bound to grow greater. The clockface tells her that one and three-quarter minutes have passed, that she must stay for twenty-eight minutes, twenty-five seconds. She knows that willing a clock to go faster is the worst way to pass the time, but cannot stop straining to see movement in the hour and minute hands while seeing nothing but torture in the slowly sweeping second hand. She tries to blind herself by shaking her hair over her face but her position prevents that. With the free hand she rakes some hair over her face but the steel ring bites so deep into the other hand that it is a relief to cling to it again and stand exactly as she was before with only one eye partly covered. She hears Senga say wistfully, "Wildcat has lovely hair."

yes

"Longer and thicker than Dona's."

yes

"Are you jealous of it, Miss Cane?"

very

"Excuse me again," says Donalda, squeezing sideways past June and carrying a bag in each hand.

From one bag a bottle of good champagne is produced, also a small leather case of crystal goblets with stems.

"Only the best for Miss Cane," says Senga, releasing the cork and pouring.

her health murmurs the bald woman, raising her glass.

"Here's to Wildcat," says Senga and drinks.

"That's you!" Donalda tells June.

As the trio stand sipping and contemplating her it strikes June again that they are the performers, she the audience of this show and she starts feeling a dazed acceptance of her position. This vanishes when Senga puts down her glass, removes a smart camera from a bag and says, "Will you take a few for the album, Miss Cane?"

As the lean woman squats low and flashes the dazzling box at June, prowls closer and does it again, slips past the side of her and flashes her from behind, returns and directs Senga and Donalda to pose on each side of her, gets Senga to embrace June and kiss her armpit again, then finally flashes four dazzling closeups of her face, June twists her head and body about with many little choking outcries. Every bit of her body and soul hates, fights against being *taken, caught, kept* in prints which many others may see and enjoy. Shock and exhaustion at last leave her hanging in a daze of pain she accepts. Dimly and without protest she sees the lean woman recline full-length on her bed, sipping from a crystal glass and glancing from June to Donalda and Senga and back. Donalda and Senga are emptying June's wardrobe of all her clothes, holding them up, trying them on, whirling about in them with little squeals of excitement.

"Wildcat knows what to wear—she really understands glamour—she doesnae give a damn for ordinary fashions!" cries

Donalda wrapping a silver sari round herself, "I'm too wee for this, you should wear it, Miss Cane."

The bald lady smiles.

"Notice something?" asks Senga, holding a scarlet flamenco dress to her body. "No trousers! No jeans, tight or baggy; no shorts, slacks, harem pants, not even a divided skirt. She definitely hates trousers. She'll look gorgeous in them."

"Yes, you've brought her the right present," says Donalda.

Senga says, "Tidying up time." She and Donalda pack June's dresses, suits, skirts, jackets, coats, hats and shoes into black plastic sacks taken from one of the bags. They then empty all the drawers in the room onto the floor and pack the contents into more sacks: underwear, letters, photographs, jewellery and everything except the cosmetic articles. These are piled on the dressing-table. For a moment Senga pauses with a pair of dolls in her hands which June has never discarded, a teddy bear and a cloth Dutch girl, so dilapidated that only a very poor child would play with them now. Before stuffing them into a sack Senga looks thoughtfully from one to another then tells June, "If you and I get to be pals—real pals—I might give you them back one day."

June nearly laughs aloud but aborts the laugh in a gasp and headshake. Laughter would destroy the stupor, the exact balance of pain and acceptance she now clings to as tightly as her free hand clings to the handcuff.

Donalda and Senga tie the mouths of the sacks with tape and pile them against the wall. The clock starts twittering. Senga silences it with the press of a fingertip and says, "All right, Miss Cane. Give me that cheque."

She is given the cheque, reads it and pockets it. She says submissively, "Thank you very much, Miss Cane. Can we give her a rest now?"

no says the lean lady, laying down her glass and standing up. She faces June and smiles slightly, then draws the thin cane from her hip-pocket, flexes it then suddenly slices the air with it in a swish which is almost a tweet. June starts wakening from her stupor. Senga takes another set of handcuffs from her skirt pocket, steps up onto the stool, cuffs June's free wrist to the ring also then steps down saying, "More comfortable?"

It is more comfortable. June's fingers are freed from the strain of clinging and the strain in her arms is now equal, though she stands rigid with dread.

"I don't like this," says Donalda loudly. She sits on the bed with her back to the others. "I don't think she needs it."

"She needs it," says Senga soberly. "Go to the bathroom and run the water. Don't make it too hot—test it with your elbow—and remember the salts."

Donalda gets up and takes a jar of coloured crystals from one of the bags. She does not look at June but mutters "Sorry" while slipping past her. The bald woman, with a beseeching look, puts her free arm round June's neck and tries to kiss her mouth, but despite her dread June twists her head from side to side and prevents this.

tell her, the lean woman whispers sadly to Senga, then slips past June to stand behind her. June is confronted now by Senga standing with legs wide apart and arms folded, looking angry.

"Our headmistress wants you to know," says Senga in a hard sarcastic voice, "that she is about to make you feel that her and you are the only two in the universe—the only ones alive. But before she makes you feel that, and after she makes you feel that, remember that no matter how much she hurts and loves you—no matter how much you get hurt and love her back—you are wearing the skirt you ordered from me, so she can't draw blood and you can't faint. Start when you like, Miss Cane."

The pain which follows is so astonishing that June does not try to scream but jerks her body at each hard regular stroke with a small indrawn cry of "ah." After the second stroke she feels nothing exists but her body and Miss Cane. After the twentieth she feels only the strokes exist, nothing else, not even her body, and when only the strokes exist each one evokes, as a kind of echo, a sensation of luxury. The luxury grows until she chokes with laughter and is about to faint. Someone shouts, "Stop!"

The strokes stop. June feels the luxury fade in her womb, a terrible burning start in her arse and upper thighs, but the beating has nearly stunned her. She is softly embraced around knees and waist and lifted. Gentle hands release her from the cuffs, take the gag from her mouth, strip off the skirt. Face down, kindly supported under shoulders, waist and legs she drifts above a floor she does not recognize, then is gently lowered, knees first then belly then breasts, into deep soft warmly soothing water. An arm supports her face above a layer of sweetly smelling foam. She sobs with relief and gratitude, soaped and sponged with no pressure at all on her sore parts. The foaming water drains from the bath, she is lifted gently to her knees and sprayed clean with more warm water, then wrapped in her fluffiest towels. She is helped back to bedroom, laid on the bed and moved gently about to let the warm draught from the nozzle of a hair-dryer play on every surface, enter each nook of her body—she giggles as it probes her armpits. This relief from all strain keeps her in a deeper daze of astonishment than the pain gave. She cannot remember having enjoyed such delicious peace in every part of her body yet the sensation is surprisingly familiar. Was being a baby like this? Stripes of pain across her bum and upper thighs still tingle but a small hand strokes on soothing cream, then two small hands (Donalda's) work it gently in and start massaging more intimately. June moans with pleasure. A voice says stop.

"Why? She's earned some fun for herself," says Donalda's voice.

i want her glamorous again

"But she'll have a drink first," says Senga.

June hears cork pop, finds glass of frothy dry sweetness tilted against her lips, sips, feels thirsty, drinks it all and feels drunk. Giggling slightly she is helped to her dressing-table and placed on the seat before.

The table is low, the mirror large and hinged to give three reflections. She sees herself naked enthroned with the lean lady kneeling on one side, Senga on other, Donalda standing forlornly behind. Senga and Donalda wear nothing but unfastened skirts, the bib of the bald woman's overalls hangs so her breasts also are bare. June chuckles. Multiplied by reflections they seem a Turkish harem painted by a lewd Victorian artist, filmed by an uninhibited de Mille. The lean lady nods to Senga. June feels her knees pressed apart and kept apart by handcuffs chaining each ankle to one of the chair's front legs. Senga takes another two pairs of handcuffs from her big pockets ("Where do you get them all?" Donalda murmurs) and each of June's wrists is drawn behind her and chained to the nearest back leg of the seat. Senga says, "You don't need all this bondage, Wildcat, but Miss Cane is afraid you'll scratch her. Don't worry. *You* won't be spanked again this weekend."

"I hate the way you said *you,*" grumbles Donalda, "I suppose that means I'm goanty get spanked?"

"Don't be a pessimist, Dona!" says Senga maternally. She takes Donalda's hand and leads her to the bed, glancing back to say, "I'm feeling randy, Miss Cane. Can I tell Dona to give tongue?"

but watch me says the bald woman, taking lipstick tubes from her pockets and adding them to those on the tabletop.

"I'll watch every little thing you do!" cries Senga, taking the pillows from the bed-head and piling them in a heap near the foot. "You're my favourite show, Miss Cane, and I'll make suggestions and give help when needed."

Senga strips off her skirt, flings it in a corner, sits on the bed-foot with her knees very wide apart and, with a luxurious sigh, lies back on the pillows. The hour is close to midnight. What follows is in twelve parts:

### 1 MAKE-UP

With foundation cream, face powder, blusher, mascara, eye-shadow, lipstick, nail varnish, Miss Cane makes June like one of the mature yet glamorously vulnerable film stars of the nineteen-forties with a difference: her breasts are tinted as carefully as her face, hands, toes. Her glorious hair is tenderly spread, combed, brushed out over her shoulders and back, then delicately scented. June's position allows her pubic hair also to be combed, brushed, scented.

### 2 MIRROR ENVY

Soft caressings that seem easy continuations of the brushing and scenting become urgent, intimate, exciting. The excitement is increased by Senga's face staring out at June from the mirror, not an ordinary face now but beautiful with wonder and longing. June now knows that it is Senga who desires her most, desires her so much that if Senga and she ever became lovers June would be the mistress, Senga the humble one. So Senga also fears her. That is why she sent Donalda to seduce June, then sold her to Miss Cane. By responding delightedly to Miss Cane's caresses June can be revenged on Senga, so with half-closed eyes June moves her head languidly about, whimpering with a pleasure she does not greatly feel. Her eyes are just wide enough to see Senga's reflected face growing more frantic, to see Senga seek relief from misery by pulling with both hands Donalda's pleasuring head harder into her crotch. At which Donalda coughs and chokes and June, giving up all pretence of rapture, laughs aloud. Miss Cane slaps June hard on one cheek, then the other.

### 3 HAIR TREATMENT

Miss Cane has been kneeling. Grinning maliciously she now stands and unloads from her pockets on to the dressing-table shears, a shaver, pointed instruments, cotton wool, a bottle of surgical spirit, some rings.

"Photographs first," says Senga, getting up and taking photographs, then she and Donalda hold parts of June perfectly still while Miss Cane clips and shaves her bald all over, including eyebrows and armpits. June has to be gagged again for this: again she thinks she cannot bear it, and does. Miss Cane then photographs June while Senga gathers her hair from the floor, holds the fragrant mass in her arms, suddenly bows her face into it and weeps. At which Miss Cane snarls, flings camera upon bed, grabs the hair and hurls handfuls round the room.

"Oh stop it!" cries Donalda. "Stop her, Senga, she's gone mental!"

"No, let her. It's good for her," says Senga, drying her tears, "She's never gone wild like that before."

## 4 PIERCING

June's body is now marked in permanent ways but she does not care: the rape of her hair has numbed her. Miss Cane calms down, pierces the wing of June's right nostril, clips a small gold ring through it. She pierces the gristle of June's right ear and puts two silver hoops through it, one six inches across and one four inches. Miss Cane uses her instruments with the assurance of a practised surgeon, Senga aids her with the efficiency of a trained nurse. Donalda collects the locks of hair strewn around the room, packs them in one of the plastic sacks, brews a pot of tea, pours it into cups. She cannot persuade anyone else to stop for a cup so sulks instead of drinking one herself.

## 5 WASPS

June is unshackled, ungagged and helped to the bed where she at once falls asleep. While sleeping she feels things being done to her body which are partly real. A wasp is stinging her shoulder repeatedly as it crawls around a spot on it. The stinging throb is also ticklish, but June is sure waking will not cure it. She sleeps until Senga shakes her awake saying, "Look! Isn't it real-looking?"

She touches June's throbbing shoulder and June, looking there, sees a small black-and-yellow trembling wasp.

"That's the best you've ever done," Senga tells Miss Cane, who rests on the bed edge, a small smug smile on her mouth and a tattooing needle in her hand. Senga says to June, "She's going to give you more—one on the tit, one inside the thigh near your thingummyjig, one on the bum and mibby others."

"Mm," says June, falling asleep again.

## 6 DREAMING

She dreams she strolls by the lake in the garden of Versailles, pestered by wasps, arm-in-arm with her husband, Tom, the baldheaded but leonine king of France. He wears a huge curling wig made from the hair of his previous queens: "Very nice if you can afford it," he tells her, "And when the revolution comes I can use it as a passport. But what do I know about hats, shoes and the neighbour's dog? Why should I care if our wallpaper is pink to harmonize with the new carpet or green to contrast with it? Life is too short."

"I wasn't interested in these things either," June admits sadly, "I just felt our marriage should have some conversation in it."

"But a man needs peace. I wish these wasps would fuck off."

In a dim room she, a baby, is sponged, dried, powdered, has her nappies changed by Mummy and Granny. They then dress her for Holy Communion, which is puzzling; they were never religious. The clothes have a lot of studs, zips, belts which take a long time to press, pull and buckle. When this is done she feels very snug and tight under the waist, looser above, her stomach quite naked. She supposes the Catholic Church requires all this. Things are done to her face. Someone seems to be trying to put a comforter in her mouth, she pouts toward it and always misses. Then she realizes they are applying lipstick and thinks, "The Catholics are wicked to do these things to a wee girl."

After that they let her fall into warm dreamless blackness.

## 7 WAKENING

A mug of liquid black warmness is held to her lips by a motherly stranger who has raised her head by an arm behind her shoulders. The liquid smells of coffee and something peculiar, tastes sweet; she always hated sugar but drinks eagerly.

Another full mug is offered. She takes it in her hands and drinks more slowly, feeling she has wakened into another dream. She can see nothing familiar. The pair of legs stretched along the bed before her move when she moves them but cannot be hers, as she never wears pants. The room is like a display bedroom of a sort seen in big furniture shops. It holds no objects of personal use or ornament except a clutter of things not hers on a dressing-table. In a corner is a sinister heap of fat black plastic sacks. There are three strangers. One beside her on the bed supports her shoulders. One sits sideways on the bed-foot looking glum. These are big-bummed, big-breasted little women with hectically messy hair, naked but for black aprons which June eventually sees are short leather skirts fastened carelessly at the waistband. The third stranger stands on tiptoe in the open doorway with arms stretching straight up. Seen from behind the figure is that of an amazingly thin tall bald beautiful gymnast with hips perhaps a little too broad to be male. But what makes this room unlike all others past or possible is the strong tones, clear colours, distinct edges of everything, everyone in it; also an ache of sexual longing. June feels this ache like the solid presence of a fifth person who knows them all intimately, has brought them all together, who stands invisible among them but cannot be handled.

### 8 A REVENGE ANGEL

Senga says cajolingly, "Stand up and look at our Revenge Angel."

She helps June stand (there is a moment of difficulty: June has never worn such high heels before) and helps her advance to meet the fifth person in the room who is not invisible at all: has the face of a fury and a figure so suavely, proudly female in elegant gleaming black that June instinctively bends to worship and the figure bows. At which June recognizes herself, memory returns, the room and things and people lose intensity. She knows who they are, how they happened. Stepping close to the mirror she studies the face which is obviously copied from the star of *The Rocky Horror Picture Show.* The features present no problem. Her mouth can in minutes be given back its modest colour within natural boundaries. The menacing scrollwork of the thin eyebrows can be wiped off and replaced by the dark feathers of her old ones, carefully redrawn where they will grow again. With rings removed the pierced nostril and ear will have no conspicuous scar. A turban can cover her scalp until hair returns; though not fashionable, it will not look bizarre. But what can she do with the wasps? Not the ones above the hairline, the ones at the outer corners of each eye? June groans with despair and exhaustion.

### 9 DEATH OF AN ANGEL

begin says a small clear voice from the doorway.

"She's to blame!" cries Senga, eagerly pointing to the figure in the doorway and putting a cane in June's hand. "Remember what she did to you! Hit her anywhere you like! She deserves it! She wants it!"

begin says the voice.

"She's not to blame. You are, but I don't care," says June wearily dropping the cane. The thought of beating someone has never excited her much and certainly doesn't excite her now. She yawns, sits down and says, "I'm tired. Please unpack my things and go away."

"It hasnae worked," Donalda tells Senga flatly.

begin says the implacable little voice.

## 10 FINISHING THE JOB

Senga frowns and walks about the room, thinking hard, sighing and casting mournful looks at June who stonily ignores her. At last Senga tells June, "Listen, I know you're sick of us but we'll havetae be here a bit longer. We've a job to finish. But we'll be as quick as we can."

begin

Senga picks up the cane, offers it to Donalda and says, "You do it."

"Oh no. If Wildcat won't do it why should I?"

"Donalda, is this a strike situation?"

"Definitely!" says Donalda, folding her arms and pouting obstinately.

begin

"All right, I'll begin, you bloody-fucking-upper-class-dyke-bitch-bully!" shouts Senga. "As usual at the end all the dirty work is left to me so here it comes! And I won't stop till you ask to go home, right?"

begin

So Senga beats Miss Cane hard and methodically all over, eventually doing it with leather thongs, and Miss Cane weeps, sobs and in her small voice, begs Senga to stop but does not ask to go home till long after dawn has broken. Senga and Donalda release Miss Cane and help her into the bathroom. June kicks off her shoes, unties the neck of a plastic sack, tips it on to the floor and picks from the spillage a shirt she can use as a nightgown. She takes the rings from her face, wincing slightly. She unbuckles, unzips, removes the leather clothes, pulls on the shirt, slips between her bed-sheets. Bewildered exhaustion is what she mainly feels, but feels also that she will not sleep until alone in her own home.

## 11 AN APPOINTMENT

Senga enters the bedroom, glances at June, stoops and refills the emptied sack.

"Leave those things, they're mine," says June without force.

"I'm going to take them all away," says Senga sadly but firmly. "I know you're sick of me because you didnae enjoy these games much. Still, I showed you a bit of life, eh? I gave you some views of the potential. Tomorrow you'll likely hate my guts and the day after too, but in a few days you'll mibby want to see me again. Anyway, I want to see you again. I'm removing all this stuff to make sure that happens. I'll phone you near the end of the week."

June is too weary to argue and dozes while Senga drags the sacks into the lobby.

## 12 CHEERIO

June is wakened by someone kissing her brow, Senga of course, who says, "I've left a few things on the dressing-table you may find handy. We're off now. See you later."

"Cheerio!" says Donalda from the doorway. "I'm sorry if we did anything to upset you, but some of it was fun, right? No hard feelings, right?"

thank you fo a very agreeable night says a tall person behind Donalda. though three thousand is ratha steep, I must have been mad to sign that cheque

"It's bought you credit with the firm for weeks to come. All out everyone," says Senga briskly switching off the light. She leaves.

June hears the front door slam. And sleeps.

## CHAPTER 13

# New June

June wakes in dark, feeling robbed of something essential to life and dignity. Aching muscles in arm, leg and shoulder, various throbs and ticklings in the skin recall what happened. She rises, puts on light, telephones Speaking Clock, is told by rich and manly English voice that on the third stroke the time sponsored by Accurist will be two hours, twenty-seven minutes and thirty seconds. She has slept dreamlessly for over nineteen hours. She now sees the theft of her clothes, personal ornaments, souvenirs, hair, the piercing and tattooing of her skin are not the worst that happened, though they constantly recall it. Her body has been deliberately toyed with and teased into a sexual hunger she only now fully feels, gnawing and dreadful hunger. Her one hope of satisfying it is someone who said "I'll phone you at the end of the week."

The time is half-past two on dark Monday morning. If she had hope of finding where Senga lived she would hunt her up, break in on her, DEMAND satisfaction, spank her till she yielded it. Is there nobody else she can break in on? A man is not what June wants but would be better than nothing. However, for three years she has tried to give men up, and succeeded. The only man she knows who can be reached by taxi and would love to be invaded is her ex-husband. She shudders at the thought of him—better use her fingers. Which she does, but not at once.

First she wanders through the flat with a sheet twisted round her. She gazes at wardrobe mirror where she watched Donalda seduce her, the rug where they made love. She now knows it was opportunity missed, wonders why she was so passive. Like lonely old woman recalling childhood game she stands on tiptoe, reaches up toward two holes in lintel of bedroom door then goes to bathroom, wipes make-up off, has warm bath which fails to soothe as last one did. She goes back to bed and caresses herself as Donalda caressed her before Miss Cane said stop. June tries caressing herself more than that, but the extra caresses don't feel right. She goes to dressing-table, sits naked before it, legs wide open as if still manacled there. With half-closed eyes she imagines the hand caressing her is Miss Cane's, that the face in the mirror is Senga's loving face before she (June) turned revengeful and pretended rapture she did not feel, rapture she now tries to create. She gets pleasure from this but too little. A sandwich would be more satisfying. The rapists did not steal her food. She gets up to visit kitchen; halts at sight of shoes, garments strewn by bed, the only clothes left her. Sitting crosslegged on carpet she examines them closely.

Pants, jacket have been made with love: all stitching in double rows, thread black as the leather but done as neat as if white: pure silk milk-white linings, exquisitely quilted, unstained by sweat from when she wore them last night. Embroidered on lining between jacket shoulders two small scarlet hearts both pierced by gold arrow, TO J LOVE FROM S underneath. June smiles, kisses embroidery, slips on jacket, zips up the long sleeves, fastens studs of front. A lot of her chest is bare, yet padded shoulders give warm protected feel. The pants have big outlined heart embroidered on lining of seat with IT ALL STARTS HERE! inside. Putting on pants takes many minutes. Seams down the legs are joined by small buckles and straps. She takes great care to exactly tighten each. The tightness comforts. She stands turning about before wardrobe mirror admiring side of each leg: from waist to mid-calf an inch-wide lane of her naked self shows under the buckles and straps. Between belt and jacket most of her stomach appears, two brave little wasps crawling left and right from her navel. At last she faces her head, staring hard at what she feared to see clearly before: bald weather-beaten head of plastic doll once seen on rubbish heap beside roofless cottage when she was wee and wept at the sight with pity and dread but now she knows what to do.

Go to dressing-table. Sit. Choose cosmetics but not Miss Cane's. Draw on eyebrows like her usual eyebrows, only darker. Ignore wasps. Paint lips, tint cheeks, shadow eyes just as usual. Unframed by dark hair this face is now definite as Rocky Horror film face and more bony, subtle, alluring. Baldness and wasps still give this head discarded doll look but look of *expensive* doll discarded because it is a *dangerous plaything able to act for itself.* June once took nightschool ballet lessons, stopped after third. She leaps up, pirouettes wildly round room, wonders why she feels free, happy. It comes from *no hair:* hair was half of her once, why women envied her, why men looked twice. It framed her head, curtained and cloaked her, a soft warming house she could move with. Hair was religion learned from devout mother who taught her to love it, worship it, serve and suffer for it, handfuls grabbed and twisted before she was twelve by boys, also girls. A new life is starting without it, one she cannot imagine nor can anyone else—not even Senga. Yes, this is freedom. She strides to telephone, again dials one two three. On the third stroke the time sponsored by Accurist will be ten hours, forty minutes and thirty seconds. She is over an hour late for work. She is about to dial her office when the phone rings.

Phone rings. She lifts receiver. Clear little voice says, hello?

June knows that voice. Her heart starts beating differently, a fact which astounds her more than the voice does.

hello, a you tha, can you hia me?

"Yes."

I'm phoning to thank you fo a truly lovely evening.

A silence.

I say, can you hia me, a you still tha?

"Yes."

good. you see I feel I owe you a lot so in yaw case I feel bad about stopping that cheque I say a you still listening?

"Yes."

I stopped the cheque first thing this mawning because three thousand pounds is much too much fo one night and the good bits wa just you and me we don't need these otha little people, don't you agree?

June nods. Her heart changed rhythm when Miss Cane's voice reawoke this bodily hunger for love.

I say, a you tha?

"Yes."

I'm besotted, I need to see you. I've money if money mattas, I suppose it does, can we meet to discuss it—but three thousand was too steep.

Silence.

when can we meet?

June's body wants to shout NOW but the eager woman pressing her had better be treated with the same caution as an eager man. June draws a deep breath and asks, "What do you suggest?"

I'd love to buy you a meal in The Ubiquitous Chip or Pumphouse or Rotunda or anywha.

"I've never eaten in the Rotunda."

not great but good fun. will I collect you by taxi, say, about seven?

"If you like."

Silence.

my name is harriet shetland. I love you.

Click of receiver put down.

"It is important not to go mad!" thinks June. What she most needs is going to be provided, but she is still a working woman, not a kept woman, and had better keep her job. She phones the senior executive of her department. He is delighted to hear June must stay at home today, maybe for several days. June has not said she is sick but, "I've overworked you, no wonder you're sick!" he says happily. "I hear it in your voice. Yes, you're tired, listless, completely worn out. Am I right?"

"Yes," says June.

"Good. I mean, it's good that you recognize your sickness, because sickness is the body's way of telling the mind, *leave me alone for a bit.* You've been too conscientious, June. When we started this thing together you had only me to advise. Now you have Bleloch, Tannahill and the new publicity officer. You need an assistant, June. It's ridiculous that our office has only one trained legal mind to depend upon. Now promise me you'll take all the time you need to recover. I suggest a trip to one of those places which are at their most charming out of season: Italy, the Canary Islands, Miami. Relax. Sunbathe. A bit of romance will do no harm! You're, haha, a very attractive legal adviser, June,

if a friendly male chauvinist swine may say so, and . . . and
. . . yes, you'll be a new woman when you come back to us.
These are not doctor's orders, they are boss's orders."

This boss is worried and reticent when facing people but can
sound like another sort of man along a wire. June quiets the
gibbering receiver by saying, "Thanks, Mr Geikie," and putting
it down. Very hungry now she makes pile of sandwiches, sits
on rug before fire, wolfs food down with teacup of sherry (she
never did that before), stretches out. Dozes off.

Is wakened by buzzing entryphone, leaps to it at once, hears
Donalda say, "It's only me! I just want to tell you I've—"

"Wait there!" commands June and races barefoot down
stairs, pulls open front door. No Donalda. June leaps out and
down stone steps to pavement and glares fiercely round. Mild
autumn cloudy noon: nothing moving on terrace but old lady
with shopping bag recoiling in terror, a distant departing Citroën canvas-topped car with two blue wavy lines on the side.

"Sorry!" June tells old lady, goes angrily back up steps,
through doorway, slams door. On floor under letter slot, padded envelope, her name on it. She takes it upstairs, squats on
rug, rips it open. Inside a letter folded round thin clean wad of
new banknotes: Clydesdale Bank fifty-pound notes, each en-
graved with a bewigged Adam Smith raising a reproving forefinger. June counts fourteen such notes. The letter is written in
childishly clear, backward-sloping little words.

*Dear Dear Dear Dear Dear Dear I can't seem to stop writing
Dear Dear Dear June, I have been a cruel bitch but I am not a
financial exploiter, hence the enclosed. You may wonder why it
is not more, as a three way split between Dona, me and you would
be £1000 each. The truth is, I cannot give anyone that much, will
not have that much myself until Harry's cheque comes through*

*tomorrow or the day after. £700 is all I have except a bit in my purse to tide me over. I have not the kind of bank account which allows me an overdraft. This is deliberate. I belong to the sort of people who never get out of debt once they are in it. My mother was respectable, never in debt in her life. Dona's dad had his legs broken because he owed money he could not pay back. I would steal (food from shops) rather than owe money. Which is why I am paying what I owe you right away though I know you will not break my legs! (A joke.) I want you to know as soon as possible that I am honest with money and not an exploiter. Dona won't mind waiting a day or two longer for hers as she and me have been pals for years. Anyway, she has a very decent sugar daddy.*

*Dear Dear Dear Dear (here I go again) Dear Dear Dear Dear June, I will not be paying you £300 when Harry's cheque comes through because the firm has had to meet certain expenses. Good handcuffs cost more than you would think possible and my customers are given only the best. Plastic cuffs hold well enough but would have been an insult. You looked so lovely in real steel I'm excited just remembering it, more excited than I was at the time. As a professional I must keep a cool head when on the job or everyone else is disappointed. You stay amateur! Maybe you and me could be amateurs together one day soon? (Like Friday?) Do you like the suit? It too is of the best, I spent hours on it. I know you did not order it but it will fit nobody but you. Please wear it for me.*

*Dear Dear Dear Dear I'm afraid you still hate my guts so I dare not phone you till Friday when maybe you will be calmer and ready for more. (Love.) Yours Truly, Truly Yours, Yours Truly, Truly Yours, Yours Truly, Truly Yours, . . .*

These words are repeated to the foot of the page and end with *Senga PTO* in the bottom right-hand corner. June turns over and reads on the other side:

*PS Harry is Miss Cane's real name. She is a very famous artist.*
*PPS All your things are safe with me.*
*PPPS I am your Senga.*

This letter astonishes June. On first meeting Senga she thought her an astute small businesswoman. In the past few hours she has thought her a sexual predator, a perverse psychologist, a social liberator. The letter shows she is still a small businesswoman, a sentimental and naive one who handles money stupidly. And money in crisp clean valuable notes is lovely stuff to handle. June lives carefully but comfortably within her income while buying her flat and adding to a fund that will let her retire at fifty-six with the same standard-of-living-index-linked income. She has nearly seven thousand pounds in two bank accounts and some British Petroleum and British Gas shares. She is careful to pay for everything which costs over a few pounds by cheque, and to note all the payments down. Like Senga she never accumulates an overdraft. She has never held so much money in her hands before: unexpected money, tax-free, free in every way. Like most who start their working life with very little June will never feel rich through her earnings, but this money makes her feel rich. She will not insult this love offering by turning it into numbers in a deposit account. She will buy magic, not security with it. She cannot imagine what will happen when she meets Harry tonight, but if she gets money (£1000? £1200?) she'll make sure the cheque is cleared (may tie the bitch up to ensure it) and give some money to Senga, perhaps.

She divides the wad in two, puts £350 in each breast pocket thinking smugly, "A chap should always have money in his pockets."

Senga left a pair of dark glasses on the dressing-table. June puts these on, smiles at the result in the mirror. Her mother, sisters, best friends and ex-husband would not recognize her now if they stared in her face. She slips on the high-heeled shoes, remembers her ballet lessons and steps about in them. They are sore on the calf muscles, but the extra height is worth it. She phones for a taxi and is driven to the House of Fraser in Buchanan Street.

To the assistant in the millinery department she says, "I want to make my head less surprising."

She buys hats which cover her head from hairline to nape of neck: a black silk turban and one of black velvet, a black felt helmet with a small posy of black felt pansies on the side, and a Russian Cossack hat in black fur. In the lingerie department she buys black body stockings in fishnet and more elaborate open meshes, black silk slips and black lacy brassières. For old times' sake she now strolls to the first leather shop she visited. She carries all her new purchases in bags for she does not yet want to look less surprising. When dressed ordinarily she drew an amount of attention that mainly embarrassed her. She now draws five times as much attention and it amuses her mightily. She is surprised to notice that the cries of building workers on a construction site she passes sound as loud and harsh as usual, though the words are more aggressive. The tone of men signalling that they want to fuck her, and that they wouldn't fuck her with a ten-foot pole if they were paid a pension, sound much the same.

In the leather shop she buys a black-belted coat with big lapels and a military-looking hat with glossy skip. She contrives to be served by the assistant who first introduced her to the Hideout, and at one point removes her glasses and says, "Do you remember me?"

After a wondering stare the assistant says, "Yes!... Did you find that place you were looking for?"

"Oh yes."

"So you're happy now?" asks the assistant, smiling.

"Yes," says June, smiling.

**CHAPTER 14**

# Critic-Fuel: An Epilogue

A few years ago I noticed my stories described men who found life a task they never doubted until an unexpected collision opened their eyes and changed their habits. The collision was usually with a woman, involved swallowing alcohol or worse, and happened in the valley of the shadow of death. I had made novels and stories believing each an adventurous new world. I now saw the same pattern in them all—the longest novel used it thrice. Having discovered how my talent worked I thought it was probably dead. Imagination will not employ who it cannot surprise.

I told folk I had no more ideas for stories and did not expect them. I said it to Kathy Acker. Kathy, pointing out a new way, asked if I had thought of writing a story about a woman. I said no, that was impossible because I could not imagine how a woman felt when she was alone. Such announcements were truthful but not honest. I hoped my talent was only as dead as Finnegan, and would leap from the coffin and dance a new jig if the wake got loud enough. Meanwhile I arranged a show of paintings, began a collection of English vernacular prologues, turned old work into film scripts and came to owe the Clydesdale Bank a sum oscillating between a few hundred and a few thousand pounds. This was not poverty. Most professional folk live in debt nowadays. Banks and building societies encourage it because debts make them richer. My state only depressed me because my parents had been working-class folk who, though not religious, avoided debt like the devil. I too could have avoided it by renting a smaller flat, using public transport instead of taxis, eating at home instead of restaurants, drinking alcohol four or five times a year instead of nearly every day. Alas, I felt nostalgia but no desire for the decent carefulness which had bred and educated me. I *wanted* to be a middle-class waster, but a solvent one.

In Queen Street station one morning I glimpsed a girl stepping jauntily through the crowd in high heels and a leather suit which fitted her so snugly in some places, left her so naked in others that it seemed a preliminary to lovemaking. Soon after or soon before I began imagining how a woman might feel when alone. This came from accompanying a friend on a shopping expedition. Some women—even women who know what looks best on them—enjoy a man's company when buying clothes, though the man stops being a distinct character to them. He becomes an audience, or rather, a small part of a vaster, more satisfying audience in their heads. I penetrated *What Every Woman Wants,* the *House of Fraser* and *Chelsea Girl* with the guilty reverence I would feel in a mosque, Catholic chapel or synagogue, yet the odour was familiar and friendly. I had sniffed it as a small boy in my mother's wardrobe. I was fascinated by women pondering sombre or vivid or subtly pale colours, fingering husky or frail or soft or sleek fabrics, holding loosely or crisply or tightly tailored second skins to their bodies. I felt a long slow sexual ache in these shops, a sad ache because no earthly coitus could satisfy all the desires and possibilities suggested by the many garments. The ache, of course, was mine, but I was sure many women felt it too and perhaps felt it stronger. Most women have fewer devices than men to divert them from affection. I imagined a woman whose world was full of that ache, whose life was years of ordinary frustrations patiently endured before a chance suggestion led her further and further away from the familiar things she normally clung to. The woman need not have been beautiful or her adventure perverse, but these notions brought my imagination to life again. While writing the first chapter of this book I enjoyed a prolonged, cold-blooded sexual thrill of a sort common among some writers and all lizards.

At that time I thought *One for the Album* (then called *Something Leather*) a short story. On completing it I imagined more adventures for June, but the first episode had internal order and was a thriller of *The Pit and the Pendulum* sort, ending when the reader was likely to be most intrigued. Believing it could be popular I sent it to a famous London literary agency, suggesting they try selling it to an expensive glossy magazine with a transatlantic circulation: *Vogue* or *Esquire* or better still *The New Yorker.* After a few weeks I learned it had been sent to a couple of British literary magazines whose editors, though friendly acquaintances of mine, had not embraced it with cries of "yes please."

In 1987 Tom Maschler, the Chairman of Jonathan Cape Ltd, asked if I had started writing fiction again, a question he had asked annually since 1984. I sent him the new story. He liked it, thought it could be the first chapter of a novel, offered money in advance. We haggled. I obtained enough to live without debt for a couple of years while still eating and drinking too much. Only the need to write an unforeseen novel now depressed me. The further adventures I had imagined for June were too few to be a novel. I will describe these adventures, then how the novel got written in a way which cut most of them out.

First came the orgy with Senga and Donalda (I had not yet thought of Harry) which changed June's looks and left her nothing to wear but dark glasses, high-heeled shoes and the suit I had glimpsed on the girl in Queen Street station. The wicked thrill of imagining a modest, conventional woman forced to dress like that was followed by speculations on how it might change her behaviour. For the better, I thought, if she had health and vitality. Self-conscious conventionality is bred from vanity and cowardice. It assumes everyone may be watching us closely and must be given no strong reason for finding us attractive or repulsive. I thought of June as very lonely because she has cultivated reticence to compensate for her beauty. She evades or retreats from nearly everything she dislikes, never opposing or changing it. Conventional cowardice has imprisoned her intelligence, so the discovery that her mere appearance disturbs conventional, timid and stupid people feels like release. Stepping jauntily through the streets in her defiantly sexual suit she enjoys a freedom which is far more than sexual. Next day, instead of brooding over Senga and what will happen when they meet at the end of the week, June returns to work as if nothing had happened. Her office job prevents loneliness and earns money, but today she approaches it with a mischievous interest in how her workmates will cope with her.

She is legal adviser in a government office created to help

poorly paid folk who have been badly treated by other government offices. Efficiently run, it would trouble several high-
ranking public servants. If run by a clever ambitious Senior
Executive Officer it would trouble them often. They have given
the post to Mr Geikie who never expected to rise so high.
Toward colleagues and superiors he feels sensations of inferior-
ity mingled with adoration. If they smile and call him by his
first name he feels perfectly safe. He is sure he can best serve
the public by giving such people no trouble at all. When June
joined his office he told her in a worried, preoccupied voice,
"Our main job is to defuse potentially painful confrontations by
arranging alternative procedures. This is not easy. It cannot
always be done quickly."

She discovers he deals with troublesome cases by postponing
decisions until the applicant's legal aid fees expire, after which
most of them have lost hope and accept a very small sum in
compensation. If applicants have a generous lawyer who sticks
by them and complains more vigorously, Mr Geikie frankly
admits that the fault is his, says the delay has been intolerable
but cannot be helped: his office is under-staffed. When June
started there she worked with Mr Geikie and three clerical
assistants. The clerical staff are now twice as many, their type-
writers have been replaced by word processors and their title
changed to Administrative Assistants. The office has also been
joined by two Higher Executive Officers who have nearly
learned Mr Geikie's methods, but if one looks like bringing a
troublesome case to a conclusion it is given to the other with
instructions to tackle it differently. The office hums with activ-
ity and Mr Geikie can still complain he is under-staffed. His
superiors have now such confidence in him that his office will
soon become a Department with himself the Principal of it. He
will also have a greatly enlarged staff and one of his underlings

promoted to Senior Officer and Deputy Assistant. He will obviously promote the most anxious and servile of his underlings, the one most like himself. June has never seemed servile, never said what she does not believe. She has avoided giving offence by being silent. Before returning to the office this morning she is trusted but not much liked by her workmates. She deliberately arrives ten minutes late, takes off coat and hat in the lift going up, carries them across large room where Administrative Assistants are working. She conveys who she is by saying, "Good morning!" in the bright curt voice she always uses. They usually reply, but not today. She enters her room and shuts the silent starers out.

This room feels as good and friendly as a workplace ought to feel after a strenuous holiday. Here are things she can tackle, routines to help her do it efficiently. She settles at the desk to which Mr Geikie sends all cases too small to worry him, cases of official tyranny she can correct or compensate for. Through the intercom she first tells the other Executive Officers that she has returned and is now perfectly well, then she studies her desk diary and the contents of the in-tray, then dictates letters into her recorder. An hour later she calls in her Personal Administrative Assistant (or secretary) and explains how she wants the letters handled. She ignores the girl's fascinated stare by sitting sideways to it, until Jack Bleloch bursts in and says, "Excuse me for bursting in June but could you tell me if—"

He then gapes, mouths silently for four seconds, mutters an apology and leaves without closing the door. As the secretary shuts it June asks in a thoughtful voice, "Do you think he prefers me in the charcoal grey skirt and sweater?"

The secretary sits down, giggling heartily. June joins her in this. The secretary, who is last to stop, says, "Did you meet someone?"

This is a daring question. June has never spoken about her private life before, though all the office know she is divorced. After a thoughtful silence June says slowly, "I did, yes. But it may not be important."

*"Not important?"* whispers the secretary, staring.

"Don't judge by appearances," says June, then they both laugh loud and long, the secretary so uncontrollably that June eventually gestures her to leave.

Shortly after this, Tannahill jauntily enters, stares hard at her and at last says slowly, "My god! No wonder Bleloch is shitting himself. I really like this new style of yours—I've got a hard-on just looking at you. When are you and me going to have our weekend together?"

June gets up, opens the door and says in a voice almost loud enough to be heard by the clerical staff outside, "Jim Tannahill, you must feel very witty and manly and daring when you say things like that or you wouldn't keep calling in and saying them so often, but I find them boring and disgusting. I should have told you that years ago. I know you haven't enough work to fill your day but I'm luckier in that respect. Clear out of here and come back when you've something useful to say, but not before next week or better still, the week after."

He goes out past her like a sleep-walker. For the rest of the morning the Administrative Assistants (all women) seem larger and noisier than usual, often erupting in untypical laughter. The Executive Officers (all men, except for June) seem comparatively rodent-like and furtive.

Ten minutes before lunchtime the Senior Executive Officer says over the intercom, "May I see you for a moment em, June, please?"

She goes to his room.

He sits staring hard at a sheaf of typed pages on the desk

before him. June sits opposite, takes a cigarette packet from her breast pocket, asks, "May I smoke?"

"Oh yes oh yes," he murmurs, pushes an ashtray toward her, stares out of the window for a while and then stares back at the sheaf. These shifts let him see June briefly from left to right and later from right to left. He blushes at the first glance, starts sweating at the second, eventually says to the sheaf of papers, "I'm em very *glad* you've recovered from your trouble, Miss . . . em, June, I mean."

"Thank you, Mr Geikie."

"Are you *sure* you have recovered? I overwork you shamefully and em you are perhaps too em em con con conscientious."

"Quite sure, Mr Geikie."

"But!—" he looks up for a second "—there is a *change* in your appearance, Miss em em June, I mean."

"I have been shaved bald for medical reasons but that will not affect my work," says June briskly and without forethought. This is the first lie she has deliberately told. She is surprised how easily it comes.

"Alopecia?" murmurs Mr Geikie, taking another peep.

"I refuse to discuss it," says June serenely.

"But there are *other* changes in your appearance, Miss em June, I mean."

She realizes he keeps calling her Miss because she is giving him the sensations of a very small boy with a mature schoolmistress. She draws thoughtfully on her cigarette, tips ash into the tray and says, "If I dressed as usual with a head like this Mr Geikie I would look pathetic—pitiable. This way every bit of me looks deliberate. You don't think I look pitiable, do you, Mr Geikie?"

"No but surely . . . a wig, perhaps?"

"I hate wigs. I hate all kinds of falsehood," declares June, so amused by how easily she lies that to prevent a wide grin she compresses the corners of her mouth, producing a smile which probably seems scornful. He cringes before it. Then rallies, straightens his back, places clasped hands on sheaf of paper, clears throat, gazes half an inch to the right of June's head and says, "However! The image our *office* (which will soon be a Department), the image our *office* presents to the general public is not consistent with your em . . . new and em . . . disturbing aspect."

"Our office presents *no* image to the general public, Mr Geikie," says June firmly, "Our clothes and hairstyles are as unknown to the people we deal with as our faces and personal characters. The public contacts us through lawyers who contact us by letter and occasional phone calls. And since we work in a commercial office block forty-five miles from Saint Andrew's House* not even our civil service colleagues know or give a damn for my appearance."

"True, Miss em June, I mean, but! Suppose!" says Geikie so eagerly that he now looks straight at her face, "Just suppose! As might one day happen! I fall ill and you have to represent our office before an arbitration tribunal! Or at an interdepartmental function! It might even be a *Royal* Function! Holyrood Palace!"**

"I never knew you were considering *me* for promotion, Mr Geikie!" says June, opening her eyes wide. The idea is new to

*St. Andrew's House in Edinburgh holds the head bureacrats who manage Scotland for the government in London.

**Holyrood Palace is the ancient home of Scotland's monarchs. Since 1603 they have also ruled England and usually live there, but sometimes visit the old home.

him also. He gets up, walks to the window, looks out, turns and says mildly, "Nothing definite has been decided, Mm . . . June. Many things are still possible, I trust?" His face shows unusual vitality—his imagination has started working. June feels inclined to pat him on the head but shakes her own head, smiles and says, "You're a wicked man, Mr Geikie. You're toying with me. How can you think of promoting me when you have Bleloch and Tannahill to depend on?"

"I am *not* toying with you! I never *toy*. Surely you've noticed, June, that you do all the work which justifies the existence of this place? I and Bleloch and Tannahill do nothing but defuse potentially explosive confrontations. The fact is (and you must know it yourself) Her Majesty's Government is cutting back the social services so vigorously that it is *detaching itself* from many it is supposed to govern. All I and Bleloch and Tannahill do is erect façades to the fact. Don't think I'm proud of myself."

June stares at him in wonder. She does know the truth of what he says but did not know he knew it.

He sits down behind his desk again looking as ordinary and dejected as he usually does but watching her wistfully sideways. She has always known he thinks her dazzling. He sometimes starts conversations aimed at asking her out for a meal, managing them so circumspectly that she easily changes the subject before he reaches it. He is the kind of married man who jokes about how much his wife dominates him. June decides she can do him good without granting sexual favours. She says carefully, "You are a stronger man in a stronger position than you've noticed, Mr Geikie. May I call you David?"

"You know that option has always been open to you, em em em June."

"An office is not the best place to discuss office politics. Can we meet for a meal tomorrow night in the Grosvenor Steak-house? Nobody we know will see us there. I'll wear a turban, David, and dress so conventionally nobody will notice me."

He pays her a predictable compliment.

So when June returns home from work she has more to think about than Senga. (Remember there is no Harry in this develop-ment of the story.) On the following night she starts persuading Mr Geikie that he will be in no social or financial danger if he prefers the public good to the comfort of his colleagues and superiors. When they bid each other goodbye with a handshake she knows the post of Deputy Principal will be hers.

On Friday Senga phones June and asks, "Do you still hate me?"

"No."

"And you'll meet me? Not just to get your things back? But I promise I will give them back!"

"Oh yes."

Senga tells June to go that evening to a street where a car will collect her. June says firmly, "No, I want to meet you without your little friend." She tells Senga to meet her instead in the lounge of a hotel, then goes to the hotel with a suitcase and books a room. She spends an hour or two in it making herself as beautiful as possible. She puts on a little black dress she perhaps bought that afternoon. It distresses Senga, who comes to her in the lounge saying sadly, "Why aren't you wearing it?"

"Do you mean the suit? My work suit? I felt like wearing something romantic tonight."

"Work suit?"

"Yes. I wear it to the office to frighten the men."

"You've changed!"

"Yes, you changed me and I'm glad—I'm grateful. Why are you looking so worried?"

"Mibby I've changed you too much. I was always scared of you, June, you were so lovely. And now I'm terrified." Senga is trembling. June says kindly, "I've booked a room upstairs—let's go there."

They go to the room, kiss, undress and make love nervously at first, then relax into gently exploring caresses which they prolong with variations for three or four hours.

"We don't need to be cruel to each other, do we?" asks June at one point and Senga says, "Not when it's just you and me now, like this. We're just starting together so we're fresh and equal. But sooner or later one of us will be up and the other down because nobody in love ever stays equal, and I'm the one who will be down this time because all my days I've managed to keep up and I'm so tired. I'll be forty next week. Oh, I love you."

She weeps and June, who has never been happier, cuddles and comforts her, says they will love each other always and equally no matter what happens, and while she says so truly believes it.

And that was all I could imagine happening between June and Senga, but I easily imagined June and Mr Geikie three months later.

They are in Edinburgh, attending the session of a tribunal arbitrating on the first case brought before it by Mr Geikie's new Department. It concerns an honest, hardworking woman who loses her ability to earn money. Her hands get scalded in a restaurant whose owner has not provided the protective gloves required by health regulations. Her schooling has taught her nothing about health regulations or employers' responsibilities so years pass before she learns she should have claimed compensation; meanwhile she loses her home, her four young children and most of her sanity with the assistance of officials paid to help her keep them. June has drawn up a detailed history of the case, given a précis of it to the judges and would gladly give further details if asked, but the tribunal finds her Principal's statement of the case satisfactory.

"Cutbacks in social welfare funding are no excuse for incompetence!" Mr Geikie concludes, "The main cause of this tragedy is a sinister absence of contact between the five offices dealing with the case, contact which could have been made at any time by the simple expedient of lifting a telephone. These offices—and the officials staffing them—work hard and long at the grass roots level of their Departmental em em em Remit. It would be invidious to single out for blame the names of particular individuals. But my esteemed colleagues, the Departmental Heads—and some of our more highly esteemed superiors—cannot hold themselves aloof from some measure of responsibility. My department can only work by drawing such facts to their attention. May they attend to them!"

"Well done," says June as they leave the building, though she thinks he should have mentioned some individuals by name.

"Yes!" says Geikie, "I was astonished to hear myself lashing out so vigorously in every direction. Yet in the men's washroom only five minutes later Macgregor of Industrial Injuries smiled and nodded to me as if I had left him quite unscathed! What a remarkable man he is. I say June, can I buy you a meal tonight to celebrate? I'll take you to my club. I'm a member of a very posh Edinburgh club. I was *astonished* that they let me join."

They are staying at the Sheraton Hotel and arrange to meet beforehand in the foyer. Since June's promotion she has not worn the leather suit but keeps it near her as a talisman. Feeling mischievous tonight she puts it on, and as her hair is again a conventional length has it shaved off by the hotel barber. On meeting her in the foyer Geikie says, "Oh dear I doubt if they'll let us into my club with you looking like that."

She takes his arm saying, "Nonsense, Dave. Women can look how they like and you're respectable enough for both of us."

The club is five minutes' walk away on Princes Street. Fewer passers-by stare and pass comments than would happen in Glasgow, but enough do it to stimulate Geikie's adrenal glands. His spine straightens. His face takes on a look of stoical endurance. His noble bearing and her careless one carry them past the doorman, past the the cloakroom attendants, and up a stair to the dining-room. Through large windows they see the lit mansions and battlements of the castle standing high in the air between black sky and black rock. At a corner table sit two businessmen with a lawyer who attended the tribunal that day, and a Scottish politician who was once a cabinet minister and famous for interesting but unwise announcements. The first three exchange nods with Geikie. The fourth turns completely round and gazes at June, who deliberately sits with her back to him. She and Geikie consult menus.

Then Geikie murmurs, "Oh here comes Lucy."

"Lucy?"

"Short for Lucifer—that's what he likes to be called."

"Excuse me for butting in unasked and unannounced," says the politician pulling a chair to their table, aiming to sit on it and almost missing, "Oopsadaisy David! David you MUST introduce me to your charming companion, even though she is staring at me as if I'm a kind of insect. And she should, because I AM a kind of insect. Looper T. Firefly, exiled President of Freedonia at your service Ma'am."

He blows her a kiss.

"June Tain, my Deputy Principal," says Geikie coldly.

"God's boots, Geikie! You are kicking out in EVERY direction these days. I hear you've actually brought a case to arbitration! Remarkable. BUT! The name of Geikie will enter the history of our race through your courage in promoting to senior rank a lady who has destroyed the STUPID old fuddy-duddy notion that our civil service is staffed by desiccated spinsters of BOTH sexes who dress to *show* they are dedicated, desiccated spinsters. Too few people have realized that a dozen years ago a new age dawned for Britain, HEIL MARGARET! She has given Britain back its testicles by turning government offices and free enterprises into businesses run by the same people. Highly profitable. And now every man with money and initiative can enjoy his woman and his bottle and his woman and his tax-avoidance scam and his woman and his special boyfriend (AIDS permitting) without having his fun spoiled by hypocritical spoil-sport neighbours and a ghastly spook called PUBLIC OPINION. Because at last at last *at last* Public Opinion recognizes what poor Fred Sneeze told us a century ago, God is dead. So now we can all do what we like. By the way, when I say God is dead I don't mean every God is dead—that would be Blasphemy and I am a Believer. I refer only to Mister Nice-Guy in the sky, the wet-eyed, bleeding-heart bastard who told us to love our neighbours and enemies because the scum of the earth are going to inherit it. *That* God, thank God, is AS DEAD AS SOCIALISM and even the Labour Party is delighted, though it can't openly admit it yet. You are still looking at me as though I am an insect, my dear. Quite right, quite right. A glow-worm. My little tail is indeed aglow. Your fault, my dear."

"Lucy," says Geikie, "We want to eat."

"Not yet, Geikie!" says Lucy firmly, "Because I have something important to say. Fin de siècle! End of age, start of other and what rough beast, June Tain, shambles toward Bethlehem to be born? I'll tell you at the end of my next paragraph. I talk in paragraphs. Please remember all I say because tomorrow I won't recall a word.

"Now a lot of idiots think that the British spy system sorry BRITISH INTELLIGENCE system is full of Russian double-agents. Nonsense. We've had a lot of these but our relationship with the Yanks ensures that it's the CIA who know most of our secrets and we have learned quite a few of theirs. Do you remember Scottish Referendum, June Tain? When it looked like London might let us off the hook, haha? Well, a friend of mine—a fine fellow and a brave soldier—showed me the CIA plans for Scotland if it won some independence for itself, and the astonishing thing was—"

Mr Geikie, who has become restless, mutters, "Better not tell us these things Lucy."

"Pipe down, Geikie, you are not in the same LEAGUE as your charming assistant and me, she is a Hell's Angel and I am a DRAGON-FLY, a bright spark spawned by the burning breath of the Beast of the Bottomless Pit. A fine statesman, Pitt. Do you know, June Tain, that the Yanks were going to be quite kind to independent Scotland? A lot kinder than to Guatemala, Nicaragua etcetera. They were NOT afraid of us becoming a socialist republic because they felt we'd be even easier to manip-ulate than England—*fewer chiefs to bribe* was how my friend put it—and no trouble at all compared with Ireland, especially the north bit. And what I want to tell you is this."

Lucy leans across the table and tells June in a hissing whis-per, *"The CIA scenario for an independent Scotland has not been scrapped and you are filling me with mysterious insights."* He stands and speaks in a solemn and quiet voice which grows steadily louder: "I am a Douglas on my mother's side, a de-scendant of that Black Douglas who was Stabbed to The Death by The Hand of A King. And if you tell me it was some other

Douglas who was stabbed to death by Jamie the First or Second or Third or Fourth or Fifth I DON'T CARE! I STILL FEEL PROPHETIC! I PROPHESY THAT JUNE TAIN—" He points a finger at June and says more intimately, "I prophesy that you, June Tain," then notices his friends are beckoning him and more people are entering the restaurant. He murmurs, "Forgive me—I'm boring you," and returns to his friends.

That was all I could imagine of June's story. I thought of extending it by having her use Senga and Donalda to entangle and corrupt important legislators, thus provoking a feminist socialist revolution. I could not believe in it. Yet from June visiting the leatherwear shop to Lucifer's speech was less than a quarter of what I had been paid to write. If I could not expand that by imaginative growth I must expand it by mere additions. June's story had a pornographic content. Such fancies come easily to me. Could I add more of them? I wrote the dialogue between the American women which I later used in the "Culture Capitalism" chapter, but tired of it. Such fancies are repetitive, and I had already written a novel using them. I decided to enlarge the book with anything interesting I could put on paper, however irrelevant: essays, bits of autobiography, perhaps a play or two. More than a decade ago most of what I earned had been payment for television and radio plays. I had long wanted to give them new life in a book. In the early seventies a one-act play called *Dialogue* had been broadcast by Scottish BBC radio, networked by Granada television, taken on tour by the short-lived Scottish Stage Company. I prosed it into the present tense, called it "A Free Man with a Pipe" and found I could easily believe the hero was June's unsatisfactory ex-husband, that he was trying to forget her by half-heartedly seducing someone else, that her voice on the telephone at the end finally demolished him.

This suggested a form of book I had not written before. After the chapter showing Senga and Donalda seducing June in the late eighties (the fashions in the streets give the date) the book would flash back to them in earlier years, each chapter showing one of my three women involved with men who failed them in very different but commonplace ways. As I dug among my forgotten plays for more material I began hoping to show a greater variety of those who make Britain than most British novels. I had tried that in my first and longest book, but had lacked the knowledge to build (as Dickens built in *Little Dorrit*) leaders of finance, government, law and fashion into a continuous plot involving the factories, slums and slum landlords, the jailors and the jailed. I had patched over my ignorance with abbreviations and metaphors. But a book of episodes showing the lives of three women converging over thirty years might do the job realistically. Once again my book would contain no real leaders of government, finance, law, fashion etcetera, but my setting was Scotland, so how could it? Like most Scots and many English I assumed most such leaders work in London and are no use to us. I should have remembered that Scotland is still very useful to them.

The chapters called "The Proposal," "The Man Who Knew about Electricity," "In the Boiler Room" and "A Free Man with a Pipe" stick so close to original plays that they contain nearly every word of the original dialogue. "Mr Lang and Ms Tain" uses half a play, "Quiet People" the start of one. If any readers of "Quiet People" feel worried for the Liddels I can show them typed proof that the Liddels and their lodgers were good for each other, separating with friendship on both sides, though very suddenly.

But Harry was an unexpected character. In the earliest version of the first chapter she did not even appear in a photo-

graph. She was invented for the "Class Party" chapter because
a quartette allowed more permutations than a trio, but she said
little because I had no idea where she came from or what job
she did when not playing perverse games with Senga. I knew
she was a rarer social type than the other women, it helped the
plot for her to be rich, it was a useful economy to think a horrid
upbringing had made it hard for her to talk. For a while I never
bothered imagining a past for her, but had a rough idea she
might be the administrator of a large hospital. One day I was
talking to a friend about what makes rich people different from
you and me, especially the rich whose wealth is a habit of mind
because it is a settled inheritance. My friend had met some in
a boarding school, also in an art gallery where she occasionally
worked. I too had met some and been fascinated by a speech
which showed how foreign they were to me. I had walked in
a big private garden with an owner who had devoted it wholly
to trees and shrubs because plots of flowers gave his gardener
too much work. I asked if he grew vegetables. He said, "Once
I did but it wasn't worth the trouble. You can get them in a shop
for a few shillings."

I had known a young woman who disliked all the people her
parents liked, saying she preferred the company of "ordinary
people." She sulked when expected to make a cup of coffee for
herself, explaining that she could not possibly do that, and
proving it by sulkily floating a spoonful of the powder in a mug
of lukewarm water. These people were individuals, not types,
but as Scott Fitzgerald said at the start of his story "The Rich
Boy," "Describe an individual and you may end with a type;
describe a type and you are likely to end with—nothing." I
remarked to my friend that perhaps the very rich found it hard
to take others seriously after boarding school, because at last
they could easily replace or escape from whoever did not per-

# ACKNOWLEDGMENTS

A pen is the only writing tool I have learned to use, so I need typists to put my words onto pages publishers will read. This once caused embarrassment. A typist refused to type part of a story which contained *fucking,* a word she thought should not be written or read. She was right to refuse. Nobody, for pay, should do what they think wrong. Luckily I met Flo Allan who could type and liked all the words I used. Being a shy soul, I could not have put chapters 1 and 12 into publishable form had I not known that Flo (a happily married mother) would enjoy typing them. So the book is dedicated to her.

The device of putting the queen's English dialect into phonetic speech is taken from James Kelman's unpublished story, "Cogmentum." I have not done it to mock a diction which perhaps a twentieth of the British islanders employ with skill and confidence, but because I enjoy its weird music.

Chapter 6 contains three men's memories of the British army. The First World War ones belonged to my father, Alex Gray. Those of the North African supply depot came from Annabel Macmillan, who got them from her father. The national serviceman's memories of Cyprus were from Charlie Orr.

The accident by which the gag writer in chapter 11 found his vocation befell Robert Wills.

The device of putting Harry's small voice in a smaller typeface is taken from the gnat in *Through the Looking Glass.* In not having her talk so in other chapters I am following The Devil's Advice to Story-Tellers in Robert Graves's poem of that name.

If British civil servants find my government office in the epilogue convincing, this is due to the advice of my friend Margaret. From Claud Cockburn comes Lucy's evocation of a Tory Britain where nothing need stop a man enjoying "his bottle and his woman." The phrase is in *I, Claud.*

# POSTSCRIPT FOR THE U.S.A. EDITION

Most English reviewers of this book were so spellbound by chapters 1, 12 and 13 that they thought the novel showed little more than kinky sex and so denounced it. The fault was mine. By calling it *Something Leather* I had pointed them straight to these chapters. I now wish I had called it *Glaswegians*. My book owes more to Sherwood Anderson's *Winesburg, Ohio* than to James Joyce's *Dubliners,* but *Glaswegians* would have pointed to the ten chapters of ordinary social kinkiness, which are the filling of my sandwich. The adventure before and after them does not even pretend to show lesbian love lives, which must be as varied as the hetero kind. That adventure caricatures (and caricatures can show truths) how the main British classes (propertied/professional/handworking/casualty) get on terribly well together. I would prefer a Britain where affections are not shaped by the unequal amounts of money we own. Meanwhile, for publicity reasons, the book will keep its present bad name until it is forgotten.

ALASDAIR GRAY
28 September 1990

**ABOUT THE AUTHOR**

Alasdair Gray's previous books include
*Lanark: A Life in Four Books* (shortlisted
for the Booker Prize), *1982 Janine, The Fall of
Kelvin Walker,* and *McGrotty and Ludmilla.*
He lives in Glasgow, Scotland.